A
Deceitful
Man

With Best Wishes
From
Vivienne Dockerty.

By the Same Author

A Woman Undefeated.

Dreams Can Come True.

A Distant Dream.

Beggarman's Cottage.

Her Heart's Desire.

Shattered Dreams.

Innocence Lost.

The Polish Connection.

Ping Pong Poms.

Clouds Below the Mountains.

A
Deceitful
Man

Vivienne Dockerty

Matador
9 Priory Business Park,
Wistow Road, Kibworth Beauchamp,
Leicestershire. LE8 0RX
Tel: 0116 279 2299
Email: books@troubador.co.uk
Web: www.troubador.co.uk/matador
Twitter: @matadorbooks

ISBN 978 1785898 945

British Library Cataloguing in Publication Data.
A catalogue record for this book is available from the British Library.

Printed by TJ International, Padstow, Cornwall
Typeset in 11pt Aldine401 BT by Troubador Publishing Ltd, Leicester, UK

Matador is an imprint of Troubador Publishing Ltd

Synopsis

Ada Moscrop, a thirty something Ward Sister from Cumbria, nursed a secret dream. It is 1922 and most of the eligible men who could have been a suitor, have either died in the recent war or succumbed to the influenza epidemic if they did make it home. Her dream of becoming a wife and mother had long disappeared.

Then along came handsome and dashing Daniel McAuley, from Westmeath in Ireland. A patient on the Men's Surgical Ward at Blackburn Infirmary and just the man that Ada has been waiting for, although she's unaware he has a hidden past.

After leaving Ireland because of the constraints of a marriage that was forced upon him and the fear of reprisals after having been a member of a dissident group, Daniel starts working at a Blackburn brewery and fills the gap in Ada's loveless life. But will his hidden past catch up with him to break poor Ada's heart, or like all strong women she will manage to survive it?

Author's Note

They say that good things can come out of adversity and I can say that has been true for me during early 2016. On Boxing day in 2015, the River Irwell broke its banks and caused devastation to the houses alongside it. Many families moved out and went to live in alternative accommodation, but we stayed put, as the damage to our property wasn't as severe as others and we could live upstairs whilst the restoration was completed.

I retreated into a sort of a dream world, which I am apt to do when I'm upset about something and feel a little traumatized. That said, I like to write about my feelings, so one day I switched on my computer, intending to sort out the jumble of emotions that were going through my mind. Then suddenly I began to write a story that I had been thinking of for many years, but couldn't quite put my mind to. So whilst the noise of the dryers whirred on 24/7 and the sound of the plaster being knocked off the downstairs walls sometimes intruded, I managed to type up the first few chapters and *A Deceitful Man* was born.

I would like to offer many thanks for all the help we were given by residents not affected, the local church who provided meals and of course the Mountain Rescue. We hope we never get to see their rubber dinghy floating down our street again.

Chapter One

It was still dark when Ada Moscrop walked along the narrow path, which was strewn with damp leaves from the overhead trees. She was on her way from the Nurses Home to the hospital and her measured steps in her black laced up shoes, told of a woman of authority. Her position as a Sister at the Royal Infirmary in Blackburn, was a great achievement for the daughter of a signal man from Whitehaven and she was proud of her status in life. She shivered a little as a gust of chilly wind whooshed down from the Pennines, causing her to draw the cape of her uniform a little closer to her tall, slender body, whilst feeling glad that her head wear was pinned on securely. She loved her job, but having to get up at this unearthly hour on these wintery mornings, sometimes irked her greatly.

She thought ahead to the twelve hour shift before her. Another one of tending to the sick, along with chivvying up the young probationer who never seemed to spend enough time on making sure the bedpans were scoured properly and keeping an eye on her S.E.N, an Irish girl from Galway. Mary Donlan tended to carry out her duties with little decorum and was often caught chatting with the porter in the locker room.

There was much to do on Mens's Surgical which had been Ada's domain for the last two years. It was in 1919 when she had come to Blackburn to take up her position as Ward Sister, which had been a just reward for the many hours she had spent tending to the wounded soldiers and injured folk at Leeds Infirmary. Now three years later in 1922, it was her job to oversee her team of nurses, as they tended to the needs of recovering men; men who had been operated on by Mr. Pearson, the surgeon.

After reading the reports at the morning hand-over with Sister Hitchen, who had been on the night shift, Ada would supervise breakfasts, take temperatures, hand out medicines, watch over the staff as they carried out their duties, making sure that bed baths, cleaning and sterilization of the instruments or changing the dirty linen before bed inspection, was performed to the highest standard. All the while her team would be working against the clock in readiness for Matron to do her rounds or Mr. Pearson visiting to inspect his handiwork.

Ada tried to run a tight ship, both with the nurses she had been allocated and the welfare of the dozen or so patients in her care, always aware that Matron might march in at anytime during her shift and find fault with something. Matron Chandler was a picky woman who should have retired before the War, but had stayed on because of the shortage of nurses.

Many nurses who had worked at the Blackburn hospital before 1914 had volunteered to go to the aid of wounded soldiers, either at the dedicated military hospitals, convalescent homes throughout the land or even scarier, in field hospitals behind the lines in war torn France. Many nurses had died along with thousands of men, but it hadn't been something that Ada had felt drawn to do. Her travels would be ended once she had taken up a permanent position somewhere as a Nursing Sister.

She supposed she would still be living in Whitehaven, if it hadn't have been for her brother feeling the need to emigrate to Australia in 1909. Their parents had died within weeks of each other the year before, both having succumbed to a nasty bout of influenza in an especially harsh Spring. Ada had just turned nineteen and was working at a Cottage Hospital in Maryport where her probationer training had begun and Charles, her brother, had been employed as a trainee surveyor at the Town Hall.

After suffering the heartbreak of his young lady reneging on their year long marriage betrothal, he had headed off to Australia leaving Ada alone. She could have gone with him, indeed he had beseeched her to go with him, as he had been nervous about going to the other side of the world on his own. But all she had wanted to do at that time was to fulfill her dream of becoming a State Registered Nurse. Working hard towards the examination at the end of a three year training period, she was rewarded with that coveted certificate when she moved to Leeds Infirmary. Then after the war she had taken up a post firstly as a ward sister on a General Ward, then on the Men's Ward at Blackburn in the Royal Infirmary. There was nothing left for her in Whitehaven once her brother had gone. No local swain who came a-courting and no close relatives, except for an old aunt who lived in Ulverston.

Still, from Charles's letters that arrived regularly once per month at the Nurses' Home, he had done very well for himself in his chosen world, having become the Chief Planning Officer in a place called Melbourne and had married a girl called Sara. A photograph, which was taken on their wedding day and sent to Ada as a souvenir, showed a shy looking girl with pleasant features.

Having reached the tall, imposing red brick building, Ada made her way along the main corridor, up the stairs and into the warmth of Men's Surgical. It was like being welcomed by a pair of open arms as she walked in through the doors. This was where she belonged. This was where a small section of humanity relied on her expertise. Especially on Men's Surgical, where left to their own devices the recuperating men liked to loll about, smoking their cigarettes or pipes in the small room allocated, or sitting on each other's beds chatting. Although at this time of day, most would be tucked up in their white iron bedsteads and sleeping. They needed strict discipline, routine and the order in their lives if they wanted to recover quickly and Sister Moscrop was the one who provided that continuity until their discharge.

It wasn't far off Christmas. It was a time that Ada disliked as it reminded her that she had no family left in England to celebrate it with. There were no relations, other than her mother's aunt and she didn't know her well enough to land on her. Esther Moscrop, her mother, was an only child and Wilfred Moscrop's family had never been discussed in front of her. Charles had once told her that their father was from a farming community near Carlisle. There had to be some mystery there, Ada supposed, but hadn't liked to pry in case it caused her parents some discomfort if they had to explain. Their father though must have been from quite a well-to-do family, she had presumed, as the semi-detached house they lived in didn't have the rent man knocking on the door. Owning part of a large Victorian residence, would have been hard to afford from a signal-man's pay.

It was a pity that there was no extended family for her to visit over Christmas, because when her parents had been alive, the day had been made much of in their household. There had always been a Christmas tree, decorated beautifully and on display in their parlour, where they had eaten roast chicken and all the trimmings after a visit to St. Augustine's church and her father's seasonal visit to the Hare and Hounds Hotel.

Though many people that year would be suffering meagre celebrations, as workers at that time were poorly paid and it was still difficult for everyone. Still reeling from the effects of the *war to end all wars,* when in 1914 brave men went off to fight the Hun to help defeat a despotic nation, ordinary people found that not a lot had changed for them. There was still poverty, still terrible diseases caused by malnutrition, still a high child mortality rate and millions of people died in the flu epidemic. Because of all this, there was a dirth of men, so people like Ada didn't have much chance of becoming a mother, as she dearly would have liked to have done one day.

She knew she wasn't outstandingly pretty, something she thought she would have to be if there were any eligible young men left to be attracted to her. Her skin was sallow, her eyelashes and eyebrows were nearly white and her ash blonde hair, which she wore severely pulled back into an unbecoming knot at the base of her neck under her starched white hat, complete with wings on either side, was dull and lifeless. Though someone had once told her that she had beautiful blue eyes and that her smile could light up a room when she walked into it, but that had been from one of her brother's friends, who had wanted her to be his girlfriend, but had not pursued her. Resigned to being a spinster for the rest of her life now, Ada threw even more of her energies into nursing.

It was quiet in the ward as Ada strode along towards the desk at the far end of the room, where Sister Hitchen was writing copious notes with a pencil and a nurse was hovering nearby. One of the patients nearest the door had lifted a hand in greeting and she smiled to herself as she felt a blush creeping into her cheeks. Mr. Daniel McAuley. The Irishman whose touch had caused her to tingle all over, when she had helped him into bed from the wheelchair on his first day. She was going to miss him once his plaster had been taken off and he was ready for home. A man in his early thirties, originally from a place called Westmeath, according to Mary Donlan, who always seemed to be hanging around his bed chatting. He had been admitted to the ward when a barrel of stout had fallen on his foot and this in Ada's opinion, must mean that he was a heavy drinker. The cheeky chappie was a bit of a joker and the type of man that Ada felt she would steer well clear of, if he hadn't been a patient and she had met him socially. He was too handsome for his own good and had probably left a trail of broken hearts behind him during the war years. The words, *tall, dark and handsome* came to mind, as she tried to concentrate on the reason that she was there on Men's Surgical. Although he wasn't tall if you compared him to Ada's five feet seven, but definitely not the same height as she was. He winked one of his dark brown eyes at her wickedly, and shouted "The top of the mornin' to yer, Sister" and her heart did a couple of somersaults as she walked passed his bed.

"Sister Moscrop." The night sister looked worn out, as she raised weary eyes from her paper work when Ada stood before her. "Good morning. Had a bit of a problem during the night. Mr. Leyton, you know the patient with the steel plate in his head, he had a convulsion and we had to send him down to theatre. Poor man, I think it was a fluid buildup that had caused pressure in his skull."

"Perhaps so." Ada didn't like to get into discussions on the why's and wherefore of the patients' operations. A nurse was there to make sure the men in her care were comfortable and it didn't do to speculate, especially as Nurse Blackwell, a young woman who preferred to be on permanent nights was waiting to be dismissed.

"You can get off now, Nurse," Ada said, "Sister Hitchen and I will go over the reports together and I'll see you this evening. It's very cold outside, so I'd hurry home if I were you."

"Thank you, Sister Moscrop," the nurse said civilly and bidding Sister Hitchen farewell, she hurried from the ward.

It took only a few minutes to be alerted to any problems that might occur after hand over, then Sister Hitchen also took her leave. A man in his forties in the bed nearest to Ada's desk, had just had his appendix out and needed a watchful eye in case he was sick from the effects of gas that he'd been given in the operating theatre. The poor man next door to him was recovering from having a piece of shrapnel removed from his arm, then further down the ward, a man in his late thirties had come in because of a goitre in his neck. He was feeling very down, because a scar would be left when he had his operation to remove it. Mr. Judd, an elderly man, had come in the day before with gout and couldn't walk as far as the lavatory and two other men each lying in their beds with a plaster cast on their legs, which was suspended by a pulley over their beds, were there because of a motor car accident.

Then of course there was Mr. McAuley, *Daniel,* he had asked Ada to call him. Not that she would, she called everyone by their surname. It was only professional to do so. He was waiting around for his discharge. His broken bones had been set, his plaster cast applied by Mr. Pearson and it was just a question of time before he was allowed to hobble.

She often wondered in times of quiet reflection, especially when she lay on her bed in the room she had in the Nurses' Home, if Mr. McAuley had any family living in Blackburn? He'd not had any visitors, although it could have been that he only had an old mother to care for him and she didn't like to travel very far. Although there was a train that ran from Blackburn to Manchester and the charabancs linked major towns, a lot of elderly people had never been outside of the place that they were born.

He had arrived one morning wheeled along by a porter in one of the hospital chairs, wearing a smart suit, a grey striped one which was double breasted, trousers with turn-ups and a nice white starched shirt underneath. The one black shoe he wore was highly polished and his dark hair, cut in a short back and sides, was slicked down with Brylcreem and he had a thick, black, moustache above his lips which had been carefully trimmed. He had brought a small suitcase with him and had produced a pair of blue striped pyjamas for wearing in bed. Not for him the hospital issued garments, one size fitting all, either too tight or drowning the body and he had produced a small, narrow, wooden box to go inside his bedside locker which held a comb and hair brush. A man who liked himself too much was Ada's assumption. A narcissus, too full of himself to have settled down with a willing girl.

Ada looked at her fob-watch impatiently. No sign of the S.E.N, nor the auxiliary, Joan Stanton, nor Valerie Mason, the probationer, although Nurse Catherine Blakely, the S.R.N had just come in through the doors. Then as Nurse Blakely reached the desk, there was a flurry of activity behind her and the latecomers burst into the ward. The three women were giggling, no doubt at some silly joke that Nurse Donlan had told them. The girl lacked gentility and Ada felt cross.

"You are all five minutes late for your shift and it will be noted." Ada's sharp tone brooked no arguments and the uniformed women stood respectfully before her, waiting for more to come. But when no further scolding came, they were puzzled by it, especially when Ada turned to speak to Nurse Blakely with a softer intonation in her voice. She went through her list of patients, telling the nurses of their patients' requirements for that day and the whereabouts of Mr. Leyton, poor man who was missing.

She impressed their need for diligence and care when handling the afflictions of the men on the ward who were still recovering, then dismissed her team briskly and told them to carry on.

"What's up with 'er, she usually acts like Miss Starchy Knickers?" Joan asked quizzically, as she and Valerie walked quickly to the sluice room to prepare the bowls of water to sponge down the infirm who couldn't be moved for the moment, whilst Nurse Donlan set off to sort out the breakfasts for the patients. "Thought we were in for a right roasting for bein' late and that. Perhaps she's found a fella and he's been givin' her some," she finished coarsely.

"Joan!" Valerie sounded embarrassed. Being a single girl, she had little experience of the opposite sex, except when she was required to give a patient a bed bath and then a blanket always covered his privates parts for the sake of modesty. Joan on the other hand had given birth to three children, who were grownup now and with a husband who was unemployed, she had come back to work as an auxiliary nurse.

"She's probably had a nice letter from that brother of hers who lives in Australia. Nurse Blakely once told me all about how after Sister Moscrop's mother and father had died, he moved over there. You have to feel sorry for her being on her own. Anyway, we were late. We should have waited for our break before we listened to Mary's wedding plans."

"Well, that as maybe, but we'd best be on our toes, as she'll be keepin' a beady eye on us, that's fer sure."

The morning sped along, as all Ada's shifts tended to do as she immersed herself fully into the duties of the day. Matron, overly critical as usual, arrived about eleven and inspected every bed, its occupant and their medical notes. Mr. Pearson, along with two medical students, strutted godlike along the ward, stopping at two or three bedsides to assess the patient's progress. Ada was glad when she was able to take a break for a quickly gulped cup of tea and a sandwich and she had time to reflect on the fact that Mr. McAuley's eyes had been following her around all morning. She felt pleased and cross in equal measures. Pleased because a man could be taking such an interest and cross that as he was a patient, she wasn't to show him that she liked his attention too.

Though what must it be like to have the love of a good man, a man to snuggle up to on a cold winter's night, instead of the stone hot water bottle that was her bed mate? Be there waiting for him with a cup of tea and a meal on the table, when he returned to their happy little home each night. Give birth to a couple of beautiful children, a boy and a dainty little girl. The girl would have Mr. McAuley's beautiful brown eyes and the boy with hair as light as hers. Mr. McAuley! Why was she dreaming about Mr. Daniel McAuley? He'd be gone tomorrow, out of her life.

Chapter Two

Blackburn, which lies on the southern edge of the Ribble Valley in Lancashire, had been a thriving mill town. In the beginning there was money to be made from the weaving of wool and many people set up cottage industries in their own homes with the aid of a spinning wheel. But later, with cotton being imported from the Americas and machines invented that could only be housed in a large building, it was textile production which helped Blackburn to become a prosperous place.

That is, prosperity for those who had become wealthy from the endeavours of the lower classes, but most families thereabout benefited from the regular employment that the cotton mills brought, enabling them to live a better life.

The boom years of the cotton industry began to decline after the First World War. This was the war to end all wars, according to the politicians who sent millions of men to their deaths. With Britain having a treaty with Belgium, it had a duty to defend their residents if the Germans decided to march through their country to France. So this thriving industry, which had transformed a market town into a place of significance and created jobs amongst the subsidiary companies which were born, found that trade begin to dwindle. Then India started to impose high import tariffs on British made goods, which resulted in many workers, mostly women who had taken the jobs of the men who went to war, being laid off and having to look for other employment. There was plenty of poorly paid work to be had though, if you cared to work in a paper mill, a paint factory, a flour mill, a steel factory or even a brewery and so Blackburn continued to be a bustling town.

It was on a bright, sunny morning in April that Ada decided she would take a brisk walk to the fruit market in the town and purchase whatever took her fancy to eat. Hospital food was bland, but nourishing, not much in variety and it had never been able to help Ada put on weight. And that particular winter had been harsh in an area which dwelt across moors and beneath the Pennines. With the bitter winds and many falls of snow, the hospital cooks had been boiling up a lot of porridge.

Ada, feeling the warmth of the sun on her cheeks, had dressed herself smartly in a cream, high necked blouse with a black, straight calf length skirt, a brown velvet coat with a narrow sable collar and a pair of chunky heeled T' bar shoes. She also wore a small, brown felt hat, which was decorated with a couple of pink organza flowers. She was looking a totally different person from the strict and starchy, no nonsense kind of woman that the patients and nurses on her ward were used to seeing, as this was her one day off that week and she meant to enjoy it.

Her thoughts were fixed on the coming weekend, as she wandered past the back to back terraced houses in the cobbled streets, though hardly noticing their existence, because much to her delight, she was to take a week away from work. Plans were afoot for her to take a nostalgic journey back to Whitehaven and then onto the little village of Colbrook where she had been born. She was to spend a week with her childhood friend, a young woman called Betty, who had been widowed during the conflict abroad. Betty had been her friend when they had attended school together and had kept in touch by letter, when Charles and herself had left for pastures new. It would be Ada's thirty second birthday the following Tuesday and this little holiday was to be a gift to herself, as she had no one else to buy her one.

Looking into the window of F.W. Woolworth on the corner of Church Street, a store where she thought she might purchase a "thank you" gift for Betty for accommodating her, she was pulled up short, when a very smart man, dressed in a black winter's coat and a black Homburg hat and who had just walked across the road from the Bay Horse opposite, stopped to greet her. It was Daniel, well Mr. McAuley, if she was to stick to propriety.

"Sister Moscrop!" he said, his eyes twinkling with pleasure once he had established it was indeed her, all dressed up like one of those models in a window of a ladies fashion shop, instead of rustling about in her starched uniform.

"Mr. McAuley." Ada replied, her voice sounding a bit wobbly after the shock of seeing the very person who invaded her dreams most nights. "I see that you have fully recovered."

"I certainly have, thanks to you and the kind attention of your nurses. I've steered well clear of rolling barrels ever since."

"Rolling barrels, Mr. McAuley?"

"Why, yes." His Irish brogue that hadn't seemed so evident when he had been in the care of the Royal Infirmary, came suddenly obvious, as if he too was nervous as he spoke.

"I work for the brewery, so I do. I check that all is well behind the scenes of various hostelries in the area. On that particular day when I was admitted to your hospital, a rogue barrel had attacked me."

"Ah," Ada had forgotten the incident.

"So, what brings you to this part of town, all dressed up as if you're off to take tea with the Lord Mayor himself in the Town Hall this afternoon?" He winked at her naughtily and she could feel herself blush.

"Just a bit of shopping. I am looking for a present for a friend, whom I will be staying with next week and I thought I would also pay a visit to the market." She began to move away from him, as the pavement was rather crowded and one or two people passing by had already tutted.

"Oh, Sister Moscrop, don't go." Daniel McAuley wasn't going to let go of this woman easily. She was a fine looking woman, rather on the thin side, but obviously had a bit of class about her which he liked. Could it be that Fate had drawn them together? Lying in his hospital bed for those few days before Christmas, watching her carrying out her duties in her calm and collected manner, he had realised that she was just the type of woman he would welcome in his life. Not the brassy types he met behind the bars in his line of work, or the young women who worked as typists in the brewery offices, he wanted a woman with a bit of class.

"Well, we are blocking the pavement somewhat, Mr. McAuley and I must admit I need to buy something for my friend fairly quickly. I am on nightshift until I leave Blackburn for a week's holiday, so time is of the essence as they say."

"Yes, I suppose I must get back to my office," he said in a reluctant voice, although it was the last thing he wanted to do. He would like to take her for a drink somewhere and get to know her, but he knew she wouldn't agree to entering the portals of a public house, as she was a respectable lady.

"Would you care to join me for a quick cup of tea and perhaps a slice of cake at the cafe just along the way here? It does a nice Victoria sponge with a raspberry jam filling and we could share a pot of tea between us, so we could." *Say yes, say yes, he pleaded with God who might be listening. I'll start going to church again. I'll say three Hail Mary's I promise. Just make her say yes.*

"I suppose I could spare the time for a cup of tea, Mr. McAuley," Ada said, feeling her stomach rumble at the thought of a slice of Victorian sponge, as she hadn't bothered with breakfast and *she* wondered why she was so thin. "Although I have to say that I don't think it is done to take tea with a former patient, but I will make an exception just this once." *And I can bask in the admiration of a handsome man for a little while. Something I haven't done for a long time.*

"Then let's do it," he said, offering her an arm to link, which she ignored and walked ahead of him.

The cafe, or rather a tea room, a pretty place decked out with white cotton tablecloths, wheel-backed chairs and organdie curtains at

13

the two small windows, was full. Mostly patronized by well- to-do people, who had spent some time walking around the market and were taking a rest or eating their lunch before sallying forth again, there wasn't a table to be had.

"Perhaps we could find another place. I know of somewhere near the market. Not as nice as this, but..." Daniel's heart plummeted, as he saw she was about to turn and continue through the open door without him.

"We're just going, Lad," said a voice nearby. A man in a tweed suit with his ample wife who had just got up from a table by the window addressed him. His saviour, he thought later that day.

"Oh, that'll be grand, so it will, thank you." Daniel ushered Ada forward once the seats were vacant.

"I would like to pay my share, Mr. McAuley," said Ada, not wanting to feel that she was beholden to this gentleman, who was making her heart go pit-a-pat every time she looked at him. Goodness, she was surprised at herself. She usually didn't behave in this way.

"I would be most put out if you didn't allow me to pay the bill, Sister Moscrop." Daniel replied, signalling to the hovering waitress that he would like her to take his order. "A pot of tea for two and would you bring a plate of your delicious cakes. Would that be agreeable to you, Sister?"

Ada nodded. She had met the eyes of the young waitress and realised that the girl had been a visitor on her ward recently. Her father had come in for a small operation on his delicate parts and she and the girl's mother had visited him twice. Plenty of gossip abounding if she were to tell her mother that starchy Sister Moscrop had been seen with a fellow!

"So, how is Men's Surgical, Sister?" Daniel watched as Ada poured their tea from an earthenware pot into two pretty china cups.

"Much the same as usual," Ada replied. "Men recovering from various operations and I happen to notice that *you* are walking very well, Mr. McAuley."

"Time is a great healer, so they say. Though I don't do a lot of walking in my job and my place of residence isn't very far away."

"Oh… would you like some cake?" Ada proffered a china cake stand that had various delicious looking slices of sponge and a couple of Bakewell tarts. What did she say now? She felt tongue-tied. Did she ask what he did for a living or ask him in what part of Blackburn did he live? Both questions sounded inquisitive and what was she doing here anyway? She should be doing her shopping, not sitting here talking to an ex-patient. It was most unprofessional of her. He saved her any embarrassment by answering her questions himself.

"I'm what you could call an Area Manager, Sister Moscrop." He began to stir his tea with a silver spoon after adding two teaspoons of sugar. "I work for Duttons. I have done for nearly three years, so I have. My father owns a small brewery near Westmeath, that's in Ireland by the way. He sent me over to learn the rudiments of running a large concern, as his greatest ambition is to have his name known as a brewer throughout Ireland. Not that it would be as big as Guinness."

"Guinness?"

"Don't tell me that you haven't heard of Guinness, Sister Moscrop. It's only been going in Ireland since the 18th century and is mother's milk to an Irishman. Begging your pardon, if you find the use of that term vulgar."

"No, I'm not familiar with the name, Mr. McAuley. If it is anything to do with alcohol, I have to admit I am from a temperance background. My parents discouraged my brother and I from drinking intoxicants. My father's favourite saying was "when drink's in, wit's out" and he only indulged himself once per year at Christmas."

Daniel grimaced. "I would be out of a job if everyone had that attitude, Sister Moscrop. And with the mention of my job, I must regrettably be on my way." He signalled to the waitress to bring him the bill for their tea and cakes, although he had only eaten a Bakewell tart himself, whilst Ada had eaten a couple of large slices of Victoria sponge. "I wonder…" Daniel hesitated. "Would it be very forward of me to ask if you would accompany to the cinema one evening? I don't know if you have seen any of these new black and white films that are all the rage, but I have heard that an actor called Charlie Chaplin is very popular at the moment." He felt in his pocket to take out a couple of shillings for the waitress, giving time for Ada to make her mind up and to Ada's consternation, she heard herself agreeing that she would.

"The only problem is that I am going away on holiday, Mr. McAuley. I won't be back until after Easter and then I would have to look at my hospital shifts."

"Then perhaps you could leave me a note with the porter in the hospital lodge, Sister Moscrop." Daniel was not going to be put off easily. "I know Alf, he drinks in the Bay Horse and his brother works in the brewery. Are you going anywhere nice?"

"Just back to my roots," Ada replied, getting up and beginning to accompany him towards the doorway. "Thank you so much for the tea and cakes. I do hope you have a good rest of the day."

"You too, Sister Moscrop," Daniel said, in a voice full of regret that he had to be parted from her. "I hope you enjoy your holiday." Raising his hat in a gentlemanly fashion, he walked away, leaving Ada to wonder if she had just been on a date, as she had heard younger people call an assignation.

Well fancy that! Ada walked back to F.W. Woolworth in a bit of a daze, wondering if Mr. McAuley had enjoyed their tete-a-tete as much as she had.

Chapter Three

Ada sat on the train as it trundled along the railway line on its way to Whitehaven. She had changed trains earlier at Preston Station and had spent the time reading. Sometimes if she felt her eyelids begin to close because of the gentle swaying of the carriage, she would stare fixedly at the beauty of the passing landscape on its way along the west coast of Cumbria.

This was one of the numerous trips she had made over the years to the little village of Colbrook where she was born. At first, when Charles, her brother, was dithering as to whether he was going to emigrate or live everyday with the worry that he might see his beloved who had spurned him, she had made her way to the village from Maryport, where she was doing her probationer training, to keep an eye on him. The house that they had lived in since they were babies and had been left to both of them in their father's Will, had been up for sale at the time with an agent in Workington and Charles, who was still full of gloom, couldn't wait for it to be sold so that he could quit the village.

Of course when the house had been sold, Charles had the funds to emigrate to Australia and Ada was able to put her money by in a branch of the National Westminster Bank. She had little to spend her inheritance on, with her employment including her accommodation and the food in the hospital canteen substantial. She didn't waste her money on frills and fripperies, preferring to keep her money for a rainy day.

She sighed as she thought back to the idyllic life which was her childhood. It had always been sunny in her world. The house that they lived in had been ample for a family of four, although Ada had sometimes wondered how her parents could afford it on a signal man's pay. She'd had her own room, as had Charles and their parents and there had been a spare one where her mother did her needlework for her family and friends. There a Singer sewing machine graced a heavy wooden table near the window, which overlooked their garden and over to the estuary. It had been a large garden where her mother had grown a mass of vegetables and fruit trees and their produce kept them from going hungry throughout the year.

Not that they had ever gone without. The Moscrops were well off if you compared them to some of the families around, although there was never actual poverty. The people of Colbrook were a close knit community, who along with the incumbent of St. Paul's Church, the teachers at the small school and the local shop owners, would have spotted impoverishment in a family and got together to help them out.

Men earned their livings in a variety of ways then. Some tenanted farms and rented their land from the local gentry. They had herds of sheep or cattle in the meadows, or grew crops on the fertile fields around, employing many labourers. There was the blacksmith, the butcher, the grocer, the cobbler, the baker and the men who ran the Hare and Hounds Hotel or the Rowan Tree Arms. There was the chimney sweep, the postman and some of the local men made their living from the sea. The Irish Sea, not far away from the Colbrook coastline, was home to a variety of fish and crustaceans, although a vessel had to be wary of the many rocks in the estuary, as they set off on the voyage.

With a backdrop of the Lakeland Fells, a beach where children could play in comparative safety and the country lanes, where daffodils grew in clumps in the Springtime, roses bloomed in cottage gardens in the summer and the beauty of the trees in autumnal colours left a lasting memory, Ada's childhood had been sublime.

Suffice to say, she had been closer to her mother than her

father. Esther Moscrop was a kindly woman who attended church each Sunday and was a member of the parish women's group. She had also spent a lot of time working in her garden, probably inheriting her love of the soil from her father, who had worked for many years in the grounds of Colbrook Hall until illness forced him to retire. Esther had been born in a tied cottage overlooking the River Col and had been one of seven children. Having been flooded out of their home when the river broke its banks, which it was apt to do occasionally, the family were taken in by a relative who lived in Ulverston. A kind great aunty, who Ada remembered well from when Esther made her annual visit with her children, to see her. Her own father, Wilfred Moscrop, who had worked on the railways since leaving school and had come from a village outside Carlisle had been a strict, but fair parent, although Ada had never felt close to him at all.

It felt chilly on that April evening as Ada got down from the train at Colbrook Station, glancing as usual towards the signal man's box which was just beyond the crossing, trying to see if it was still the man who had taken over from her father working the signals, or perhaps someone new. It was hard to make a figure out, as dusk was on its way and if she didn't hurry she would miss seeing Betty's children before they went to bed. She nodded in greeting to the Station Master, who lived in the station house with his family, after he had glanced at his fob watch to check that the train would leave his station punctually. She wouldn't tarry, there was time during her holiday to make the acquaintance of him and his wife again.

Ada picked her way carefully along the muddy lane that lead from the station, listening to the snorting noise of the engine and the rickety rack of the compartments as the train began to gather speed. Smoke billowed in front of her as she paused to look at the gates which now would remain open until the next train made its appearance. It was hard to believe that it was such a long time ago when her father had operated those levers in that box up the wooden steps. Which when she was a child had likened them in her mind as a stairway to the stars. Her father's place of work had been such a long way up to a little girl who was never allowed to enter his domain. She could only watch from safety beyond the station gate and that only if her brother was with her. Now here she was, Sister Moscrop, with her own ward in a hospital and responsible for her team of nurses and her patients of course, nearly thirty two years old and unmarried.

Of course, she couldn't be married and be a Ward Sister, she thought to herself as she wandered along, passing Applecroft House and arriving at Fox Hill Terrace, both places that she remembered from her childhood years. Although she would give it all up in a heartbeat, if she could find a loving husband as her friend, Betty had. It had been such a shock when Sam had lost his life at a place called the Somme. He had volunteered to join the Cumbrian regiment at the beginning of the war, leaving Betty to bring up a two year old girl and a little boy who was approaching five. Of course they were bigger now and went to the village school where it appeared they were bright pupils, but Betty had never looked at another man, so they didn't have a stepfather. Instead she made a living as a dressmaker and was in demand from the gentry who lived in Colbrook, but also as far away as Whitehaven too.

Ada had given her friend her mother's Singer sewing machine, once the house was up for sale and the furniture had been sold at knock down prices to the locals. It had made Betty's dressmaking business a lot easier and improved her skills as well. According to her letters, which Ada received on a regular basis at the Nurses Home, she had recently been asked to make a wedding dress for one of the daughters of a well-to-do family near Ravenglass.

"Aunty Ada!". The front door of the cottage at the end of the terrace was opened by Janet, a dark curly haired youngster, aged ten, who was dressed in an ankle length blue cotton nightdress and a blue woollen dressing gown. "We thought you weren't coming. Mother said you might have missed the train at Whitehaven as it was getting late." She put her arms around Ada's waist and gave her a hug.

Sidney, her elder brother, an older version of his sister in looks, but with short dark curls who was standing behind her in the narrow hallway, was more reticent. "Hello, Aunt Ada," he said, putting his hand out to shake hers formally. "I did suggest to Mother that we walked down to the station to meet you, but it was getting close to Janet's bed time."

"Well, I'm here now," Ada said briskly, walking into the hall and shutting the door behind her, as she knew she would be letting out the warm air from the kitchen range. "Where's your mother? Sewing as usual?"

"I'm up here in my sewing room." Betty came to stand on the landing. Smiling, she put her hands together in a form of supplication or prayer and struck a pose as if she was dealing with someone from the upper classes. "Betty Marmaduke at your disposal Madam. How can I help you this fine evening? Will it be a light cape for the summer or an evening dress for a charity do?" She ran down the stairs with a delighted smile on her face and hugged Ada.

"You never change, do you," Ada said giggling, as Betty pinched her arm playfully, then sailed off into the kitchen. "Get kettle on Missis, I'm dying fer a brew!"

Ada could see where the children had got their curls from. Betty had always had unruly hair as a child and her parents had insisted that she grew it long, so it had always looked like a cloud when she had taken it out of the plaits she usually wore. Now she wore it short to just below her ears and tried to temper the curls with a few hair grips. Her dress was simple, plain grey and long sleeved, with a white collar and the hem was just below the calf and not knee length which had become fashionable.

"I see you've treated yourself to a new coat since I last saw you," was her comment, as Ada and the children followed her into the large kitchen. " Blackburn the height of fashionability is it now?"

"Just one off the peg," smiled Ada. "Got to keep up with these young girls in the latest modes if I'm to find myself a handsome suitor." She wouldn't mention Mr. McAuley taking her to tea at the cafe just yet. Her friend would have her married and expecting a baby within a year, if she had anything to do with it.

"The children have grown," she said fondly, as Janet waited to take her coat and Sidney settled himself down at the kitchen table where he had been reading a book. "Gosh Sidney, last time I saw you, you were as big as I am, but now you are taller by at least four inches. And Janet, you've lost your puppy fat, you're going to be a very elegant young lady."

Both children blushed, as they were unused to being made a much of. As far as they were concerned, they were just village children and their Aunt Ada was from a different world. She was a boss in a big hospital, a long way away on a train. They had only been as far as Whitehaven, when their mother did the purchasing of her sewing materials at the drapers there.

"Tell your Aunt Ada the news, Sidney," said Betty, as she placed the big black kettle on the top of the cooking range, then busied herself with making Ada a cup of tea.

"Oh, what's that Sidney?" asked Ada, knowing it must be important for Sidney to tell her or Betty would have mentioned it in her last letter.

"I'm to be taken on as an apprentice car mechanic in Workington," Sidney replied, trying to stifle the pride he was hearing in his voice as he said it, because he didn't like to be thought a show off.

"Uncle Martin has opened a garage there and thought with me coming up to fifteen in the summer, I might like to have a crack at it. With Dad being a farm machinery mechanic, he reckons fixing cars might be just something I could be good at."

"I'm sure you'll take to it like a duck to water. You've always liked making things and fixing stuff for your mother. I remember her telling me you always liked to help her oil the Singer when you were a little boy."

"Aye, he's always been a good helper," said Betty. "Both of

them are. Janet made this fruit cake I'm bringing over and it's as good as any that I could make. I'll miss Sidney though. He'll be lodging with Martin and Ellie, as it would be too expensive, not to mention tiring, to go on the omnibus each day."

"Uncle Martin says I'll get a day off on a Sunday, so I can come over on the train for my dinner after you and Janet have been to church." Ada could hear how happy Sidney sounded and she was pleased, as his father's death had hit the young boy hard.

"I've got you a pie in the warming oven," said Betty, as she brought over a plate with slices of cake on, then a tray with an earthenware teapot and cups, saucers and plates. " But first I thought you might like to try a slice of Janet's cake before she goes to bed. She's been mithering that she stay up to greet you."

"Well, it tastes wonderful," said Ada, after she had swallowed a bite. "Light and airy. You'll make someone a good wife one day."

"Oh no, Aunt Ada, I'm not going to be a wife," said Janet, shaking her head after blushing because of Ada's praise. "I'm going to do something with my life first, like you have. I might be a teacher, or even a doctor or I might go travelling to Italy or France."

"She's been listening to her cousin who's off to teacher training college in Ambleside. Mary's a bit of a blue stocking and has told Janet that there's a world out there just waiting for exploration. She's been reading about these suffragettes in Liverpool and Manchester. Anyway, off you go to bed young lady. You got your wish. Aunt Ada has had some of your cake and she'll still be here in the morning, so perhaps we can all attend St. Paul's together and you can go to Sunday school."

"So what have those nurses of yours been up to lately? Betty asked, once Janet had trailed reluctantly off to bed and Sidney had taken himself off to his room to continue reading about the latest cars and their engines and the two friends had made themselves comfortable on two wing armchairs. "Last time you were here you were telling me about someone called Mary, who was a thorn in your flesh and never got to work on time."

"Not much difference there, although she's getting married soon and will be disappearing to God knows where. No, on the whole they're a good team of women and they help me to run the ward as it should be."

"And?"

"And?"

"And why are you looking so dreamy all the time? You've lost your brisk no nonsense attitude."

"I'm on my holidays. I'm unwinding. It isn't easy being Sister Starchy Knickers, as I know the nurses call me."

"Do they?" Betty started to giggle. "I wish they'd known you then when you were younger, you weren't a Starchy Knickers then."

"I was a good girl, Betty! Not like you, who I caught kissing Freddie Saunders behind the Village Hall."

"Oh, don't mention him. I think he must have kissed most of the girls in Colbrook. No, when we were young you didn't have the weight of the world upon your shoulders, which you must have now after all the years you've been nursing. Is it a man? It must be! You're not usually so dreamy."

"I'm tired Betty. It's been a long day…oh go on then. I think I may be about to form an attachment with a man called Daniel. I shouldn't do, because he's an ex-patient, but I bumped into him when I was shopping in Blackburn and he took me to a cafe for a cup of tea."

"Oh, you've gone all red, Ada. Even in this lamp light I can see. Do tell me more, won't you. Oh, this is exciting, Ada Moscrop in love."

"Not in love Betty, it's early days yet. He asked if I would go to the cinema with him one evening and I'm to leave a note with Alf, the porter, at the front door of the hospital to tell him when I'm free. Alf drinks in the Bay Mare, where Daniel often visits with his job."

"His job? He's not a bit of a drinker by any chance then?" Betty was frowning at the thought of her best friend taking up with a man who liked to drink alcohol. Both had parents who had been temperate over the years.

"No…he's an Area Manager for a local brewery. It's his job to visit various hostelries and check things over. I suppose though he would do a bit of sampling. He came into hospital with a broken foot, because a beer barrel rolled onto it."

"Oh dear," Betty couldn't help smiling at the thought. "It sounds as if he'll have to be careful in that kind of job. What's he like then? Good looking? As handsome as my Sam was?"

"No, not as handsome as Sam was, Betty and not as heroic, as I never heard of any mention of the war when he was my patient. Usually I hear the patients' chitchat when they get together for their smokes and he never said what regiment he served in. Thinking about it though, he does have a slight Irish accent, so perhaps he didn't go to the Front."

"Perhaps he was a conchie then. You'd do well to steer clear of him if that's the case."

"Let's change the subject, Betty." Ada could see the tears welling up in her friend's eyes, as they were apt to do still when she remembered her beloved husband. "Are we going to make Tuesday a day out in Whitehaven for my birthday, or have you got something else planned?"

The two women nattered late into the night as they had a lot of catching up to do and Ada found she was intrigued with what a local gossip had told Betty, when she had heard that Ada was to arrive for her annual visit. Old Mrs. Ploughman who had lived in the village forever and knew every family and their history, had said that there was more to Wilfred Moscrop than met the eye and there was skeletons in his cupboard as far as she was concerned. Ada dismissed her words as tittle tattle, but one day, she promised herself, she would travel up to this place called Carlisle, where her father had come from and see what she could find about his family.

Chapter Four

Daniel felt restless. It was Easter Sunday. The public houses had limited hours and so the town was quiet. Most people had been to Mass or to Matins if they were Protestants and families would be gathering at home for their Sunday lunch.

His landlady, Mrs. Dewsbury, a kindly woman who rented out three of her bedrooms to himself and two other men who worked in the area, had invited them all to partake of a roast dinner that she had prepared for the festive occasion, as many people of that time had fasted during Lent. Not that Daniel was feeling festive. Without his parents he was feeling glum and was beginning to miss them.

It wasn't usually so. He only seemed to miss his family if it was Christmas or like that day, the Easter holiday. Most times he was so absorbed with his work that he didn't have time to think of them and after a few pints of Guinness in his local hostelry each night, he usually fell into a dreamless sleep. Sundays, his day of rest, when all public houses were shut because of the religious mantra, "thou shalt not work on the Sabbath day", was usually spent writing up his notes for the perusal of his boss on Monday morning, but these were done. It had been an easy week, with Maunday Thursday and Good Friday giving a shortened week to the workers, there was nothing much to report about the hostelries which belonged to Duttons in the town and its surrounds.

Perhaps a walk after lunch. Perhaps a brisk walk around the lake at Queen's Park and he'd ask Mrs. Dewsbury if she had any stale bread that he could feed the swans with. He and Winnie, used to feed the ducks if he took her for a walk along the Grand Canal, but he didn't want to think about Winnie. Winnie was in his past and he was sick to his soul that he couldn't see her. His father had seen to that when he had sent him away.

Daniel lay on his bed and let his thoughts roam to the reasons he was there in Blackburn and not sitting down to Easter lunch at his family home in the county of Westmeath.

There were three boys and two girls belonging to the McAuley family and Daniel was the youngest of the boys. Before 1916 when a group of the Irish Volunteers took over the General Post office and Padraic Pearse announced his famous proclamation, he and his brothers, like most young men of their time, were enthused by a cause to fight for and had joined the Irish Republic Brotherhood. To Daniel, who was rather easily led by his two older and tougher brothers, joining this militant group was no more than flying a flag for patriotism. It meant taking a stand for a better deal for the Irish, although later he found that to be a member of the Brotherhood meant taking on a subversive role. Meetings were held in secret. Guns were being bought from foreign governments who had an interest in Ireland freeing itself from British rule and the members had to learn to defend themselves, should they be called upon to fight for the Republican cause.

Daniel suddenly found he had no stomach for it, especially when he was called upon to learn to handle a gun. But once a member always a member, although providentially he was safely back at home on the day of the Easter Rising in Dublin. It was the end of Lent and the family had cause for celebration. There was a wedding to be held in St. James' Church the following week and everyone had to get ready to attend.

He had made the mistake of falling in love with an auburn haired girl called Connie McKenzie. Well, he had supposed it had been love, when she had allowed him to take liberties with her one night when he was walking her home from a hooley. He had known her for years. She and his sister had gone to the same convent and the boys had gone to the Catholic school nearby, but they had lost touch for a while, when Connie became employed as a skivvy by a well to do family locally.

Around the age of fourteen, when the onset of his testosterone caused him to look at girls in a sexual way, he had been attracted to Connie because of her pretty face and cat like green eyes. Though it wasn't until a few months before his 21st birthday, after working hard to learn the way of things in their family brewery, that he had decided to ask her out. Connie's family lived on the main road into the village and he often saw her when they all attended Mass at weekends. But, as he recalled to himself bitterly, unknown to himself, or to Bridie and the McAuley family, she must have been secretly seeing a married bloke, although she had never mentioned his name to anyone.

And that had been it, thought Daniel wryly. *She had led him to the altar and got him hook, line and sinker, until a female older member of the family pointed out that babies usually took nine months to arrive after a wedding, not six. But at least the ceremony had saved him and his brothers, from possible execution in Kilmainham Gaol if they too had holed themselves up in the General Post Office as many had done. And the good thing to have come out of Connie's fornication was that he had fallen in love with Winnie, Connie's little girl.*

He opened his bedroom window, then took out a cigarette from his packet of Senior Service. His marriage was not one that had been made in heaven and Connie had never confessed her infidelity to him, but rumour had it that when she found out that she was expecting, she had to find herself a gullible man. And he had been gullible. He had never touched her until that night she had lured him behind Kenny's warehouse, after they had gone to celebrate his birthday in Mullingar and he'd been quite surprised when she said a few weeks later that he had got her with child.

In a small village between Kilbeggan and Mullingar, where everyone knew everyone, their way of life in a Catholic community dictated that a couple should pay for their sins and being the easy going innocent that he was then, he had no option but to pay for them.

"Dinner's ready, Mr. McAuley." Mrs. Dewsbury's voice carried up the staircase and broke into his thoughts, as he stubbed out the fag end in the glass ashtray that sat on the dressing table. He checked his hair and newly trimmed moustache in the mirror, pulled down his pinstriped waistcoat into a more comfortable position over his pristine white shirt, then went downstairs to join the others in the dining room.

"Ah, Mr. McAuley, how are you this fine Easter day? I heard you up and about early this morning. Where you on your way to Mass at the Sacred Heart?"

"I was so Mrs. Dewsbury," Daniel acknowledged, " the place was crammed to the rafters as usual. Full of us Paddy's praying for God to continue bringing peace and harmony to the world." He said it with a jocular sound to his voice, as the two other occupants at the table had never said what religion they were and from the Lancashire accents they spoke with, they were not Irish.

"So they should," said the older man called Mr. Livesey, who was sitting at the head of the long mahogany table which was covered with a white, lacy cloth and laid with good crockery and cutlery. Mr. Livesey was a dour man with greying hair, whose job was to visit firms in the area and promote the advantages of the road haulier business, as opposed to moving goods by train. "I read in the paper that there was mayhem on the streets of Dublin, even after the Easter Rising was stopped in its tracks. There was looting in the shops, shootings and buildings being blown up and so they brought in an Emergency Powers Bill to stop the perpetrators."

"Hear, hear," said the other lodger, a slightly effeminate gentleman who worked in the men's section of a local department store for a living and used his arms to punctuate any sentences that he spoke. "The Irish are a whinging nation, always looking to blame the British if they can. If it wasn't for us…"

"Now, now, that's enough if you don't mind, Mr. Preedy." Mrs. Dewsbury, a lapsed Catholic after becoming a widow in the war, was quick to stop a heated discussion in its tracks as she came through with a joint of roast beef, surrounded by crispy looking potatoes on a platter. Especially when she saw that Mr. McAuley was looking rather aggrieved. "I don't like politics being brought into this house as I've told you before. Now, Mr. Livesey, would you care to carve the beef and Mr. Preedy, hand round the potatoes."

But it was true what Mr. Livesey had said, thought Daniel, as he walked around the lake later, carrying a wrap of bread that Mrs. Dewsbury had donated. According to his father who sent him letters on a regular basis, the British government had raised a temporary army to assist the Royal Irish Constabulary. Drawing from the numbers of British Army veterans who were unemployed after the war was over, they had been recruited to seek out suspected members of the Irish Republic Army and in 1920, thirteen civilians had been shot dead in Croke Park, after an auxiliary unit had been raised to swell the military's numbers. There were incidents of police brutality and a young man called Kevin Barry, only eighteen years of age, had been hung in Mountjoy Jail for being involved in the deaths of three British soldiers. Whilst the property belonging to I.R.A suspects was being burnt and men were tortured into informing on their comrades, many people, Daniel's brothers included, escaped for a new life abroad.

Just as he had. His father, having many contacts through his line of business, had been warned that retribution was on its way for anyone who had been connected with the Brotherhood. All his sons had been sympathetic to the cause, although they hadn't broadcast it. As young men they had been excited to think that they might just help to bring about freedom from oppression for their homeland by getting involved. They spent hours drilling and parading in the grounds of an old ruined house that had been

30

abandoned by the gentry a century before and listened to the tales of the Famine and long dead Irish heroes from an elderly man, who visited them from time to time.

But once married with a few children between them and with tales beginning to come in thick and fast about the vengeance being meted out to those who had belonged to any of the dissident organisations, it had been during a family conference that the decision had been made for measures to be taken to protect their kith and kin. Daniel's father, not a wealthy man by any means, as his brewery had to compete with the larger ones in Dublin, was able to provide sufficient funds to send his sons and their families out of harm's way. Daniel chose to travel to Blackburn, where his Uncle Dickie, a distant relative, had secured him a providential job and his elder brothers had joined a branch of the McAuley clan in Chicago.

And it had been a good move for him, he thought, as he watched the swans and little ducks circling around the lumps of bread on the water and squirrels awoken from their hibernation chasing up the tree trunks and birds pecking on the left over bread crumbs and he certainly didn't miss his wife. She was adequately provided for, as he sent her a monthly banker's draft and she lived with Winnie in one of the terraced cottages that had been built on brewery property.

Connie hadn't raised any objections, when he told her of his intention to take up the job as an Area Manager for an English brewery, as their marriage had been over as soon as the rumours had begun, but at least her child had been born in wedlock. It was just Winnie that Daniel pined for. A pretty little three year old with red hair, with an infectious chuckle when he left her and would probably be an adult when he returned.

It hit him, as he walked along King William Street and passed the clock tower where he checked his fob watch to see if it was keeping good time, that pursuing Sister Moscrop wasn't such a bad idea. He'd have a bit of female company, someone to go to the pictures with, perhaps a couple of waltzes around the dance hall, though he wouldn't take her to watch Blackburn Rovers at Ewood Park. He didn't think that she would enjoy a football match like men did, probably the reading of a good book was more her style. She'd be back to work after the Easter holidays and he'd leave her a note with Alf.

Chapter Five

The air was still warm as two nurses, having finished their shifts for that day, walked arm in arm along the road outside the Infirmary. Nurse Blakely and her friend, Nurse Appleby, who worked on the Children's Ward, had changed out of their uniforms into lightweight frocks and cardigans and were on their way back to their respective homes, both feeling glad to be away from the cloying atmosphere of their hospital wards. Nurse Appleby was gossiping. She had heard a juicy bit of information that she couldn't wait to pass on.

"I mean, when our Rita told me that a friend of hers saw them together in the cafe she works at, I couldn't believe it! She must be over thirty if she's a day. She's far too old to be getting a fellow and especially as they call her Miss Starchy Knickers, or so I've heard. Well, that's what Joan calls her, yer know the woman who's our auxiliary on Men's Ward?"

"Probably because Joan's a bit slapdash and Sister Moscrop is always on her back." Nurse Blakely had always tried to model herself on her superior, as she admired her professionalism and dispassionate ways.

"Our Rita said that the bloke she was with was on your ward with a broken foot a few months ago. Isn't there some rule somewhere that nurses aren't allowed to hobnob with the patients?"

"Oh, who was that?" Nurse Blakely was all ears now, although she still didn't believe that Sister Moscrop was associating herself with a former patient. They had probably run into each other, if they were both popping in for a cup of tea after shopping in town.

"Someone called Daniel McAuley, I believe his name was. She said he was an Irish bloke who worked at the brewery."

"Ah yes, I remember him. A good looking man, who I seemed to think had a bit of a roving eye when he was a patient with us. I can't believe she'd be doing more than passing the time of day with him."

"Well, we'll see, won't we? Anyway, let's go to mine and see if Mam's got a bit of supper. I don't know about you, but I'm starving."

Ada hummed to herself, as she left the Nurses Home that evening to walk into town. This was her second date with Daniel since she had got back from Colbrook just after Easter. She supposed she could call it a date, as the young ones now had seemed to stop calling seeing a man "stepping out together" or "walking out". Certainly it was a date, because he had asked if she would be free at all this weekend, after he had taken her to the Exchange Picture Hall last Saturday night, but she didn't think they were "courting", which was another phrase that now seemed in vogue.

What a palaver it all seemed to be anyhow. She liked him and she presumed he liked her and when his note had arrived at the porter's lodge asking if they could meet and go to the pictures together, it was just a matter of penning a reply with her acceptance. All this lovey-dovey stuff and going on dates, which she had heard from the females she worked with, was the result of reading modern women's magazines in her opinion. A liberated woman such as she was, dependent on no one but herself for her daily bread, shouldn't put too much store by the words that flowed from a man's mouth, who might have dubious intentions. Until she got to know Mr. McAuley better, her heart would not be given willy-nilly, even if her sleeping hours were filled with dreams of marrying somebody like him. In those dreams she could clearly see her future with Mr. McAuley. They would settle down together in a small cottage in the countryside. They would keep chickens and she would tend a vegetable plot, just like her mother had. She would have two children, a handsome boy and a pretty girl and they would be called Harold and Grace and she'd be as happy as Betty had been, when she had been married to poor Sam.

She wondered had she overdressed herself on this occasion. Mr. McAuley was taking her to a dance hall and what to wear had taken hours of deliberation, as she had never been to one before. Even as she had stalked the ward that day, taking temperatures, smoothing a pain racked brow or checking that the nurses had done their job properly, she pondered on the frock she had chosen for such an evening. It was a calf length beaded lacy confection, over a lilac satin under-dress, with little sleeves and a built in cape to cover her shoulders. She would wear it with a pair of white T' bar shoes, along with a little gauze skull cap to cover her hair, which she would twist into a bun in the nape of her neck. She had bought the outfit at a place called Maria Modes and it had cost her a lot of money from her savings in the District Bank. She would carry a matching clutch bag and around her neck was a rope of pearls that she had long ago treated herself to for her twenty first birthday.

His face said it all when he saw her. He looked incredulous when he saw that the person before him was Sister Moscrop, or Ada that he had begun to call her in his mind. She was without a scrap of makeup, but her eyes were lit up with a brightness that he hadn't witnessed before.

"Too much? Over the top for a local dance hall?" Ada was taken aback to see him looking dumbstruck.

"Err…well no, you look so different." Daniel could hear himself stuttering. "In a nice way?" Ada asked mockingly. "Or have I got above myself?"

"Er, no, but you don't think I'll be taking you to a lowly dance hall, dressed so beautifully that I wouldn't even get a waltz there'd be so many men wanting to ask you. We'll go along to the Cumbrian Hotel and have something to eat there."

"The Cumbrian?" Ada had heard only the nobs and the well to do could afford to go there. "The Cumbrian." Daniel nodded and linked her with his arm.

As Ada suspected, the hotel, situated just a short walk from the town centre, was furnished to attract the wealthy through their portals, not mere mortals such as themselves. She stifled a gasp as they entered the luxurious foyer, where crystal chandeliers hung down from the ceiling and marble shiny tiles led up to the gilt trimmed reception desk ahead of them. A uniformed man had leapt forward initially to retrieve their baggage from them, only to raise his arm in a respectful salute when he saw that they were not carrying any. Daniel left her whilst he spoke to the man on the reception desk, then beckoned her to follow him. It seemed that he had been given a table in the dining room, as once through the door, the head waiter attired in a black jacket over a white shirt and a black dicky bow and wearing pinstriped trousers, clicked his fingers to an underling to take Daniel's coat. It was then that Ada saw he had also taken pains to dress himself up, in a black evening suit. He was a smart fellow, Ada decided, not sure now whether this was a set up and Daniel perhaps had no intention of taking her to the dance hall, but knew that if he had suggested they would eat at an expensive hotel she would have baulked at it. Although perhaps the wage of an Area Manager was more than a Nursing Sister earned.

They were shown to a table covered in a pristine white tablecloth, where mahogany dining chairs were covered in a deep red velvet. It was set for two, with sparkling clean silver cutlery and various shaped glasses for drinking from. Around the large room, where a small band was playing a piece of music from Elgar, there were elegant gilded mirrors and a pale peach silk canopy draped in folds and covering the entire ceiling. The carpet was a swirl of orange and green plushness and Ada felt as if she was sinking as she walked upon it. She could feel a certain ambience as they were seated, as the diners spoke in lowered tones which befitted the atmosphere.

"Well lad," she said, in a broad Lancashire dialect, which she decided to put on to break up the tenseness between them, whilst the waiter went to fetch the bottle of wine that Daniel had ordered. "Yer dost know 'ow to treat a lass, bringin' her to a place such as this. No pie and peas 'ull do fer this fair maiden." He laughed when he heard her taking the mickey, she was full of surprises this Ada Moscrop. It surprised him that this normally cool, unflappable Nursing Sister, whom he had the privilege of meeting through adversity, that is, his broken foot, had made such an impression upon him. He hadn't been looking for the company of another woman, as he was still bitter about what Connie had done. She had tied him down forever by forcing him to the altar like she had.

"Nothing's too good for thee lass and ye should know it." Then he laughed again, as he had sounded more Irish than Lancashire.

"Would Sir like to look at the menu?" The wine waiter was hovering waiting for Daniel to try the sample of a French burgundy he had poured into the wine glass.

"Sorry, yes…thank you. Ada, would you like the waiter to pour you a small glass of burgundy? It is supposed to aid the digestion, or so they say. Leave the bottle, would you waiter, I have had this label before."

"I'm not used to drinking wine," Ada confided, as she took a little sip, then wrinkled her nose at the taste of it. "My parents were teetotal, which I think I have mentioned before."

"Whilst me and my brothers' were apprenticed to the brewery from an early age."

"Yes, you said last week that your father is a brewer and you came over to Blackburn to gain experience in a larger concern. Are you here for a specific length of time, or until you think you have absorbed it all?" She hoped that he would say the latter, as she was beginning to grow quite fond of Daniel McAuley. In some way he reminded her of Charles, her brother, although she didn't know why. Charles was quite slight, dainty even and fair haired, whereas Daniel was stocky, well built and dark haired and a little bit shorter than her. Perhaps it was because both men were gentlemen, with an inherent kindness that tugged at her heart.

"I am not sure of the future Ada," he said, with a look of tenderness, that caused her heart to beat a little faster as he spoke. "I feel that I am as free as a bird in my occupation. I answer to no one, other than the man who has the job of overseeing my endeavors. At home in Ireland, I feel that I carry the weight of the world on my shoulders, whilst trying to find a way of increasing the profits for my father's brewery. Of course I miss my family. I miss them at special times, like Christmas and Easter."

"But surely you could catch a ferry from Liverpool or Heysham and spend your holidays with them, like I just spent some time with Betty, my friend."

"Ah, would it be so," he could only say and was grateful when the menu arrived.

They dined on roast chicken, crispy potatoes and helped themselves from dishes of delicious tasting vegetables. It was stolid fare, which was expected of a northern hotel. Their pudding was a mouthwatering apple pie and custard and then came coffee, which Daniel drank with a small measure of brandy and Ada drank with milk.

It was enough to satisfy and then some and were startled, when the hovering waiter asked them would they like to adjourn to the lounge where more drinks could be ordered from the Bar.

"Or we could dance," said Daniel, as they passed the quartet whilst following the waiter and he noticed there was a small area set aside for dancing. And they did so later, fitting perfectly into each other's arms as they waltzed.

It was when he walked her home, linking her arm through his and breathing in the smell of her, a light scent of roses and that newness of material before its had a wash, that he realised Ada would have been the one he had chosen had he been looking for a wife and not married to Connie. She would have been perfect for him. A no nonsense kind of female, practical, sensible, with a sense of humour once you got to know her and she had melted in his arms when they had danced together that evening.

"Will you be free next weekend?" he asked. " I thought maybe a visit to the Blackburn Public Hall. There is usually a musical concert on that we could listen to."

"Daniel." Ada stopped suddenly and turned to face him. "Daniel. I have to say that it is all well and good you taking me here and thither and I've enjoyed it. But it must be costing you a fortune. I've no idea how much an area manager for a brewery gets paid, but I am sure it won't be a fortune. What I am saying is, that I earn a good wage, enough to get by on anyway and I think if we are going to continue seeing each other you must let me pay my share." She stared at him anxiously after she had spoken, wondering if he would be angry at her remarks.

Instead, he suddenly took her by the hand and slowly led her to sit on the park wall, which they were passing at the time. Then as they sat, he kissed her on the cheek and then began to smile.

"Sister Moscrop, do yer know what yer doing to me? From the moment I saw yer, from the moment yer gazed upon me and asked about the level of pain I was havin' as they wheeled me into the Men's Ward, my heart was yours. I was lost. How could I ever get a woman like yourself to even look at me and here you are, offering to pay yer share towards the outings which I consider to be a dream that I'm fulfilling. A wonderful dream when I get to take yer into my arms, like I got to do this evening on the dance floor."

Ada suddenly laughed and pushed him away playfully, as he had got so close she could smell the brandy on his breath. "Give over, Daniel, you're codding me. It must have been the alcohol you've been drinking this evening, or you have your fill of Irish charm."

"No, Ada, it isn't either and do yer know, tonight you've started calling me Daniel instead of Mr. McAuley? That tells me that you are beginning to have some feelings for me. Oh Ada, will yer marry me?"

She looked at him in shock! And he in turn felt shocked that he'd asked her. He'd got carried away, swept along by the intimacy of the evening; the relaxation of her role as a formidable nursing sister and if he was honest, his liberal intake of alcohol.

But to Ada's mind, as she began to take in his sudden offer of marriage, she saw that this was her chance to become a wife, a mother, the owner of a home with a vegetable plot and some chickens. So naturally she said that she would!

She quickly kissed him on the cheek, as she would her brother, then they both walked together in a daze, but arm in arm back to the Nursing Home.

Chapter Six

He supposed he could just make a run for it. Hop on a ferry, hole up in his father's brewery, make his peace with Connie and have little Winnie back in his life, but would it really matter in the scheme of things if he repeated those vows of intention to another? Nobody here would know of his marriage to Connie and perhaps Ada could get a nursing job in another town and they could move into a little house there. He thought long and hard, whilst his working hours took him around the hostelries of Blackburn and his nights were spent worrying.

There was only one other person, besides his close family, who knew that he was married and that was his Uncle Dickie, who was friends with Mr. Fletcher, his immediate superior. But Uncle Dickie lived over in Dublin so he would never know. Perhaps they could have a small and informal ceremony, not at the Sacred Heart, but somewhere outside Blackburn and no one from the brewery would be invited to come. He would pretend he'd gone back to Ireland for a week or so.

He was dreading seeing Ada at the weekend. She'd be full of wedding plans and her thoughts would be full of orange blossom, just like Connie's once had been.

Oh what a tangled web we weave when we first set out to deceive.

On the other side of town, Ada had been in a whirl of excitement, which had to be contained during her working hours, as after all, she wasn't going to be a young and blushing bride like some. To her, this forthcoming marriage was a practical solution to a dream that she had long hoped would be fulfilled before she was too old to have children. Though that didn't mean that she didn't have her tummy turning over when she thought of Daniel. Sharing her life, sharing his bed and doing all the things that her parents had done together. To her mind her parents had been a proper married couple; being there for each other in times of hardship or crisis and even in death, which they couldn't overcome. But she had decided to put her foot down regarding the ceremony. Being Irish, he was probably Roman Catholic. Although they had never discussed their beliefs in a Divine Creator, he probably was and there was no way she was turning Catholic for him. A marriage in the Registry Office was good enough for her and she would only ask Betty and her children to the ceremony. Janet could be a bridesmaid and… oh, who could she ask to give her away, or wasn't that necessary at a Registry Office? She'd tell Daniel of her plans on Saturday. He was taking her to a variety show at the Exchange Theatre, but they had agreed that afterwards they would make their wedding plans.

It was as Daniel was walking along the corridor to his office on the Friday morning, that Freda, Mr. Fletcher's assistant called to him. She was an efficient young woman, not a fluffy one. She was small and neat in the black outfit she wore and on a couple of occasions had intimated to Daniel that she would like to be more than just a colleague to him. Her face was a wreath of smiles as she stood in the office doorway.

"Mr. Fletcher has got a surprise for you, Daniel," she said, knowing what the surprise would be as her boss had told her, but acting all mysteriously. "He asked for me to let you know that he wants to see you in the yard at ten thirty. Would you like me to make you a cup of tea? I could bring you one and then if you have any notes for me to type up for Mr. Fletcher, you could pass them over to me."

"Thank you, Freda," Daniel said, not even acknowledging that his boss had a surprise for him, as his head was still whirling around with what he was going to say to Ada at the weekend. Mr. Fletcher was probably going to ask him to have a look at one of the new lorries that the firm had begun to replace the traditional horse and cart with and at the moment Daniel had more important things on his mind.

"You'll be able to go to Bolton or even over to Clitheroe," Freda said, as she placed a china cup and saucer on his desk, then took the slim wad of hand written notes he held out to her. "I wonder if you will have to leave it here at night."

"What are you talking about, Freda?" Daniel said irritably. "I've enough on me plate at the moment without you wittering on."

"You'll see soon enough," she said, not taking offence at his words spoken scathingly. "Anyroad, you'll be able to hear the noise of it soon enough."

Sure enough at ten thirty, a lorry with its cargo covered with a large tarpaulin chugged into the yard. Then a small crowd of brewery workers, probably just beginning their tea break, stood in a group and looking on with expectancy, waited for the lorry to unload.

"Mr. McAuley, Daniel. It's here, come with me, we'll go into the yard together!" Freda stood in his office doorway, urging him to accompany her.

"Ah, Daniel, just the man," said Mr. Fletcher, a silver haired, portly man, as he saw his Area Manager hurrying out of the building along with Freda. Whilst down the ramp that the driver had created with a large piece of corrugated iron, came a black and yellow Austin 7, straight into the care of a couple of ex-army mechanics who were looking at the vehicle in awe.

"Isn't it tiny, pint sized and will yer look at those leather seats? Nothing like the monsters we worked on at the Front, nor the coaches." One of the men in his navy overalls, couldn't wait to touch it and ran a loving hand over the shiny paint work.

"But can you get it going?" Mr. Fletcher asked. He had

approached a local business who was just beginning to operate a coach company, to send a couple of their men to oversee the brewery's newest acquisition.

"If it's got a starting handle, I'm sure we can and we've even brought along a can of petrol, though I see you've got a pump."

"Then in you get, Daniel McAuley. Let's see what stuff yer made of. Let's see you drive it round the yard."

And to Daniel's pleasure, he was able to do so. Although his mouth was dry and his heart was pounding, he followed the mechanic's instructions. The pedals were given a name and the reason for them. He found out what the metal stick near the steering wheel was used for and something called a choke and after a couple of judders and jumps, he shot away from them all. To cheers and air punching from his audience, he managed a three point turn and brought the vehicle back to a standstill before them.

"Well done Daniel, a natural, though I think you must have done this before." Mr. Fletcher was delighted. "Now that our company is beginning to acquire one or two of the other smaller breweries in the area, we need someone who is willing to travel around their tied houses too. Park the car by the bottling shed and then come in to the office, will you?"

A car! A car of his own. Well, a car he had to leave locked up in the yard at night for safety reasons. Although Mr. Fletcher had said that the only reason it was to be left in the yard at night was because of the many wazzicks in the town, it might get damaged if he parked it in the street. He would be allowed, with permission, to use the car for leisure pursuits, but then he would have to fill the petrol tank at his own expense. Daniel would have loved to drive it to the Nurses Home and given Ada a surprise on Saturday, but the risk of having it scraped or scratched wasn't worth it.

Ada dressed this time in a dark blue suit. It had a long sleeved fitted jacket and a kick pleat in the calf length skirt. Her shoes were black patent leather with a T' bar strap and she had twisted her hair into a stylish bun, which she wore under a small brimmed dark blue hat.

She felt nervous. She had suddenly begun to doubt Daniel's intention. Why would he want to marry her anyway? She wasn't a beauty, wasn't a loving kind of person who would hang on his every word and make him feel good. She was practical, forthright and spoke her mind and once he got to know her, it might cause all sorts of rows if she wasn't allowed her own way. She wondered if she should tell him that, as he had only known her as a strict no nonsense nursing sister, but she wasn't going to change a thing about herself for him.

"Change of plan," he said, kissing her briefly on the cheek, after they had met up outside the theatre, where they had intended to watch a Vaudeville Show. "I think that we have much to discuss, me darlin' and I don't know about you, but I fancy a run out into the country."

"Well, you're not getting me on an omnibus at this time of night, Daniel." Ada sounded indignant. "It'll be dark in an hour." She had been looking forward to watching the variety show, as it had got a good review in the Blackburn Times.

"Ah, but we're not going on an omnibus," he said, tapping the side of his nose. "Come with me, me darlin', your carriage awaits yer." He gripped her hand, then walked her along the street, until they turned a corner and lo and behold, a puzzled Ada saw a small black and yellow motor car parked on the road outside a fish and chip shop. She noticed that it had a registration plate, which said ACB 820 and Daniel took a key from his pocket and unlocked the passenger door. "Can't be too careful," he said, a little pompously, noticing the glances of envy from the people who were standing in the queue outside the chip shop. Then with a flourish, he beckoned to Ada to be seated within, before he busied himself with the starting handle.

As the engine burst into life, he heard an uncertain clapping from one or two of the men in his audience. Whether it was sarcastic or not, he didn't care, he felt so happy, although his happiness was tempered. Mr. Fletcher hadn't sanctioned the use of the car.

Ada meanwhile, was staring in awe and with a little spasm of fear at the dashboard. It had a leather trim and a clock, which she didn't know was a speedometer and shiny things on the floor that looked like pedals and something that looked like a stick. Then Daniel jumped into the driver's seat, pulled out the valve that controlled the inflow of air and gripped the leather trimmed steering wheel. She began to feel relief that whatever it was under the hinged cover in front of her hadn't caught fire and Daniel appeared to know what he was doing, once he had set off along the road.

There was a bit of a judder, as the wheels bumped over the cobbles and some grating noises from the gears from time to time as the car began to increase in speed, but after a while she could feel herself relaxing, so freed her hands from the front of her seat, which she had been gripping it tightly.

"How are yer feelin'?" Daniel asked, acknowledging that he had probably given her a bit of a fright, as it was possible she had never been in a car before. Perhaps he should have warned her, but he had been carried away with a reckless impetuousness that afternoon and had wanted to surprise her. Now he felt exhilarated, then fearful in equal measures, as he worried that if Mr. Fletcher got to know that he had used the car without permission, there might be hell to pay.

"Alright," she acknowledged, feeling the colour coming back into her cheeks, as she was sure if she had looked into a mirror, she'd be deathly white. "Wherever you're taking me to, it had better be worth it."

"Not knowing the local area, I asked my secretary if she knew of somewhere not too far away, but out in the country for a nice run. She told me about a place called Tockholes and I believe there is a hostelry where we can be alone." Poor Freda must have thought it was she that he was taking for a run out in the country, as she had seemed rather flustered during her reply.

"Oh, you've got a secretary,"Ada joked, as for some reason there appeared to be a bit of barrier between them. It had come upon her after she had met him outside the theatre hall. "My, my, it seems that a successful businessman has suddenly come into my life."

"No, no. Freda belongs to the company, but she writes up my notes when I've been out visiting the pubs that Duttons own and organises Mr. Fletcher's day with meetings and the like."

"Ah, but you've got a new car out of it, so you must be doing something right."

"Only because Management has bought a couple of other places and they want me to visit their hostelries and check that everything is running how they want it to. It'll make a change, so it will and once the newness wears off the thing, I'll probably be able to drive it out of hours."

"Oh don't tell me you're driving it without permission, silly sod. You'll have the bobbies after you." She kept her voice jocular, but deep down she was thinking that there was lots of things she didn't know about this man and here she was thinking of making a life long commitment to him.

"No, Mr. Fletcher won't even know about it, there was no one in the yard when I got there."

It wasn't long before they arrived in the village of Tockholes, a place full of history in the countryside. Before the steam powered looms had arrived in the town of Blackburn, the villagers in Tockholes made their living from either working in the coal pit, hand-loom weaving, spinning or dyeing and had tenanted the cottages there. Situated in a valley, most of the farmland, farms and some of the early buildings including a manor house, had been flooded by the Liverpool Corporation in the middle of the 18th century, so that they could make a reservoir. It was then that most of the population, having lost their homes and livelihoods, headed off to work in the cotton mills in town.

It was becoming dusk, as the little car chuntered down the hill and came to rest outside a public house called The Victoria. It was a stone built place, small and snug looking and hopefully it would have somewhere that Daniel could talk to Ada in peace. To his relief, although the Bar was filled to capacity with the locals, all enjoying their Saturday night, the highlight of their working week, he spotted a room just off the main one where a couple of elderly ladies were drinking glasses of stout.

"We'll go through there, Landlord," he said to the man, who smiled inquiringly as they entered the premises. "A pint of bitter and a glass of shandy for the lady."

"A glass of lemonade would have done," Ada said, as she sat in an upholstered chair near a fireplace, where coal was burning brightly in the grate. "Sit here next to me, it's lovely and warm. You wouldn't believe that it's almost the end of May."

"Perhaps a June bride then, nearly Mrs. McAuley," he said, trying to keep up the pretence that everything that they planned to happen, was going to do. Although he still questioned his foolishness, or was it weakness, in proposing to her. "I suppose you've spent all week dreaming of our wedding."

"Probably not in the way that you envisage," she said, giggling a little, as she could see the elderly ladies pricking up their ears as he said it. "How about us marrying in a Registry Office? I've no family here, although I suppose your family might object to the ceremony not being in a church."

He kept his counsel for a moment, whilst his heart soared at the thought that he wouldn't have to say his vows before God again. If there was a God in Heaven that he would have to confess his sins to when he went to meet his Maker, then that would be a lesser one to get off his chest. Marrying in the Town Hall this time couldn't be counted as a sin.

"Thank you, Landlord," he said as their drinks were set upon their table and he passed over a silver florin and told the man to keep the change. "That suits me, Ada," he said, lowering his voice, then taking a sip of his pint. "Do yer want me to do the necessary?

Yer know, book a date, do all the official stuff and then all you'll have to do is turn up looking pretty."

Ada nodded, though turning up looking pretty was the last thing on her mind. What about his family? Would they like her? Would she like them? Would they mind that the ceremony wasn't in a church? His next sentence answered her question.

"I won't trouble the folks to come over. They're getting on a bit and my sister Bridie has just given birth. I'll write ter them and let them know what a wonderful woman I'm marrying."

"Then we'll travel there for our honeymoon, Daniel. It'll be a nice surprise."

It surely would be, he thought, feeling a little agitated as he pictured the looks on his parents' faces if he turned up with another bride on his arm. There would be holy hell to pay and Connie wouldn't be best pleased either.

"No, me darlin'. I was thinking of somewhere we could be alone for a few days. Get to know each other better. We don't know a thing, other than you're a nurse and I'm from a family of brewers. How about a few days in the Lakes or even Scotland?"

Chapter Seven

The nightmare began as he lay in bed that evening. It could have been the whiskey chaser that he had before taking Ada back to the Nurses Home. It could have been because he'd been uptight before parking the car safely back in the brewery yard. Or it could have been that what he was proposing to do by marrying Ada was a great big sin after all and the guilt of it would spoil their "wedded" bliss.

The girl who invaded his dreams that night wore a long white floaty dress. She had orange flowers in her brown shoulder length hair and was walking ahead of him towards the altar with her head bent in prayer. He was following, acknowledging the smiles that came from the well-wishers who were watching them. His mother, father, sister and two brothers and all the village people who had come to see him marrying this woman that day.

His heart was drumming loudly, he could hear it as he lay there and it seemed to be threatening to come up into his throat and choke him. The girl turned as they reached the altar and it wasn't Connie or even Ada, it was a death mask head staring back at him. It smiled to show blackened teeth, below hollow eyes and no nose to speak of, then it tilted itself forward to place a kiss on his lips. Daniel heard himself scream. Whether he did or not, it was enough to propel himself out of bed and with shaking hands light up a cigarette, from the packet that he had put on top of the chest of drawers near his bed. He opened the bedroom window and stared up at the moon that was looking down upon the Earth, which was populated with millions of frail humanity. It was then that he knew that he couldn't go through with this marriage to Ada and he had to tell her so.

His conscience wouldn't allow him go through a ceremony that was a falsehood. He'd hate himself and what would he do if his father wrote and said that his life was not now in danger? By then he and Ada might have started a family and he knew that he couldn't leave his children then, as he had done with Winnie, his little love.

Ada ambled slowly amongst the clothing rails in the department store. It was her day off on a Thursday that week, so she was spending some of it looking for an outfit for her wedding day. Then later, she was to meet Daniel in the little cafe. The cafe that he had insisted on taking her to after they had met outside Woolworths on that fateful day.

"Can I help you with anything?" asked the young woman, who had been arranging some gloves in a display on top of a nearby counter. "Is it for a wedding? There are some Mother of the Bride outfits over by the window that have just come in."

A mother! Did she look old enough to be someone's mother? Ada felt shocked and then annoyed. Perhaps the assistant needed spectacles. Surely she didn't look like someone's mother at aged thirty two.

She nodded her thanks politely, then wandered over. A Mother of the Bride outfit would do admirably for a Registry Office wedding.

Daniel looked his usual dapper self, as he waited outside the cafe waiting for Ada to appear. She was late and he didn't like being kept waiting and what he was about to tell her couldn't wait, as he had been like a cat on a hot tin roof all morning. He had been picturing her face when he told her. Would she be shocked? Would she be like most women and burst into tears? Would she get angry and make a scene in the cafe and have everyone looking towards their table. He wished it was an hour ahead and it would all be over by now.

"Hello Daniel." Ada had sneaked up behind him and caught him unawares. He jumped two feet in the air and swore as he turned to look at her. "Jesus, Mary and Joseph, don't you ever do that again, yer scared the shite out of me!"

"Language, Daniel," she said, puzzled and taken aback that he should use a bad word in front of her, as he had always been such a gentleman in her presence before. She was used to the word, hearing it used many times by the men on her ward, when they thought that there was no female present to hear them, but she never thought she would hear that word from his lips, especially as they were meeting to discuss their marriage plans.

He looked ashamed for a moment, but gestured impatiently that she must go ahead of him into the premises, like the gentleman he was supposed to be.

"What was all that about?" Ada asked bluntly, as they sat at a table near the window and Daniel fiddled with the menu, after putting his hat down on the chair beside him. "Bad morning? Your boss didn't find out about you using the car, did he?" She put out her hand towards him in an affectionate gesture, but he remained with his arms folded on the table as he looked at her.

"There's no good way of saying this Ada, so I'll have to tell yer as it is. I've not been to the Town Hall like I said I would. I'm married already yer see."

"Oh."

What had he expected? Had he thought that she'd start foaming at the mouth, need some smelling salts, shout that he was an underhand bastard and she might have known it, seeing as he hadn't agreed to her meeting his family on their honeymoon? She'd gone pale, but she was usually pale when he thought about it, but he could swear that there had been a look of pain in her eyes for a moment.

"What are we going to have to eat, Daniel?" she asked briskly, as the waitress sauntered over with her notepad in hand. " I would like a roasted chicken balm cake with salad cream please." She ordered a pot of tea for two, then as it seemed he had been struck dumb, she ordered a balm cake for him as well, then coolly looked him in the eye.

"Why didn't you tell me you were married?" She spoke as if she was talking to one of her patients, which he had been once, in a soothing voice after taking his temperature or administering a spoonful of medicine.

"I couldn't. I just couldn't bring myself to shatter your dreams, when I knew that all you have ever wanted was to settle down and have children. I thought I could go through with it, but you know us Roman Catholics, I couldn't live with the sin."

"Then we'll think on it. Let's enjoy the barms that I see are being brought over. Perhaps with a lining on our stomachs we'll be able to focus our minds."

It gave her thinking time, when all around her people were eating their meals, drinking their beverages, chatting and gossiping. With tantalizing odours wafting from the kitchen and the smell from the smoke of many cigarettes causing a haze in the room, Ada's mind flashed to many possibilities, whilst Daniel looked into the distance after finishing, with nothing much to say.

"This doesn't have to be the end, Daniel." Ada looked at her watch, then asked him if he was in a hurry to return to work. "We can find a bench, it's a pleasant day, or perhaps you'd like to walk a little. I'm sure we can work out something if we really want to."

He nodded, then paying the hovering waitress, he ushered Ada through the door of the cafe, still not sure what there was left to say on the matter. There wasn't much point if he was to be honest and they should say goodbye today.

He had reckoned without Ada's determination. Sister Moscrop, she who supervised her team of nurses with a rod of iron and saw to the welfare of her patients with an unemotional calmness, was not about to see her golden opportunity slip away.

"I have a little money, Daniel," she said, as they sat on one of the benches provided by the Corporation, away from the busy pavements of the shopping area. "And when we were travelling in your car on our way to Tockholes the other evening, I was thinking that now you have transport and can travel to work each day, that I could purchase a small cottage. Somewhere that no one would know us and you could visit me, or perish the thought, live with me. But tell me, what has happened to have caused your marriage to break up? I presume that your wife lives in Ireland along with your family and that is why you didn't want me to go across and meet them."

Daniel nodded and proceeded to tell her his story. Although he didn't mention that Winnie didn't know that she wasn't his real daughter and it wasn't that he felt obliged to rear her, because he loved her.

"But why here? Why Blackburn and didn't you say your father has a brewery over there?"

He wasn't going to mention his parents fear of reprisal for their sons, now that the Black and Tans were looking for dissidents, of which he was one if he was honest. Let her think that he'd been cowardly and left his missis for a better life.

Ada seemed to accept his explanation that he had felt obliged to marry, because of pressure from his family, when they heard that the girl he had been courting was expecting a child. She patted his hand kindly, but deep down in part of her practical mind, felt glad to hear that he indeed could father a child. It would only be a matter of time then, before she held a little baby in her arms.

"It happens. You wouldn't be the first couple to have a shotgun wedding, as I have heard the situation called. So what do you think? To be honest, I would like to take a break from the nursing profession, seeing as I have been toiling in the job for nearly twenty years. I would like a place to call my own, grow some veggies, keep some chickens and go for brisk walks in the country air. Are you with me Daniel, or shall we say goodbye now and put it all down to experience?"

She held her breath and waited for his answer and when there was only a non committal grunt to say he would think about it, her spirits soared.

Daniel was still feeling stunned, after he had escorted Ada to the Nurses Home and heard her chattering on, about how she was going to give them notice at work when they had found a cottage. Perhaps he could ask permission to borrow the car and they could ride out, to say Tockholes or maybe Whalley. She had heard it was very nice out there. It wouldn't be too far away for him to travel each day and think of the money he would save on lodgings. Once she had got that bit between her teeth, Ada Moscrop would be moving heaven and earth to make it happen.

She didn't notice that he hadn't kissed her as they said goodnight and she had said that she would leave a note with Alf to say when they next could meet. Although she was in charge of the staff rota, it wasn't fair that she should be off too many Saturdays, but if he could be looking around the town to see if there were any postcards in shop windows saying that there was a property for sale. Or he could keep his eye on the adverts in the Blackburn Times, that would be very helpful.

He stopped in a pub' on his way back to Mrs. Dewsbury's and ordered a pint of bitter and a whiskey chaser. Not sure how he had got himself into it, other than he felt he was being swept along by this strong woman and he wasn't sure he liked it, he drowned his thoughts with alcohol, then weaved his way home.

Doubts began to creep into Ada's mind, just as soon as she had kicked off her shoes and sat down on the chair which she used for draping her clothes upon. What was she doing? Why was she prostituting herself to the first man who had shown an interest in her? Because that was what it would be, a form of prostitution if he didn't marry her and they went ahead with her plans for domestic bliss. He was already wed to a woman back in Ireland and for all she knew there might be a cart load of little McAuley's over there, not just the one he had mentioned.

For a few moments she felt anxious. She was committing herself to someone she knew little about. Was she losing her mind by grabbing the first opportunity? Or could it work, perhaps better than a conventional marriage would? They could both have their freedom if they wanted, in the years to come. She wouldn't be relying on him financially, although he would have to pay his whack. And no one need know that she wasn't Mrs. McAuley, as long as they didn't slip up.

"Give over worriting, Ada," she said out loud, as she took the pins from her hair and began to brush it vigorously. "You've risen to some challenges before in your life and this will be the best you've risen to yet."

When Daniel awoke with a thick head the next morning, regretting his lack of control in the amount of drink he had consumed, it was to the knocking on the bedroom door by Mrs. Dewsbury. He must be late, he thought, as he shot out of bed and put on his dressing gown over his pyjamas.

"Coming, Mrs. Dewsbury," he answered, as he stumbled across the room in an effort to get there before she pushed a key into the lock, which she had done once before when he hadn't been quick.

That had been embarrassing, as he had noticed that his willy was sticking out of the gap in his pyjamas. Luckily it wasn't standing to attention, when it could have been.

"Sorry if I woke you, Mr. McAuley," she said, " but it's nearly time for breakfast anyway. I have the bacon keeping warm in the oven as we speak and it's just a question of frying a few eggs for all of you. No, why I'm here…" and she produced a letter from a pocket in her pinafore. "This has come fer you and it's marked Private, so I thought you would like to read it away from prying eyes."

The letter could only be from his father. No one else wrote to him from his family. Just his father and they were never chatty letters; just a line or two asking how he was? This letter was a bit more serious.

Son, how are you. No names, no pack drill, but I heard that
someone in the village has been carted off to God knows where and
we all know what a loose lipped eejit this feckin person can be. I
am letting you know because there's a rumour going around that
there are fellows in pursuit and one or two of them may be heading
over to the mainland. Don't write again. There could be traitors
up in Dublin at the sorting office and seeing an English postmark
might alert them.

From your Dada.

So it had come to that then. He was on the run, even though
he had never fired a rifle or murdered a man. Even though he
hadn't even been in Ireland when things had got heated and
Michael Collins had lead the war against the British for Irish
independence. He'd been a sympathizer, that's all, but now
it seemed he was on the Wanted list. Jesus, Mary and Joseph,
what a feckin' eejit he had been when he had tried to ape his
older brothers. They'd be safe over there in Chicago. Though
knowing them, they'd probably be trying to raise some money
to send across a glut of guns.

Well, that was going to change a few things in his life, he
thought, feeling panicky as he dressed himself quickly, not
bothering to even shave or spend a few minutes checking his
appearance in front of the mirror like he normally did. Bloody
hell, he'd have to disappear. Start over again somewhere and be a
wanted man for the rest of his life!

His breakfast was tasteless, as he mulled over the possible
destinations where he could vanish to, as it were, into thin air.
Maybe down South, a big city such as London might be just the
place. Or perhaps he could get on a ship from Liverpool and join
his brothers in America. They were sure to find a job for him. It
didn't have to be in the brewery industry, perhaps in a car making
factory like Ford.

"Penny for them." Mrs. Dewsbury looked concerned as she
poured Daniel a second cup of tea, as the one she had given him

earlier looked as if it had gone cold. Whatever was in that letter she had given him must have been bad news.

"Oh, the letter? No, it was just news from home as usual. Dada letting me know about the family."

"From County Antrim, that's where you're from, isn't it, McAuley? Mr. Livesey poked his head out from behind the Telegraph and regarded the Irishman curiously, whilst Mr. Preedy looked on. "Says here that those dissidents in the south are being given a run for their money. Another one's been executed at Mountjoy Gaol."

"Is that a fact, so," Daniel put on a disinterested face, then got up from the table. "Got a busy day, so will yer excuse my haste. Livesey, Preedy, Mrs. Dewsbury." He hurried to his room and within a few minutes was walking through the front door.

Chapter Eight

"Ah, Daniel, just the person I wanted to see. Freda was just telling me that you might be doing a spot of courting. Someone she knows said she saw you in the Springfield Cafe with a fair haired lady. Wedding bells on the cards, maybe?" Mr. Fletcher was a great believer in matrimony, having been happily married for the last twenty eight years.

"Something like that, Mr. Fletcher, but as it happens I wanted to have a word." Perhaps his boss could come up with a solution, although he wasn't going to tell him the truth of the matter. "Have yer got a minute that you could spare fer me?"

His boss nodded and gestured to Daniel to follow him into his office, then when they were seated, Mr. Fletcher at his mahogany desk and Daniel on an office chair, he asked had Daniel got a problem?

"Not really a problem as such, Sir, but as you rightly said a little earlier, I do have a betrothed now. She works in the nursing profession and she has applied to work at another hospital, which would mean that I would probably have to do a lot of travelling each day."

"But you have the car. The hospital can't be that far away. Where is it, over in Preston?"

"I believe it is on the other side of Bolton, Sir." Daniel gathered his wits quickly, trying to remember where it was that Ada had said, when she mentioned that she had applied there before she came to work in Blackburn.

"Well, there are two hospitals there as far as I know. There's the Royal and there's a place called Townley's. Neither of them wouldn't be so far away. And where were you thinking of living, may I ask? Bolton has an excellent football team, good enough to win the F.A Cup."

Daniel shook his head. "We haven't discussed where we would like to live yet. But if I can still have the car for travelling, I suppose Bolton is good as anywhere.

"I wonder…" Mr. Fletcher looked thoughtful, then he turned away. "Call back in later, Daniel. Let's say after you've done your rounds and then you'll have the weekend to mull things over. About three o' clock then…I'll make a couple of telephone calls." And with that he walked along the hall on his way to the bottling plant.

Daniel picked up his briefcase and followed him into the brewery yard, glancing fondly over to where he had parked his car. There must be a solution to his predicament. It was just a question of finding one.

Ada hummed to herself as she walked along the row of beds, checking that her patients were looking comfortable and ready for their afternoon sleep. Visiting wasn't until the evening on a weekday, so this hour, she insisted, was for resting and recuperation and not for sitting around smoking, playing poker or whist.

She had just taken a note for Daniel to the porter's lodge and was looking forward to seeing him on the following Saturday, as Sister Hitchen wasn't too adverse to working on a Saturday and had agreed to take over Ada's shift. In fact, she preferred to attend church on Sundays with her brother and his family.

Ada had decided that she and Daniel would take a trip out in the country, that was if he had access to the car again. Perhaps this time they could drive through the market town of Darwen and across the moors to a place called Bolton. And on their way she could keep a lookout for a small cottage that might be up for sale. Because when she found one, the plan was to give in her notice and explain that as she was getting married in the near future, she wouldn't be able to work.

She would explain that her marriage was to a widower, who didn't want any of the fuss, friends or family and any of the rigmarole at the ceremony. Hers wouldn't be anything like the wedding that she'd heard Mary Donlan was to have. Mary was travelling back to Galway and being married with all the pomp and ceremony in the family church.

"Ah Daniel, come in," Mr. Fletcher face was wreathed with smiles, as he saw his Area Manager hovering outside his door, just as his secretary was getting up from a chair after taking dictation.

"I just might have the solution for you. Sit there and I'll tell you all about it. Freda, we'll have a cup of tea if you don't mind and some of that shortbread you gave me this morning. I am sure that Daniel would welcome some refreshments too."

"Certainly Sir," she said, scuttling past Daniel and giving him a look of rancour, that might have boded ill if he thought on it. But his mind, geed up with the hope that his boss had come up with a plan so that he didn't need to pack his bags and flee, wasn't about to worry about the feelings of a secretary.

"As you know, the Directors have been in talks with smaller breweries in the area, with a view to a takeover at some point in the future. They have their eye on one further afield in Bolton and as soon as you said this morning that your young lady would be going to work at a hospital there, I thought perhaps the Directors would like me to arrange an insider. When I say insider, I don't mean like a spy, going undercover, you would still hold your position as an area manager. It would all be above board. So I had a word with Mr. Halligan, you've heard me speak of him before and he thinks it would be a good idea if you were to spend some time there as our consultant. Do everything you do for us here in Blackburn. Make notes, sample the quality of their beer in the brew house and it goes without saying that you should see if you can discover any of the recipes they're using. Look around their hostelries, their premises, then bring a report to us in say a month or so. If in your considered opinion, a proposed takeover would be worth our while, we could begin our negotiations with their management."

"And I believe they have an excellent market in Bolton," Freda remarked, as she brought in a tray with two cups of tea and a plate of biscuits. She had been obviously listening at the door.

Daniel felt as if he had sprouted wings as he walked out of the brewery yard and strolled back to his lodgings. A month! A month where he would be given breathing space to make any plans for the future. He could get Ada settled in a little place where no one would know them and then…no he couldn't begin to think beyond that; his mind was in danger of cracking up as it was.

It was a sunny morning, as Daniel and Ada drove along in the Austin in the direction of Bolton. It had been agreed on meeting that they would travel for thirty minutes and wherever that would be, they would stop the car and look around them. Ada was in a giddy mood. Released from her world of patient suffering and with a whole new future ahead of her, she remarked that she wasn't going to live on a pig farm, if that was where they found themselves to be.

"Or near the bleach works, Daniel said blithely, picking up her mood, as he had heard about various industries on the way to Bolton, from Mr. Fletcher. "Or a cotton mill. Do you know, that this place we're travelling through called Darwen, started out as a centre for textile manufacturing as early as the Industrial Revolution in 1793. And for a time, the creator of the spinning mule, called Samuel Crompton lived here."

"Yes, I've heard said that the reason this area has so many cotton mills is because of the weather. The damp we get makes it ideal, I believe. Anyroad, I thought perhaps we could find a cozy little cottage," Ada continued happily, more interested in looking for a home than thinking of the area's historical past. "And now that you will be working for Magees, where did you say it was, a place called Derby Street? Well then, we'll need to be near enough to this road, so that you can go back and forth across the moors."

The road between the moors which they had begun to travel on was quiet, except for an occasional horse and cart that passed them by on its way to Darwen and sometimes a lorry, it's engine straining loudly as it chugged up one of the inclines, transporting a load to one of the warehouses there. The moors looked beautiful with clumps of purple heather mingled with yellow gorse and sheep grazing upon the outcrops with many thickets of rowans, silver birch and oak trees standing behind the walls that lined the road. Ada looked at her wristwatch and felt glad that there were still another ten minutes to go of their journey, as she wouldn't have wanted to live in one of the roadside cottages or up a track leading to a hillside farm. It wasn't far before they reached a village.

Egerton, named after Sir Thomas Egerton, a local landowner, had been a purpose built village to house the workers belonging to the cotton mill, which had been built by John Ashworth for his son Edmund. The Ashworth family were Quakers and known for their benevolence, so along with the Eagley Mill, built by John on the banks of Eagley Brook for his son, Henry, they were able to provide work for over one hundred people. The Egerton Mill specialized in spinning, crochet and sewing cotton and the operatives there were treated outstandingly. There was a village doctor, a school, and a library and the stone cottages provided, were very well constructed and had been financed by Edmund's father-in-law, Thomas Christy.

Of course none of this was known by Ada or Daniel, as the little car sped down the hill. Passing the King William tavern on their right, a handsome place built of local stone, near what looked to be a small chapel in a field, then the Cross Guns Inn, a low lying establishment built on the left near Cox Green Road and an imposing United Reformed Church in its own grounds, which was surrounded by mature oak trees. On the corner of an unmade road stood the Globe Inn, which made Ada think that the villagers were well served by the hostelries which she had been passing by.

She glanced at her watch again. Here was a pretty little village, with a few shops and stone built cottages lining each side of the road, but it hadn't quite reached the thirty minutes that they had promised themselves, although Daniel had his foot on the brake and had begun to travel more slowly.

"Three more minutes," Ada said laughingly, " although I must admit this place does appeal to me. I wonder what it's called, do you know?"

"I saw a signpost as we were driving down the hill back there. It said Egerton. What say we go into that grocers and tell them why we're here. They might know someone who wants to sell their property."

"Oh shall we?" Ada felt exhilarated. This was her first step to becoming a wife and mother. Well not a wife, but certainly a mother. And they had agreed that they were to be called Mr. and Mrs. Moscrop. She didn't bother to ask why they couldn't be called Mr. and Mrs. McAuley, as her own name would be easier to remember when she thought about it. She was finding out that Daniel McAuley was a bit of a mystery, but really did she mind what he got up to, as long as he did the deed and gave her a child?

Daniel parked the car and then they walked across the road to the grocery shop. Ada felt pleased that she had put on her dark green drop waistline dress with the pleat in the skirt and had worn a little jacket to cover her shoulders, a matching cloche hat, white gloves and black T' bar shoes. She felt stylish and thought she looked the part of a well heeled lady. Just as Daniel with his well-groomed appearance looked every inch the gentleman. He had prolonged the mystery during their journey, when he had insisted that if they found a house that day it should only be put in her name.

She hadn't argued, in fact she felt quite liberated. Just like one of those suffragettes, who had been fighting for women's freedoms and wasn't it her money that would be buying the house anyway.

"What can I do for you today?" The grocer, a small man with

not much hair to speak of, dressed in a cream shirt and brown waistcoat with a large white stained overall covering his paunch, asked Daniel. He ignored Ada, so she tried to hide her temper by examining what was in the hessian sacks that lined the wall behind her. The smell of coffee and perhaps a haunch of beef that someone was roasting in the kitchen, made her realise that she was hungry and she thought she might purchase a couple of the pies that were displayed on the marble counter.

"Well just for the moment, my wife and I are looking for information. We are new to the area and are looking for a dwelling where we could live. The name's Daniel Moscrop."

Ada drew in her breath. Already he was using her name… Moscrop.

"Could be a bit of a problem there, if you don't mind me saying so. The cottages you see around you belong to the Ashworth estate and as far as I know they are all tenanted. They were built for those who work at the mills around and about and even I have to pay them rent for this place. Perhaps you could try a bit further yonder. If you continue on, say another quarter of a mile beyond the bend there, just beyond the Mason Arms and past the church, you'll see the footings for the War Memorial they're planning to build. If you take the left fork in the road, it will being you to a place called Dunscar, where there might be a couple of properties for sale."

"Champion," said Ada, putting herself in charge of the situation. "Would you like to get us a couple of those succulent looking pies, Mr. Moscrop and then we'll be on our way?

Ada banged the door as she got back into the Austin. "Who does he think he is, the ignorant little man? I hope he comes onto my ward one day, I'm very handy with enemas!"

"I bet you are." Daniel gave a mock shudder. "I'm glad I never needed one when you were nursing me! Here, have yer pie and be careful it doesn't choke yer. Changing the subject, there seems to be a lot of hostelries in this village. I've counted three already and the shopkeeper mentioned another one on the bend."

"They must be heavy drinkers round here then." Ada swallowed a piece of her pie, before she answered him. "Anyroad with the pubs being close together, that means you won't spend a lot of time travelling and then you'll be able to come home early to me."

"They might not even belong to any of the breweries that I'll be overseeing, Ada, but before we set off on the last leg of the journey, I think you should listen to me." Daniel brushed off the bits of pie crust that had landed on his trousers. "Is this what you want? I mean, we won't be married, we'll be living in sin. I'll be your lodger rather than your husband, cos' I don't have any savings to give yer, only me wages at the end of the week. I'm a married man and whilst I'm living on this earth, I always will be. So tell me if you've changed yer mind and I wouldn't hold it against yer."

"Just drive Mr. Moscrop. Another three minutes around the bend, then we'll see what we can see."

Dunscar Fold consisted of a gentleman's residence, a farm, a beautiful view across to the Smithills Moor, if you stood on a hillock, a fast flowing brook as there had been a couple of rainy days and plenty of grazing land within the dry stone boundary walls. As the car drew up outside another public house called the Dunscar Arms, Ada felt that she might be coming home.

It felt right somehow and after she had wound down the car window and she breathed in a lung full of country air, it felt a long way away from the smoky atmosphere and industrial buildings of Blackburn. In fact it felt a lot like the village of Colbrook where she was born. Of course there was no sounds of the sea lashing onto the shore and there was no seagulls wheeling around above waiting for a fishing smack and there was no mountains in the distance. But as she got out of the car and looked around her, there were open views and the sound of lowing cattle and if she looked over to her left, there was a hill of sorts with a couple of cottages upon it. Even the row of cottages which were attached to a fine hostelry, were built in a similar stone to the ones she'd known at home.

She suddenly felt overwhelmed as she looked at the pretty

scene. The sun was high in the sky and there were no clouds to cast dark shadows. Everywhere was bathed in sunlight and she could feel the warmth of it upon her face as she stood there in a kind of daze. And in the gap between two rows of cottages, she could see a driveway up to, what appeared to be a gentleman's residence which was nestled within a stand of trees.

"It looks grand here, Daniel," she said softly, after he had joined her and took her hand in his, companionably. "I think that we could be happy here, if we can manage to find a place, don't you?"

Daniel nodded. "Let's go across to that tavern and speak to the Landlord, shall we? Landlords know everything about what's going on and the whereabouts of everything anyway."

Chapter Nine

The Dunscar Arms was a small hostelry with a rather gloomy interior. It had low beams, a dark wooden counter and sawdust on the floor. But the landlord looked a jolly man and greeted them warmly.

"What can I fetch yer?" he asked, as they settled themselves comfortably at one of the two wooden tables in an alcove. There was no one else in sight, but that was possibly because the doors of the place had only recently been opened.

"A drop of Guinness if yer have some," Daniel stared over at the counter to see if he could see the brass handle of a pump, which might contain his favourite tipple. "And a shandy fer me wife. Is that all right fer yer, me darlin'?"

"Ah, is it a drop of Dublin's finest, yer wantin'?" The landlord smiled and adopted an accent which was a good impression of a man from Irish shores. "My Da was from Ireland," he explained. "I don't usually speak this way, but hearing you made me want to. I've only got the bottles, Sir. I need ter speak to the brewery about it."

"Bottled will do it," Daniel said, making a private note to himself that should this place come under the banner of a takeover, he'd be the first to recommend they supplied it with barrels of Guinness. After all, if this was going to be his local, he'd need it to stock his "mother's milk"

"So what brings you to this part of the world?" the landlord asked, as he brought over a glass of the black stuff and a shandy for

Ada. "Is it a touring holiday? I noticed you'd parked your car over yonder when I opened the front door."

"Yes, something like that," Daniel replied, before Ada had a chance to explain why they were visiting the area. "We've just come over from Ireland and we're having a look around for a place to purchase. We've recently married, but we haven't decided yet whether to live in Ireland with the family or branch out on our own." He took a sip of his freshly poured drink, then sighed with satisfaction. "Not so bad, landlord, considering. Though if you've ever tasted it straight from the barrel, you'd have noticed the difference."

"So, what kind of dwelling are you looking for?" Changing the subject, the landlord addressed Daniel, occasionally smiling in Ada's direction, but turning to Daniel for an answer. At first she couldn't understand the reason behind both men, him and the grocer, deferring to Daniel and ignoring her, but it came to her suddenly that it was probably how things were done in the country, especially as she was now a "married" woman and as such belonged to her man!

"She's set her heart on a little cottage, haven't yer me darlin'? Do yer know if there is anything going hereabouts?"

"Well," the landlord considered. "I did hear Reggie Thornton saying the other night, that his old mother isn't doing so well since she fell down the stairs and twisted her ankle. He was going to ask his wife would she be prepared to take her in and the money that was got for the place would come in handy. Old Mrs. Thornton lives in one of the cottages up by The Flag. It'll probably need a bit of repair and a lick of paint mebbe and she's a stubborn old devil, so it might be a bit of a chore getting her out of there."

"Me wife's a nurse," Daniel said proudly. "She's used to dealing with stubborn old cusses, aren't yer love?"

"Where could we find this Mr. Thornton?" Ada asked, after pricking up her ears, thinking she might get the place a little cheaper if it needed a bit doing to it.

"He'll more than likely be in here in a minute or two, with

it being Saturday and Bolton is playing at home today. He likes a couple of glasses before he sets off on the chara and you never know it might be your lucky day! One for the road yerself then?"

The landlord busied himself behind the bar, as neither Daniel nor Ada wanted another drink. Indeed Ada had to visit the lavatory in the yard outside. Then a small group of men, all dressed in cloth caps, collar-less shirts, waist coats and hobnail boots, came walking into the pub' in a jaunty fashion, their voices sounding excited as they arrived.

"Set em' up Landlord," said a man, who looked the elder of the party. "The usual for me and whatever Mick and Ralph are having and Fred will have a glass of stout."

"There's a chap and his missis who'd like a word with yer, Reggie. I was telling them about your mam having that fall."

"Oh aye and who wants ter know about it," the man asked, thinking that the inquirers must be the people sitting in the corner, as they were the only other ones there. He sauntered over, whilst his companions stood by the bar chatting and waiting for their drinks.

Daniel stood up and held out his hand. "Mr. and Mrs. Daniel Moscrop," he said politely. "The landlord seems to think that you would know the whereabouts of a cottage that might be up for sale. We are in the market for buying one, if yer have the details."

"Ah, well yer got me there. I've not brought up the subject with the wife yet. It's me mother's house. We were brought up there. She had a bit of a fall and hurt her ankle. She's a tough old bird, but I think the fall shook her a bit, cos when I said she should consider movin' in with me and Dolly, she didn't put up her usual excuses about how her and Dolly wouldn't get on."

"And is it near here?" Ada was anxious to be off, even if she only got to see the outside of it. It would be a start to see the outside of the cottage anyway.

"Fred, I'm just taking these people over to ours fer a minute." Reggie suddenly appeared eager and left his newly poured drink on the bar counter. "It'll take me two seconds then I'll be back."

"She's never got over losing our Billy at the Somme," he said, after they had crossed the road and began to walk up a lane. "Out of the five of us who went over, only Billy didn't come back to her and it's made her old before her time, I reckon. Did yer see much action yerself, Danny?"

"No, poor Daniel wasn't able to enlist," Ada jumped in quickly. "I was his nurse. That's how we met when he had his operation."

"Oh, right," Reggie looked embarrassed, not wanting to ask anymore questions. "She might feel better when the War Memorial's unveiled at Dunscar next year. We all will be, I'm sure."

Ada looked around her as he was speaking. Apart from two large old houses on the right hand corner and another public house at the top of the lane, there were fields on either side. There were two small cottages joined together, then a row of stone built dwellings, all mullioned windows and wooden gutters and small gardens behind the walls. There was a field nearby, where a wooden fence ran along the perimeter and a small herd of goats frolicked within, then another two cottages at the top end.

"It's that one," Reggie said, pointing to the second cottage before the terrace began, "but she might be having a nap." He looked a bit worried as he stood at the garden gate and considered. "Mebbe yer could come again after I've had a word with her. Is there anyway I can get in touch?"

"Well, it's like this," said Daniel. "We're only over here on a short holiday. The wife and I have only recently wed and we were hoping to find a place around here, before we decide where we're going to live."

"Oh and where do yer…? Reggie was about to ask, when the cottage door flew open and a white haired woman in her seventies, wearing a pinafore over her long black dress and leaning heavily on a walking stick, came out.

"What yer doin' here, Reggie? I thought yer were off to Wanderers on the twenty past."

"Oh, I were, but this couple's lookin' for a house, so I

was bringin' them over to see yours in case you've come to a decision."

"Well, you get off and I'll see ter them meself. Tell your Dolly I'll see her later."

"Pester, pester, pester, that's all I get from my lot," Mrs. Thornton said, as Reggie strode off back down the lane and Daniel and Ada stood on the doorstep. "Come in and I'll make yer a brew. I haven't made me mind up yet if I'm sellin' or not, but ye can have a look around whilst I'm about it."

"Oh, thank you," said Ada, pushing herself in front of Daniel in her haste to be the first to see inside what could possible be her new home. She found herself inside what she supposed was the living room, all dark low beams, a flagged floor with a couple of ancient rugs upon it and a large stone fireplace wherein sat a cast iron range. There were gas mantles on solid walls which still smelled of recently applied distemper, an ebony display cabinet and old horsehair sofa and a small kitchen beyond. The kitchen had a Belfast sink, a storage cupboard, a wooden table and a couple of heavy looking chairs.

"The tea shouldn't be long," Mrs. Thornton said, after she suspended the nearly boiling kettle to a trivet on top of the fire and motioned her visitors to sit on the comfortable looking sofa which was covered with an old fringed blanket.

"Now, I'm not saying that I want to sell me house, but my lads tell me that after I had that fall down the stairs the other week, I should be thinkin' of movin' in with one of them. They've all got wives, even our Billy, God Bless him, left a widow. Yet it's our Reggie that's got the room. Him and Dolly have a house just around the corner. He's only renting, but there's a spare room that I can have and its got an inside lavatory and a bathroom and I suppose I can help him out a bit with the money I get for this."

"What do you think, Daniel?" Ada asked, thinking that if she was to have a family, it was a little on the small side and until she saw the size of the bedrooms she couldn't be sure.

"It's up to you, Ada. Tell me Mrs. Thornton, what kind of

money were you lookin' for?" At least Ada would know if she could afford it or not.

"Reggie thinks I could get around £50 to £60 for it, as it needs a bit of work if I'm honest. It needs new guttering, as some of its rotting and probably another down pipe. There's a bit of damp in the back bedroom and the drain outside needs someone to take a look. Besides all that, it's given me and me family a roof over our heads for the past thirty years. We've always lived around and abouts. Me and me husband, God Rest His Soul, met when I worked as an Assistant Mistress at Walmsley School. He was a joiner and did very well for himself when those cottages on the road got built."

"Mmm." Ada was elated with the price that Mrs. Thornton had suggested. With the money from her father's Will and the money she had saved from her wages with having always been accommodated in a Nurses Home, she could well afford it. Although time was of the essence if Daniel was soon to begin his new job in Bolton.

Then a little voice inside her, the practical Sister Moscrop voice, began to ask if she was really ready to settle down so quickly with Daniel? She didn't know him, didn't really know anything about him, except he was Irish and worked for a brewery in Blackburn. She pushed her qualms away, when the little voice began to tell her that he might be her only chance.

"Would it be possible for us to have a look around?" she asked, conscious that both Mrs. Thornton and Daniel were looking her way. "I would like to have a look at the bedrooms if it is possible."

"Of course, yer can, there's three of them. They're this way, up the staircase."

It had begun to rain, after Daniel and Ada had come down from their tour of the upstairs rooms, causing Mrs. Thornton to mutter that it always rained on match days and she didn't know why men wanted to hanging around watching other men kick a football.

"So what do yer think," she asked of Ada, as something was

telling her that it was the woman who would make the decision in this relationship. The man had only given the bedrooms a passing glance, whilst his wife had even examined the width of the window sills.

"They're a bit small," was Ada's only comment, although inside she was warring with herself. One of the bedrooms could have its wall knocked out to make a bigger one and it wasn't as if she was thinking of giving birth to a multitude.

"Well, at one time I had five boys living up there and the size of the rooms didn't seem to bother them." Mrs. Thornton sounded indignant as she set about making the tea.

"Oh, I'm not complaining," Ada said hastily, thinking that if she wasn't careful they'd be out on their ear and the cottage did have possibilities. Even after she had paid the money that Mrs. Thornton might be asking, they'd still be plenty of money in the bank.

"Well, like I said, I'm still thinkin' about it. It's a big decision giving up my independence, but I don't want to end up in Blairs, that's our local convalescent home. Sooner I was with family, than be stuck in there."

She brought over two china cups on a wooden tray and placed it on a small table beside them, along with a matching plate full of homemade biscuits. "Help yerself and I'll get a piece of paper and a pencil. You can tell me your address and when I've made me mind up I'll get our Reggie to post yer a letter."

"Ah," said Daniel, thinking again that he must cover his tracks in case of retribution in the future.

"We're touring, we don't have an address at the moment."

"Yes, but she could send it care of your sister who works in Blackburn." Ada suddenly had a brain wave. "She works as a Sister in Blackburn Infirmary. If you send it to the Nurses Home, she could pass it on."

Chapter Ten

It was over a month before a letter addressed to Mr. and Mrs. Moscrop, c/o Sister Moscrop, was delivered to the Nurses Home. In that time Daniel had begun to travel daily across the moors to the brewery on Derby Street in Bolton, but still kept his lodgings with Mrs. Dewsbury for the time being. He liked it there, his landlady was a good cook and except for the two eejits who shared their mealtimes with him, he was feeling quite fortunate. Always at the back of his mind though was the warning that one day his past may catch up with him, but in his more logical moments he felt it unlikely, as he had always been a small cog in the wheel of the I.R.B.

Ada had been working on a day shift and although aware that she might never receive a letter from Mrs. Thornton, she was tickled pink when she did. It was time to get her plans into action and when she read that there were legal papers available for her to sign in a solicitors office in a place called Water Street, in the town of Bolton, she began to feel that she could.

It had been strange, she had to admit, that before saying their farewells to Mrs. Thornton, on the afternoon when Bolton Wanderers was hammering the opposition, that Daniel had insisted that the cottage be put only in her name and on their way home later, he had explained why he didn't think it would be fair not to. He was a married man and it was her money not his and like it or not, they might go their separate ways in the future. No one knew what the future held for anyone.

His words hadn't worried her unduly. What he had said was true, it was her money after all. And as time went by and she became more familiar with his masculinity, she began to liken their relationship to that at a stud farm, where he was the stallion and she was the mare. There was no declaration of his love towards her, nor any enthusiastic discussion about their future life together. Not since the night he had got carried away with himself and asked her to marry him. And except for an occasional kiss on the cheek, there didn't seem to be a physical attraction between them either.

One Wednesday morning, a day off in the week for a change, Ada dressed in her dark green dress, jacket and matching brimmed hat, set off for the railway station. She had inquired at the ticket office a few days earlier and was told that she could catch a train to Bolton and that they ran every hour throughout the day. Picking up a timetable, she had decided that she would visit the solicitors on the following Wednesday and insist that Sister Hitchen have a Saturday off instead of her. During a quiet moment when she felt that there would be no one listening, she used the telephone in the almoner's office and rang for an appointment.

She was in good spirits as she set off from the Boulevard, to travel in one of the second class carriages through the moors, little stations and verdant countryside. In her handbag was a banker's draft from the District Bank for fifty guineas, which was the price agreed with Mrs. Thornton a few weeks before. It would be a fait accompli, when next she saw Daniel, as what was the point of bothering him with the legalities?

Daniel, at that moment, was wishing himself anywhere other than Blackburn. Having made a few notes to give to Mr. Fletcher, only this and that, but enough reason for him to have a ride out in the car from the Crown Brewery as it was a sunny day, he thought he might check up with Ada and see how the sale of the cottage in Dunscar was faring. He planned to take her out, maybe treat her to dinner one evening, once she had checked her roster and they could talk over their plans for moving.

"Good morning, Mr. McAuley," Freda stood by the office door, after hearing Daniel's foot steps coming long the hall. She was dressed in her usual black dress, but today she wore a bit of a secretive look on her face, as if she knew something he wasn't privy to.

"How are you enjoying all this travelling you're having to do each day? You must be very tired when you return to your lodgings each evening."

"Yes, but I don't mind it really. Perhaps when the winter comes it will be a different tale. Is Mr. Fletcher around or is he in the bottling shed?"

"Oh, he's gone off to a meeting this morning. Can I get you a cup of tea whilst you wait? Oh, I nearly forgot. Wilf at the gate, said that a man turned up yesterday asking was there someone called Danny working here? He said that he knew this Danny used to work in a brewery over in Ireland and he'd heard that he might be working in one over here. He didn't give his name, but said he could be contacted at the New Inn, as he has a room there. I thought with you being Irish too, you might know him."

Fight or flight. Those were Daniel's first primeval instincts.

What the hell was he going to do?

"Wilf could have told him that *you* worked here, but he didn't think it was his place, especially with you being management. But I could take this fellow a message to the New Inn, if you wanted me to." Freda put a friendly hand onto Daniel's arm, before walking away to make him a cup of tea.

He dithered. They were looking for him. The I.R.B had finally sent someone to get him or it could be them Black and Tans who were after retribution. He must go, he must get away. He had to go somewhere and hide until the nightmare was over. They couldn't stay in Blackburn forever waiting just for him. He'd go any place, anywhere, but first he must go to see Ada and tell her of his flight.

"Ah Freda," he said, " thank you." He began to sip at the cup of tea which she had placed on the table in front of him. " I was hoping to see Mr. Fletcher to tell him something, but I'll have to tell you the problem and you must pass it on to him. I need to go back to Ireland as soon as it is possible. Me granny's ill. Me father sent a letter, so he did. Touch and go, or so I am believing. So I must travel on the train to Heysham and catch the boat."

"Oh, Mr. McAuley." Freda's face was a picture of compassion. "You should have said… there was me going on about your visitor… Perhaps he had come to tell you about…you know, your poorly grandmother."

"I'll have to pack me case." Having finished his tea, he quickly grabbed a couple of sheets of paper, wrote brief notes to both his boss and Ada, then announced to Freda that he could be away for two weeks or longer, but it would all depend on the state that his granny was in.

As he dashed along the street, with his mind in a blur and with no idea where he was going to spend the next few weeks in hiding, his only hope was that the Irishman would be long gone on his return.

Fergal McKenzie whistled to himself happily as he walked to the station to catch the train back to Manchester, where he had started working as a brickie a couple of weeks before. His job in Blackburn was done. With a bit of luck that gob-shite Danny would have got the frighteners on him and think that someone had come to get him from the Brotherhood. It was only what he deserved, in Fergal's opinion, as Danny McAuley was the one who'd done the dirty on his sister Connie, who had been left back in Ireland with her little girl to rear.

Ada walked along the busy street, looking in the windows of the shops in Deansgate, Bolton. Safely in her handbag were the deeds of her newly purchased cottage called Daisy Nook. A major achievement for a woman of her time, when women were subservient to the man they were married to. But in Ada's case she was the epitome of the liberated woman. She wasn't married, she had risen through the ranks of nursing to fulfill her ambition and the only thing that was missing in her life, was the dream that hadn't yet been fulfilled. Her own little child. How she longed to hold a baby in her arms. She was made for motherhood. She would be kind and caring. Her training to look after her fellow man had prepared her for that, although she wasn't sure that she was ready for the mechanics involved with baby making. She had never tried it before and didn't particularly want to try it neither, because she had heard from various women across the years, that the process involved with the prospective father, wasn't really good for you at all. It could cause all sorts of strange things to happen and there was a possibility of losing one's life after giving birth. But if that was what it took to hold a baby in her arms, Ada thought purposely, she would grit her teeth and try.

Daniel stood outside the porter's lodge waiting for Alf to check if Sister Moscrop was available to speak to. It was beginning to rain, a summery kind of rain that only drizzles for a few moments. He moved to an overhanging roof for protection, pushing his bag with his foot and cursing when he saw that Alf had returned without her.

"It's 'er day off accordin' to Sister Hitchen. Said somethin' about taking a train ride to Bolton. Are yer off somewhere yerself?" He looked pointedly at the leather holdall, which held a few of Daniel's clothes, as he had left most of them behind at Mrs. Dewsbury's.

"Would you give her this?" Daniel handed over the note that he had sealed into an envelope and ignored Alf's awkward question. He didn't know where he was going himself, although he knew it involved a train station. Somewhere quiet and somewhere as far away as possible and with the hope that on the day that he returned, the threat that was hanging over his precious life would have gone.

Ada sat on her bed in the Nurses Home later, pleased as punch that she had the deeds to the cottage in her possession. Now all she had to do was give in her notice to Matron Chandler, find a man who could carry out the repairs of Daisy Nook and a little redecoration, write a list of all the things she would need for furnishings and write a letter to her best friend, Betty, to let her know her new address.

She felt for the little black box that was nestling in her handbag. Its contents held a small gold wedding ring that she had bought at a shop called Prestons, whilst she visited Bolton. Until that day she had never thought she would be purchasing her own wedding ring, but left to Daniel, they would be moving into Daisy Nook without one, she was sure. To their neighbours, they would be known as Mr and Mrs. Daniel Moscrop and their child or children that they would hopefully produce, could never be called a bastard. It was such a horrible name. After she'd had a little rest, she would take a walk over to the hospital. Daniel would have left a note with Alf by now and they could set about planning the rest of their lives.

Ada stared in disbelief at the porter's words when she saw him later. "Gone, what do you mean gone, Alf? Gone where? Didn't he tell you?"

"It were only about an hour ago, Sister Moscrop and 'e never told me where 'e was goin'. Just said to give yer this note and off 'e went. He had a traveller bag, but not a suitcase, so perhaps 'e isn't goin' very far."

"Well, it's the first I've heard of it. Though perhaps he had a letter from his family in Ireland. I believe that is how he communicates with his father."

"Aye, that'll be it. He'll be back before we know it and 'e'll be standin' me a drink at the Bay Mare."

My dear Ada, (Daniel wrote)
I have had some bad news from Ireland and I must away back to

my family. I don't know when I will be back, but please don't let this interfere with your plans. Go ahead and I'll catch up with you later.

   Daniel.

So that was it. He expected her to get on with things without him. Well, so be it. Or was this a way of letting her down gently and he'd gone back to patch things up with his wife? He'd given her a sketchy tale about his family. Something about his father owning a brewery and he'd been sent across to Blackburn to experience how things were done over here. He had been rewarded with a brand new car and he had comfortable lodgings with a woman called Mrs. Dewsbury, so it wasn't as if he was from poor beginnings or had a country bumpkin life. But that was all she really knew about him and if she was honest with herself, recently she was finding she didn't care. All she had ever wanted from a man was for him to be a supplier of the necessary. Being love struck was a bonus and who was she to complain?

Daniel, by the time Ada had got his note, was standing on the platform at Preston Station, waiting for the Carlisle train to appear. Still nervy, still jumpy, he had recalled the tales of Ada's idyllic childhood and had decided to give himself a little treat. The Lakes had sounded a beautiful place and he hoped his visit there would give him peace.

Handing in her notice to Matron Chandler the following afternoon had caused Ada a lot of heart searching and a lot of thought about her future, before she had asked for an interview. If she was going to change her life, now was the time to do it. Before she knew it she'd be forty, without much chance of ever becoming a mother and a wife. Though she had be careful with the truth, Matron would have dismissed her on the spot if she thought that she was going to cohabit with a man.

   Matron Chandler, a portly, silver haired woman who could

stop a marauding tiger in its tracks with just one glance and could reduce a person to a snivelling wreck after one of her lectures, stood with hands on hips and nostrils flaring after she heard of Ada's intended marriage.

"I find it hard to believe that you of all people, Sister Moscrop, would give up your successful career and throw it all away for the sake of a marriage. Indeed I would go as far enough to say that you are a woman after my own heart, dedicated to the profession and your commitment to your staff and patients have done the hospital proud. As you know, when retirement knocked on my door, I turned it away knowing how bereft I would become if I were to choose it and I was of the impression that you might think the same as I did one day."

"I'm sorry Matron," Ada looked the irate woman in the eye resolutely. "I realise that I will be leaving you in the lurch and I know it might be difficult for you to find my replacement, but as my intended isn't local it means that we must move away. But if I am assured of a good reference, it means I don't have to give up my profession until such time when I have to. Indeed I would be grateful if you could furnish me with a copy and then I won't have to bother you again."

"And will your nuptials be imminent or will I be allowed a decent length of time to find your replacement, Sister Moscrop? As you know, I have to find someone to replace Nurse Donlan too."

"I am sure we can work something out, Matron."

After all, there was no hurry, was there? She might never even see Daniel again.

Her announcement of her "forthcoming nuptials" to her team of nurses was met with incredulity. Though it was mostly the younger women of course, when they saw she didn't have a ring upon her finger to prove her claim. And annoyingly she was confronted with a barrage of questions and speculation on whom her intended might be, especially as one of the nurses recalled the gossip regarding Mr. McAuley, a former patient on the Men's Ward.

Ada stayed tight-lipped and continued in her usual formidable fashion, whilst keeping her team firmly in their place. The most she would reveal was that the ceremony was being held in her home village of Colbrook. They would probably look around the Lakes to find somewhere to live and she wasn't wearing a ring, because it was too precious to wear whilst working.

Chapter Eleven

Alf, a fountain of knowledge having lived in Lancashire since he was born, was pleased to help Sister Moscrop with directions for her trip on the following Monday morning.

"I know Dunscar well," he said, when Ada told him that due to Daniel having to go away so quickly, he had forgotten that they were to visit a relation of his, so she thought that she would go along and introduce herself. " I have a cousin who works at Eagley Mill and sometimes we have a drink in The Flag. It's a nice little place. A bit too quiet for me and the Missis, but worth a trip on the train if you like all that countryside. Pity about Danny though, Sister Moscrop, it'll put your plans back a bit, I dare say." *And he only dared say it because Danny was his mate, Ada thought, as she nodded wryly. She knew she'd be the talk of the hospital grapevine now!*

It had been a pleasant journey to her destination. At first calling at Darwen, a busy market town, then rattling through the moorland and along side the Entwhistle reservoir, to stop at Turton which was the station for the hamlet of Chapeltown. During that summer of 1922 the weather had been cold and although some people were looking forward to their annual holidays from the mills, it was with the hope that it would get warmer. Wakes Weeks, where some northern mill towns had an allocated week in June or July, would see the masses leaves their homes in droves. Blackpool being the usual magnet for a relaxing few days on the sands with the family, or a weekend if the mill owner was a stingy employer, incorporated a stay in a lodging house and a trip up the famous tower. Though some people caught the train to the Lake District, where bed and breakfast was offered in the many small hotels.

Bromley Cross where Ada alighted, was another small hamlet in the Lancashire countryside and had been named after the Bromley family, who had been landowners in earlier years. Except for the hostelry called the Railway Arms, which had served generations of tenant farmers, minor gentry and cottage dwellers from the surrounding farmland, Ada found there was only a country lane for her to follow until she came to the main highway.

She felt glad that she had chosen to wear her dark blue suit with her knee-length woollen jacket, had shod her feet in comfortable shoes and wore her brimmed hat on her tied back hair, as it transpired, according to Alf's instructions, that she still had at least a mile to walk to the Dunscar Arms and it was feeling rather chilly. Once there she was to meet Mr. Thornton, who had agreed in a recent letter to carry out a few repairs. In her handbag was her prized possession, a set of large brass keys, which jingled as she walked.

"He's gone, I'm afraid," the landlord explained to Ada, as she strode briskly into the Dunscar Arms ten minutes later and inquired of Mr. Thornton's whereabouts. "He waited as long as he could, but he needed to get back, as his mother has been taken into Blair Hospital."

"Oh…" Ada wasn't sure what she should do now. Wait around or…?

"Have you come on your own today, Mrs. Moscrop? It is Mrs. Moscrop, isn't it? I remember your husband saying so." The landlord, hoping for new customers in the future, was very conciliatory. "Can I get my wife to make you a cup of tea and perhaps a sandwich? Reggie was saying that you were coming by train from Blackburn today. Did you stay at the hospital with your sister-in-law?"

For a moment Ada looked at the landlord blankly. What did

he mean…she was the Sister? Then she remembered that Reggie Thornton would have given him that information, because she and Daniel were supposed to be on a touring holiday.

"I'd love a cup of tea and a sandwich, thank you." She looked around for a table to sit at, which would ensure that she wouldn't have to tell anymore lies if she was sitting away from him.

"He said he shouldn't be long. Just to get his mother settled and then he'll be back again."

Phew, Ada thought, so she wasn't going to have to keep coming back and forwards then.

"A bit on the coolish side for June," the landlord said, after he had brought her a pot of tea, cup and saucer and a small jug of milk on a tray. "Will the weather be better over in Ireland at this time, do yer think? Me Da was always saying that the summer months were beautiful."

"It's sure to be and Mr. Moscrop will be very fortunate if it is. Would it be possible to have a bit of sugar, do you think?"

She waited then with bated breath. He was bound to ask more about Daniel, but luckily his wife arrived with a plate of cheese and pickle sandwiches, so his unspoken questions were avoided. After all, it was only polite to allow his customer to eat without talking. Soon after, Mr. Thornton appeared full of his apologies and they set off along the lane to Daisy Nook.

"It's only for a short while," Reggie Thornton replied to Ada's inquiry as to how his mother fared. "The doctor thought that she wasn't resting her foot enough. Yer know, with all her packing and getting ready to move in with us. She's left some stuff, she didn't know if it would be of any use to you. If it isn't, I'll pile it in the back yard and get one of me brothers to shift it later. We fixed the guttering and the down-spout, but we'll have to ask around for someone to have a look at the damp, but it might have been because of the guttering."

"That's very kind of you, Mr. Thornton," Ada felt pleased that she wasn't having to pay out for the repairs. She might have a good amount of savings in the District Bank, but once she had left her job at the hospital, it might suddenly begin to peter out on her.

"Is there a shop where I may purchase food and perhaps a mop and other cleaning items, Mr. Thornton? I plan to move in within the month, but it won't harm to get used to the area whilst I'm here."

"Is Mr. Moscrop not moving in with yer?" Reggie looked puzzled. He had thought it strange when his mother had told him that the deeds of the cottage, according to the solicitor, had been put in the wife's name. It was usually the man who had his name on the deeds.

"Not at the moment, Mr. Thornton." Ada was rather brusque, as she walked through the cottage gate ahead of him. "He has business in Ireland that he must see to. He's a rather busy man."

The man in question was indeed rather busy. He'd had to decide whether to spend a couple of weeks as a guest in one of the hotels in Bowness, after alighting at the Windermere railway station, or get a job? He was conscious of perhaps not having enough money with him to pay for many nights in a hotel and at that time of year when the Wakes Weeks were just beginning, maybe one of the hotels in the area would be in need of some extra staff. It didn't matter if the job was a porter or a waiter, he was sure he could do either jobs if he was required to do.

He chose a hotel called Lakeside Manor, which looked across Lake Windermere and had been a gentleman's residence. It had twenty five bedrooms, was built from local stone and had a large mature garden, where guests could sit and admire the stunning views.

He was greeted at the Reception desk by a pretty young lady with a welcoming smile and a rather chic bobbed hairdo and after his inquiry as to whether the hotel was in need of of any staff that week, permanent or temporary, (although he had to bear in mind that Mr. Fletcher would go mad if he didn't return after a couple of weeks) he had waited in the foyer for the Manager to arrive.

It was as he had thought, they did indeed want someone

temporary. They were in need of a porter, as the person who had filled that position earlier in the summer, had gone down with a bad dose of flu'.

"I suspect it's because of the weather," Mr. Greenwood, a tall man with a London accent confided in his southern tone. "I have worked here since the war and at this time of the year the weather has always been glorious. No wonder people are suffering with coughs and colds with the temperatures plummeting. I take it you have done this kind or work before or you wouldn't be asking."

Daniel had nodded. He wasn't dressed in his usual attire, which denoted that he was a man with a prestigious career, he was dressed for travelling. He was wearing a striped collar-less shirt under a brown knitted tank top, a pair of brown corduroy trousers and shiny brown leather shoes, with a black three quarter length jacket to keep out the cold. He had shaved off his moustache, much to his dismay, but it was needs must at that moment if he wanted to look like an ordinary bloke. All in all he presented a clean cut appearance, which was necessary if one was to be the first person a guest would meet on arrival. It was enough to persuade Mr. Greenwood to give him the job that day.

It was strange how quickly he and the young lady had become attracted to one another. The saying of how *their eyes met across a crowded room,* could have been invented just for them. As Daniel carried travel bags, suitcases and the bits of paraphernalia belonging to the guests on their way from the front door to Reception, the girl with the chic hairdo and sparkling blue eyes would be waiting to book them in.

Her name was Millicent Pearson and she came from a small place called Stoneclough, which was on the way to Manchester. She was Milly to her friends and it wasn't long before Milly became the stuff of Daniel's dreams.

It was as Ada was travelling back to Blackburn on the train after agreeing with Reggie Thornton which pieces of furniture that she would keep and which could be discarded, that the thought hit her that she didn't have to give up her nursing career just because she was getting "married" and moving away from the Infirmary. She could inquire at this place called Blair Hospital, where Mrs. Thornton was having respite care for her injured foot, according to her son. Now that one of her dreams had been fulfilled, due to the fact she had risen through the ranks to become a Nursing Sister, a dream she'd had since beginning as a probationer, it wouldn't matter in the slightest if she was to work there as a S.R.N.

Besides, she couldn't be sure that Daniel would appear in the next few weeks as he had said he would, for she had heard that these were dangerous times in Ireland with all the rebellion going on. Far better to get on with her life whilst she had the opportunity, or she may not have the chance of living how she wanted ever again.

Matron Chandler seemed relieved when Ada told her of her inspiration.

"Well I thought it seemed strange when you said you and your husband would be leaving the area. You seemed unsure, especially as I have heard on the grapevine that he has a good job with a local brewery. I'm not one to listen to gossip as you know, but I do feel that it is part of my job to know what is going on around me and if you prefer to travel from your new abode each morning, I can take my time in looking for your replacement. An ideal situation for both of us."

The first time making love to Milly gave him feelings which he hoped would last forever. They had kissed before, once or twice in the storage cupboard when no one else was around, but had never been alone together so they could be as one. Her flesh was warm when he lay above her partially clothed body, being allowed the liberty of searching for her breasts beneath her bodice. His fingers stroked her taut nipples as he began to kiss her neck and listened to her sighs as he did so. He felt as if he had been transported to heaven, as they lay together on his jacket beneath a dark twinkling sky, sheltered within a small copse near the lakeside. Away from prying eyes, they indulged in a passionate pleasure.

Ada awoke early one morning and after using the bathroom which she shared with a host of other nurses who slept in dormitories on her corridor, dressed herself carefully in the brown linen suit which she had chosen for travelling in, brushed her hair until it shone, then cramming a large hat which sported a colourful feather, headed for the railway station carrying a suitcase.

This was the day that, if Daniel had made an appearance, they had chosen to spend some time away together, to give their "marriage" credence. But he hadn't come back and rather than Ada facing the pitying glances, which she would have had to brazen out, if the other nurses had thought she'd been dumped by her fiance, she decided to visit Betty and her family in Colbrook.

First though she was going to do something that she had promised herself since her parents died. She had the time, as she had told Matron that she and her new husband would be back at the end of the following week in Blackburn. She was going to make the journey to a place called Carlisle, which was a town at the top end of Cumbria, look for any members of the Moscrop family and she would wear the wedding ring on her third finger whilst she was there.

Chapter Twelve

Ada stepped down onto the platform at Dalston Railway Station. She had been informed by the ticket clerk at Carlisle, that Dalston was only a couple of stops away and she would be there in the wink of an eye. She felt hungry, unusually so, until she remembered in her haste that she hadn't had breakfast and if she didn't eat something soon, she might expire.

The grocer's shop on the road that lead to St. Michael's and All Angel's Church and village school was busy, when Ada stepped through its portals. As she glanced around she saw that there were delicious looking pies sitting on a slab upon the marble counter and bottles of homemade lemonade for sale. The woman serving behind the counter was a fount of knowledge Ada found, after she had explained she was looking for members of the Moscrop family who were related to her.

"Well for a start, I would go to the graveyard down yonder," she said, after she had placed a succulent looking pie into a brown paper bag and reached for a cloudy looking bottle. " Though did yer say the name was Moscrop? Plenty of Moscrops around here, love and generations of them in St. Michael's graveyard too. What was your father's name? My Dad might have gone to school with him, yer never know."

"His name was Wilfred, but that is all I ever knew. I don't know anything about his family, he never said."

"I bet he was one of the Moscrops from Gaitsgill. She were a nursemaid for the Tomkinson family and married Ted Moscrop, who had a farm up in Gaitsgill years ago. I remember Hilda left the farm after Ted died as it was tenanted and lives in a cottage across from Caldew Brook."

"Is this Gaitsgill far away from here? Could I walk it? Or is there a bus which could take me there?"

"It's over five miles away and so I'd wait fer the bus if I were you, love. It looks as if it might rain and I see yer haven't got a brolly."

Ada knocked on the first door of Brookstone Terrace. She had been told by the local postman that a Mrs. Hilda Moscrop lived there, although most people around called her Nana. It was quiet within and Ada felt her spirits plummet. If she had come all this way for nothing, she would feel heart broken.

"Yes?" The door was opened slightly and a silver haired old lady, dressed all in black and looking to be in her early eighties, peered around the door. She stared at her caller suspiciously, then suddenly her face broke into a grin, showing a lack of teeth in her gums.

"I knew you would come one day. I just knew it. You're our Wilfred's lass, ain't yer, I can tell? You look just like him, skinny as a lath, not a pound of flesh on yer. What am I doin', leaving yer on the step? Come in, come in!"

Ada followed her into the large, but gloomy room, where the staircase went up into the upper storey and was separated by an archway from a small room beyond. It had high ceilings, whitewashed walls, a flagged floor with a couple of small, mostly tatted rugs upon it and a wooden cabinet. There was the usual cast iron range within a large stone fireplace, which was used for cooking on. Although the fire was barely in, making the room feel on the chilly side, but Ada also noticed that the back door was wide open.

"I wouldn't have heard yer knockin'. I was out in't coal shed getting a bucket full, but summat made me stop for a moment and come back in. Well, sit thee down, what did 'e call yer? I can't remember the name he give yer."

"Ada and I also have a brother named Charles." Ada sounded surprised as she sat down gingerly on a big old fashioned sofa, as one or two springs were sticking out above it. "Did you know about us? My father never spoke about his family. I only knew that he came from Carlisle."

"Aye, that'll be Wilfred. Kept his cards close to his chest. I knew about the both of yer and one time he brought little Charlie up ter see me. That was when Ted was alive, so we met down in Dalston. At the time, it was better that way."

"Oh." Ada sensed there was a story to be heard, but it could wait for the time being. She suddenly decided not to visit Colbrook until the following day.

"Is there anywhere I could stay in the village?" she asked, keeping her fingers crossed that there might be a spare bed in the dwelling, save her paying out for a hotel.

"Aye, yer can stay at our Moira's. Her Jimmy's got a job over in Whitehaven and 'e only gets home ter see her once a month."

"Oh, you had other children besides my father, I didn't know." Ada hadn't thought that she might have cousins, nephews, nieces. More family than just her and Charles then.

"Aye, I had another three after our Wilfred. There's Moira, Jed and Franny. I don't 'ave any sugar, do yer tek it in your tea?" The old lady walked carefully from the range holding two white cups in trembling hands.

"You should have let me do that," said Ada, leaping up and taking the cups out of her hands and placing them both on an ancient looking table. "What am I thinking, I could have made the tea."

"Nay lass, I can still mek a cup of tea." She looked at the Grandfather clock that was over by the stairs. "Our Moira'll be over soon, then yer can get ter meet 'er. She's a bonny lass. Took after her Dad for her looks, she doesn't look like Wilfred."

"Tell me," Nana Moscrop made herself comfortable beside Ada and took hold of one of her hands.

"Didn't Charlie tell yer that he wrote to me when yer mother and father passed over? I only saw the lad the once, but he did write to tell me when they died."

"No, he didn't." Ada wondered why he hadn't. She thought that she and her brother had no secrets between them.

"It'll have been yer Dad then, must 'ave swore the lad ter secrecy. Ashamed he was when I told him that he wasn't Ted Moscrop's son, but that was how it had to be if he wasn't to be called a bastard."

"My Dad? You mean he was illegitimate, we never knew."

"No one did and if yer staying the night, I'll tell yer all about it. Now *you* tell me what has happened in your life."

Ada was just in the throes of telling her tale, how she had worked her way up to being a nursing sister and was living in Blackburn, when a small, plump woman, dark haired and in her late fifties, came bustling through the back door, carrying a baking dish and had a large bloomer under her arm.

"Only me, Mam," she shouted into the living room. "I'll stick it on the table. Sorry it's late, but our Jenny came natterin'. I told 'er, I had yer dinner warmin'. Oh! Who are you?"

Ada stood up and held her hand out politely, as the woman hurried across the room to meet her. "My name is Ada Moscrop. I believe that you and I are related."

It was later that day when Ada heard the story. After Moira had gone, taking with her the empty baking dish and half the bloomer, as her husband Stan was bound to eat the rest of it, Ada and Nana, as she had been told to call her grandmother, settled down to chew the fat. It appeared that Hilda had been a nursemaid for a local family called Tomkinson. Her employer, William Tomkinson had made his money by buying up shares in the railways and as a result had become part of the minor gentry.

His wife, a frail woman, having felt that she had done her matrimonial duties after the birth of a fourth child had nearly killed her and William, not wishing to visit the slums in the nearest town for the services of a prostitute, in case a willing girl was carrying any diseases, turned to Hilda for a little loving instead. It seemed to suit them both. Hilda, a practical girl, who like Ada hadn't seen a queue of men waiting for her hand in marriage, had been carrying a torch for William Tomkinson, ever since he had interviewed her for the position of nursemaid to his growing family.

"And there yer have it," explained Nana Moscrop. "Not a lot more to tell, other than the unavoidable happened and I began to carry his baby. But William was a kind man, a decent man and didn't treat me like a pariah like many a married man would have done.

He had a word with Ted Moscrop, a tenant farmer on his property, and persuaded him to marry me. Ted was a widower and we knew each other from when we were little ones and he never did throw it back in my face that Wilfred belonged to Tomkinson. But the father and son bonding wasn't there for Wilfred, like it was with my other son and when Wilfred was old enough I took him aside and told him the nub of it. He got offered a job on the railways and was glad to take it, though he never knew of the strings that were pulled by Tomkinson so that he could have an apprenticeship. Nor where the money had come from when he wanted to buy his house. I didn't tell him, nor anyone, but William still gave me a little sum of money now and again. I kept it aside for Wilfred, in a box under the floorboards at the farm. I suppose it was meant to keep me quiet, so that I wouldn't mek his life difficult, but I never would 'ave done that, because I loved the man."

"It was all such a long time ago and they were happy together, he and my mother," Ada said soothingly, patting her grandparent's arm as she would one of her patients, after Hilda had turned away so that she could wipe her eyes with the hem of her dress. *And who was she to pass judgment on another soul, when she was about to embark on a similar undertaking.*

It was early the next morning when Ada called to say goodbye to Nana Moscrop. She'd had a refreshing sleep on the comfortable feather mattress in the bedroom belonging to Jimmy, her newly found second cousin. She had met Moira's husband Stan, who worked as a gardener at Dalston Hall and he had told her of their eldest son who was away in Whitehaven, working for a coal merchant who used to deliver the loads by an old horse and cart. Jimmy had delighted in delivering to the local population of the seaside town, but he wasn't so happy now. The owner had him delivering the coal by lorry and his beloved horse called Jess, had been put out to grass. Jimmy was a country lad at heart and was sad when his Nana had given up the farm, the way she had.

"But that's the way of the world, I keep telling him. He was lucky to come back unharmed from the war, because many of his mates didn't come back at all. Such is progress. All this modern transport, the factories that are springing up all over the place bringing work to them who couldn't get any before and do yer know, I swear I saw one of those aeroplanes, flying over Dalston the other day."

And besides Jimmy, Moira was mother to Jenny, Phil and Dorothy, all with families of their own in and living around Gaitsgill. Franny, Moira's sister, who had two grownup children to add to the growing list of Ada's new family, had gone to live in Newcastle and had married a man who was now a head teacher in a village school. Franny had met him when she had worked as an assistant teacher in Dalston.

"So when will we get to meet this new husband of yours?" asked Nana Moscrop, when Ada called to say goodbye, as she was on her way to visit Betty in Colbrook. "I can't believe you only got married a few weeks ago and he's had to go back home." She leant up to kiss Ada on the cheek and hug her warmly. "And don't forget, next time you write to that brother of yours in Australia, tell him I'm waiting to hear from him as well."

She shook her head in disbelief, once Ada had started walking down the lane towards the bus stop. A Town Planner and a Nursing Sister in the family. Well neither of them would have got their brains from her, so they must have got them from William Tomkinson!

It was raining when Ada climbed aboard the train, not heavily, but she could hear the sound of pitter pattering on the window as she took her seat. There was no one else in the compartment and she sighed with relief. She had much to think about that morning. Finding her father's family had been a shock in itself, but she could understand now why he had never talked about them. Except to Charles, her brother, she thought with a pang of envy, remembering how he had been allowed to sit within the signal box and she wasn't.

So she had a family. A whole lot of family if she counted all the cousins, first and second and probably third if she had stayed at Moira's longer and found there was more on the list. What must it have been like, to always have someone there to play with, argue with, have secrets with and be there for you when you needed someone to talk to? Of course she'd had her mother and to some extent, her friend Betty, but there had been no one else that she could confide in when childish troubles caused anxiety.

She slowly twisted the wedding ring round upon her finger and began to feel a sense of dread, as the train steamed slowly along the track towards Colbrook Station. Everything had turned out fine when she had presented herself to the Gaitsgill Moscrops as a married woman, wed to a man with good prospects, but who unfortunately had gone off to Ireland to see his granny who was ill. But Betty was a different kettle of fish. She was bound to see through Ada's story. She always had, as Ada always went pink in the face if she told a fib.

The rain had stopped by the time she had alighted on the platform, though in the distance she could see that the clouds hung low below the mountains and she felt that the air was cool upon her face. The station clock was showing just after half past ten and Ada wondered if Betty would be waiting for her. She usually attended morning service on a Sunday, but Ada had written ahead and said that there was a possibility that she and her husband Daniel would call in on their way to the Borders, where hopefully they might come across some trace of Wilfred's family. It would be nice to introduce them to Daniel as well.

Ada rammed her hat more securely onto her head, as the wind was blustery and she had forgotten to secure it with a hat pin. She scurried along the lane, dodging puddles and occasionally standing under a dripping tree, whilst she debated on what she was going to say to her friend. She felt annoyed with herself, she wasn't usually a ditherer. Sister Moscrop made firm decisions every day, so she couldn't understand why she was suddenly feeling apprehensive.

"Beard the lion in it's den" was the maxim that suddenly popped into her mind as she stood there. *"Nothing ventured, nothing gained"* came right along behind it. Resolute, she picked up her suitcase and walked along briskly, smiling to herself at her silliness in view of who she was going to tell.

Chapter Thirteen

The door was slightly open as Ada stood on Betty's step, waiting for her to answer her tap tap tapping.

"You're here," came Betty's delighted voice from somewhere within, causing Ada to walk into the hall of the cottage uninvited. "Well, where is he? Is he parking the car? Oh, I can't wait to meet him Mrs. McAuley. Show me the ring!" Her friend, flushed and excited came rushing into Ada's arms and hugged her tightly. "I made you a set of bed linen. I know you'll need them when you move into a place of your own."

She suddenly looked puzzled and went to the cottage door and poked her head through it, looking around. Ada called her back, than sat on the sofa in the living room with a thump.

"He's not here, Betty. He's had to go back to Ireland, his granny is ill."

Her friend's face was a picture. "You mean to say you got married yesterday, then he left you to visit his sick grandma instead of going on your honeymoon. Well, what a kind man, what a hero. There's not many men…"

"Betty, we didn't marry, he's married already. He didn't tell me until after I had made all the arrangements, even after I had sent a letter off to you. So what could I do? I would have died if my team of nurses had found out that I'd been jilted. Well, I wasn't really jilted, was I?"

"What!" Betty in her turn, sat down beside her, looking astounded. "He was a married man? What a nerve. So how did he think he'd get away without you knowing?" She patted Ada's arm, her poor friend must be distraught.

"Well…" This was the bit that might just put Betty against her. Her friend was a very religious woman and would not sanctify fornication. In her eyes, the coupling of a man and woman was confined to the bedroom and only performed then for the production of a child.

"Well, I think that it was his intake of alcohol that played its part the night he asked me to marry him. It seemed he was carried away by the moment and had forgotten that he was already spoken for. I believe that his marriage was forced upon him, as I think that she was already in the family way."

"Dirty dog." Betty was the epitome of scorn for the man. "Couldn't keep it in his trousers. Well, I hope you told him where to go."

"Actually Betty, there's no two ways of saying this… I've bought a cottage and we're going to set up home together."

If it hadn't been such a serious situation, Ada would have laughed out loud when she saw that her friend had her mouth hanging open in disbelief, but it didn't take Betty long to recover her senses.

"Have you gone mad? You've bought a cottage and you're going to set up home together? What live over the brush, as they call it? Sister Ada Moscrop cohabiting with a married Irishman?"

"Well, as you know Betty, I've always wanted a family. You of all people know what it is like to have two bonny children to care for. That is something that I've always wanted too." Ada waited in trepidation for a reaction, as she could feel the anger slowly rising in her friend.

"Yes, but my children were conceived with a thoroughly decent man. My man never touched me until we were respectably tucked up in our marriage bed. Janet and Sidney are the offspring of a hero, who gave his life for his country. Tell me Ada, did this Daniel go to war? Put himself at risk in order to defeat our enemies?"

When Ada shrugged, Betty stood up and beckoned to Ada to do the same. "I think you should go before Janet comes back from

Sunday School. It's lucky that Sidney's away at Martin's, because I wouldn't want them knowing what you're planning to do. I'm surprised at you. Throwing your career to the wind, after you've worked so hard to get were you are, just for a Johnny Come Lately who will probably drag you down in the end. I'll not give you the bed linen I made for you either. I'll give it to a properly married couple instead." Snatching her wedding present back after Ada had picked up the parcel unintentionally, along with her suitcase and handbag, it was then that Ada realised that she would never see her childhood friend again.

It was cold in the cottage when Ada arrived late that evening, after trudging into the unlit lane and feeling eternally grateful that it didn't go dark so early in the summer, or she would have felt very nervous entering the place without a light to see. She stifled a scream, as something ran over her foot and rushed through the open door, as she dumped her suitcase on the floor and felt in her handbag for a box of matches. A field mouse, a rat maybe. In the gloomy interior she couldn't tell.

She proceeded to light the two gas lamps, then looked around at the sparse furnishing in the room. Mrs. Thornton had left her the old sofa and an old peg rug in the living room and the table, which was covered with a green chenille table cloth, had two heavy looking chairs underneath it in the kitchen. Luckily for Ada, she had also left a pair of brown velvet curtains hanging at the windows at each end of the room.

She quickly drew them. Her intention was to curl up on the sofa as soon as possible, though first she must check if there was any slack left in the coal hole outside. She'd be dead in the morning if she spent the night in the really low temperatures that the summer of 1922 had turned out to have. But needs must, she couldn't trail back to the Nurses Home, report for duty next day and pretend that everything was good in her world. Her staff, the nosy beggars, would want to know all about the wedding and why she had returned home early from her honeymoon.

She found it hard to sleep as she lay on her makeshift bed, still fully dressed, with her feet wrapped up in a towel that she always took in her suitcase, whilst listening to the sounds of dying embers falling in the grate. There was the sound of a cat mewing on the doorstep and her mind kept going over and over the events of the day.

She had felt numb as she had dashed back along the lane to Colbrook Station, with tears from her eyes mingling with heavy drops of rain. She had felt sorrow that her friend had stood resolute against her impropriety and her lack of morals, when it came to living with a man. And what if Daniel never returned from Ireland anyway? Had she lost her friend for the sake of wanting her dream fulfilled by him?

The man in question walked along a Blackburn street to his lodgings the following morning. He had a dejected look about him, because it was only the night before that Milly had spurned his advances. It had been inevitable that the man who had the job of porter would get over his influenza and report for duty, which he had done the day before and so Daniel was made redundant. His return had come at a price, as without a job there was nothing for it, but to return to the brewery and pick up the reins, or at least his car, once more.

Daniel and Milly had walked along the waterside together, where elegant necked swans mingled with geese and mallards, waiting for the many tourists to feed them with pieces of bread. A paddle steamer, its horn tooting as it pulled away from the jetty in readiness to take its passengers to Hawkshead, caused a lump in Daniel's throat as he realised that this might be goodbye for him and his girl, if he couldn't get her to change her mind.

"You can't mean it, Milly," he said, trying to pull her closer with his arm around her, as they sat on a wooden bench together, which overlooked the lake. "I thought we had something special. I mean, you've allowed me liberties that a young woman of your calibre wouldn't usually allow. I thought it was because you loved me and we would be together for always. You know how I feel about you and if it's because I've lost my job as a porter, I can always find another."

"Daniel, my love." Millicent looked sad, as she lifted her blue eyes trimmed with curling black lashes to look into his own. "Working as a receptionist in a beautiful hotel is all I have ever wanted, since coming here with my sisters and parents on holiday. When my parents died just after the war from that damned Spanish lurgy that so many people succumbed to, I promised myself that I would be my own woman and come up here to live in the Lakes. I didn't want to marry a village boy, have lots of children and be beholden to my husband for ever and a day. I enjoy my job, I get to meet lots of different people and the money that I earn goes straight into my pocket. I'm sorry Daniel, I have worked here for three happy years and this is where I want to stay."

"So, you're saying that even if I was to find another job and we had a long courtship, you still wouldn't marry me one day?"

"That is what I am saying, Daniel. I do love you, but perhaps not in the way you expect me to."

Ada awoke to a tapping sound. She groaned at the noise and hoped whoever was at the door would go away and leave her to doze a little more. The night before had been fraught enough, with the fire going out and the temperature dropping in the room she was lying in and her mind in a constant whirl as she relived the events of the weekend.

The tapping continued and Ada, feeling annoyed at the intrusion and desperate to go to the lavatory now that she was on her feet, walked briskly to answer the door. A woman who looked to be in her sixties, dressed in an olive green dress, a little on the plump side and with grey hair styled in a bun as a top knot, stood on the step. She looked as if she was ready to take flight if the person who answered wasn't very nice. She had heard from Mrs. Thornton, that the cottage attached to hers had been sold to a new occupant and when she had seen that the curtains were still drawn, even though it was half past eight in the morning, she had come to investigate.

"Yes?" asked Ada, sleep deprivation causing her to sound hoity toity to the listener's ear.

"Oh, I'm sorry," said her neighbour's voice apologetically. "I'm from next door and I couldn't help but hear moving about in here last night and so I came to have a look in case there were burglars."

"Burglars?" Ada looked at the timid looking woman in amazement. "You mean to say you get burglars around here?"

"No…no, we haven't ever had any burglars, but yer never know… That's why I came ter have a look anyway."

Ada felt a bubble of laughter, causing her face to split into a grin.

"Much good you'd be against a great big burglar. Anyway, come in, you can see there's only me."

"Oh, I didn't mean to intrude." But the woman followed Ada into the living room anyway and Ada pulled back the curtains as she passed them. "Oh, she left the furniture. I wondered what she was going to do with it."

"Sit down, sit down," Ada moved the towel away and beckoned her neighbour to sit on the sofa.

"The name's Ada Moscrop. My husband and I have only just moved in, as you can see. It seemed sensible to keep what furniture there was, until we can replace it."

"I'm Hetty Robinson, pleased to meet yer. Is Mr. Moscrop upstairs? I don't want to intrude."

"No, but would you excuse me for a minute or so, I just want to use the lavatory." Ada went outside to the brick built outhouse which held the porcelain and promised herself as she hovered, that this place and every part of the cottage was going to be scoured by the end of the day. You would have thought that somebody would have put themselves out and given everywhere a bit of a do. Especially in the lavatory, which was stinking.

"No, he's away on business," Ada explained, after she had

washed her hands under the running water from the kitchen tap and then went to sit at the side of her neighbour. "He works for a brewery and gets to go all over the place. So, Hetty, how long have you lived in Dunscar?"

"All me life. Although having said that, me and my hubby moved here to the cottage years ago when we both worked at Eagley Mill. That's down the brew by the way. We got this when Norman was made a foreman, but before that we lived with me mother on Cox Green near the quarry. Me Dad were a quarryman and we were brought up on the hill."

"And have you got children?"

"All grown up and moved away, except for me eldest boy who fell in the war. The girls got married and one lives on the other side of Bolton and the other lass lives at the bottom of Tonge Moor. And yerself, do you have any kiddies?

"Not yet. I work as a nurse, but I am sure we'll have children in the future. Now, perhaps you can tell me where I can get a bit of shopping. I'm clemming for a cup of tea and I haven't eaten since yesterday."

"Mr. McAuley!" The door of the lodgings flew open, as Daniel walked up the path. "I wondered where you'd got to. I got your note to say that you were going back to Ireland, but you didn't say when you would be back!" Mrs. Dewsbury sounded most put out as she spoke, to Daniel's dismay, as she had always been very pleasant with him.

"I didn't know when I'd be back, Mrs. Dewsbury. Me granny was ill and unfortunately she died whilst I was across there." He crossed his fingers behind his back as he said it. His grandma had died many years before when he was just a lad, so that would be another sin he would have to confess when next he was in the Confession box. The sins he'd been committing were colossal and his knees would be worn out when he got around to visiting the Sacred Heart.

"Well, I don't know how to tell yer this, Mr. McAuley, seeing as how yer granny has died so, but Mr. Preedy was of the opinion that you were getting married. He said that a lady that you had been seen with in the town had been into their store and purchased an outfit suitable for a wedding. So we put two and two together and I allowed his friend Malcolm to have your room. As you know, Mr. McAuley, this is my only income and I depend on it and with you going off the way you did, it put your rent into arrears."

"Oh." Daniel couldn't believe his ears! No sooner had he left his lodgings, that rat, Preedy, had moved his friend in. He felt his anger growing stronger as each minute passed him by.

"I take it yer didn't throw me stuff away, Mrs. Dewbury. A good Catholic woman like yerself, I'd be assured that you kept my belongings for me."

"It is so," Mrs. Dewsbury looked relieved that her ex-lodger hadn't bitten her head off after hearing her news. "I'll go and fetch them. I'm sorry, but you left me no choice and I have to say that you have been a model lodger, if you want a reference off me."

"No, yer alright, Mrs. Dewsbury." Daniel pulled himself together and spoke haughtily. "I was going to tell yer that I've purchased a little place fer meself in the country. However, I was going to give you a bit of notice before I left."

Chapter Fourteen

It had been a productive day. Everywhere in the cottage smelt of vinegar, beeswax and ammonia and the cast iron range had been cleaned with a mixture of water and bicarbonate soda. The curtains had been taken down and washed with a handful of soap flakes that had been dissolved in water in the kitchen sink. They were hung to dry over a piece of rope, which had been tied between two posts at each end of the yard. The outhouse smelled strongly of Lysol.

It had been warm for a change that morning and the sun was high in the sky. Ada could hear the blackbirds singing in the trees, as she had set off to walk in the direction of Egerton. She had a list of basics, mostly cleaning, sanitary and toiletry supplies. A saucepan or frying pan and a little flour, sugar, porridge oats and an ounce of yeast, as she had noticed there was a warming oven within the range where she could proof a loaf of bread. Perhaps she would buy one of those delicious pies that she had eaten on that fateful day with Daniel. She pondered, not for the first time, on where he had got to and if he was ever coming back.

The grocer, this time sensing he had got himself a permanent customer, was polite to the point where Ada wondered if he would lick her boots, if she asked him to. Perhaps he had remembered his arrogance towards her and was trying to make amends.

"I could have these things delivered if you wish, Madam," he said, after piling her purchases upon his counter and mentally deciding that he could shut the shop that afternoon with the profit he had made. "There are rather too many purchases for a delicate lady such as yourself to be carrying."

"I think you're right," Ada replied. "I'll just take the things that I will be needing in the short term. Oh, and one of your delicious pies."

It was cool sitting on a wooden bench later, under the ancient trees that grew in the churchyard. She ate her pie and listened to the children's happy voices, as they ran around in the grounds of the nearby school. One day, it might be her little children's voices that people could hear, when they played in Walmsley Church School's playground.

It was around seven o' clock, when Ada, worn out from her walk to the grocers and feeling every muscle in her body from cleaning the cottage from top to bottom, not forgetting the porcelain, felt her eyes drooping as she sat on the sofa staring into space. She had cooked herself some eggy toast in the small frying pan that had been delivered, along with the cleaning materials and groceries on a cart by the man himself. She had made herself a cup of tea, after scouring the coating from the rusty old kettle and the teapot, both having become corroded over the years. Then surveyed the room with satisfaction, though the rehung velvet curtains looked rather plucked and worn.

She sighed, as she mentally ticked off all the things she was going to have to buy to make the cottage comfortable. A bed to begin with and a chest of drawers and wardrobe to hang up her clothes, when she brought them back with her from the Nurses Home. The upstairs rooms were empty, although she had found them easier to clean with there not being any furniture and Reggie Thornton, true to his word, had fixed new guttering and treated the damp.

Hetty, her neighbour, had advised that there would be a coal delivery each Friday and the local farmer had a daily milk round, except on Sunday and as Ada sat there contemplating the need to visit a furniture shop in Blackburn and a letter needing to be written to Charles in Australia to tell him of her new address, a knock came on the cottage door.

Thinking it was her neighbour and not wanting to encourage Hetty to drop in at anytime she chose, Ada rose slowly from the sofa and wandered over to the window. She was taken aback when she saw who it was that was standing on the doorstep, with his face clean shaven and his hair newly trimmed. It was the man whom she had thought might have gone from her life forever. And as she opened the door, he stretched out his arms to enfold her and after noting that she was wearing a wedding ring, began grinning from ear to ear.

"Ada me darlin'" Daniel said, his eyes beginning to glimmer with tears, when he saw that he was welcome at least by her, after finding his room had been given away. Sister Ada Moscrop, his only hope, would give him succour like no other woman would.

She felt delighted! Here he was, standing there with his arms circling her tightly, telling her how much he loved and missed her with that silver tongue of his. Listening, as he whispered that he never wanted to let her go and seeing that sitting on the pathway were two black holdalls and a small suitcase, it was obvious that he was intending to stay.

"Yer wouldn't believe the time I've had today," he said, after dragging in his heavy bags and sinking down on the sofa. "After the bumpy night crossing from Dun Lagaoire and then an early train up to Blackburn, I found that Mrs. Dewsbury, that's me landlady, had packed all me clothing and left it in the hall. It appears that the Preedy fella, one of the other lodgers, had bagged me room fer his mate. I'd left her a note, said that I was going to Ireland to see me sick granny and that is what happens. I was waitin' to see if you'd got this place before giving her notice, yer see."

"Well, you're here now and I hope your granny's feeling better," said Ada, walking briskly to the range, her spirits high with the sight of him, to put the kettle on. "I've only got some eggs and a bit of bread if you would like me to make you something to eat."

"No, you're alright," Daniel replied, looking around the

room and thinking it looked a bit neglected, though he couldn't have faulted its cleanliness. "I had to wait ages for a bus at the Boulevard, but they had a little cafe there and so I went in. What I really need now is a couple of pints of Guinness or failing that, a glass of stout. What do yer say, Mrs. Moscrop, are yer up for it?"

Lurching, staggering, giggling at nothing at all, at least Ada was, Daniel being well used to the amount of alcohol he had drank that night, they wended their way back to the cottage, after the hand bell had been rung by the landlord in The Flag, to call time.

Ada, unused to drinking three glasses of port and lemon in succession, was as the term goes "anybody's" and made no protest when Daniel, having checked out upstairs and finding that there was no bed to lie on, pushed her lightly upon the sofa and began to undress her. It was time for "Miss Starchy Knickers" to find out what a shag was all about, although he was certain she would know all the mechanics of what was involved. Didn't she see a man's willy on a daily basis at the hospital, but he bet no one had got close enough to give her a shag before.

Her slender body trembled under his touch, as his hands eased off her skirt and bodice and as he struggled to remove her drawers and stockings she helped him, giggling as she did so. She lay naked, as he stood up to shrug off his trousers and watched as he fumbled with his shirt buttons and yank off his tie. For a moment, it hit her that she was giving up her virginity to a married man, instead of waiting for a single one to come along.

Then Betty, stern and anxious, came leaping into her mind, as she felt his weight come upon her. His warm, fleshy body smelt of sweat and his breath was stinking of the stout he had consumed earlier, whilst he probed around with his fingers to find the place he was looking for. It was too late for thoughts of morality though when she felt the hardness of his baby maker, as he first tried to enter her, seemingly without much success. So she guided him, primevally desperate to feel this hardness within her. She shuddered with pain as his penis parted the walls of her vagina and she felt it push. Then exhaling her breath she began to pant, as her heart had begun to throb violently. When his actions caused such ecstasy which she couldn't control, she instinctively wrapped her legs around his waist, until something inside her exploded. It was over for him, as he lay on top of her out of breath and glassy eyed, gone to goodness knows where in his mind, whilst she felt wet and sore. But on reflection, it was worth all the bother if it resulted in a pregnancy.

He stood on the back step later enjoying a cigarette and giving himself a pat on the back, as he knew he hadn't disappointed. He had heard her gasps of pleasure as he grasped her bony bottom and pounded in. She'd feel beholden. She'd let him stay and he wouldn't have to go cap in hand to another mercenary landlady like Mrs. Dewsbury.

Ada looked exhausted when he looked down upon her sleeping form and wondered how they were both going to fit on the sofa. For a moment he felt a wave of tenderness. Much like he felt when he was in his mother's company, who was a kindly lady but could give it out if her boys were ever bad. He bent down and kissed Ada's cheek, then made himself comfortable across a couple of chairs in the kitchen.

It was on the following Monday that Daniel presented himself to Mr. Fletcher in his office. Both Daniel and Ada had travelled together on the train to Blackburn, as before Ada could continue working at the Infirmary, she had to have an interview with Matron.

"Good morning Daniel," Mr. Fletcher said, after Freda had inquired after Daniel's granny and if she was now in good health. She busied herself at the filing cabinet, so that she could hear what Mr. Fletcher had to say to his area manager.

"I don't know whether this is good news or bad for you, Daniel, but in your absence, things have been moving apace and

Management has decided to put in an offer for a smaller brewery than the one in Bolton. It will now mean that you will have to travel to Colne."

"Colne?" Daniel's spirits slumped. He could hardly ask Ada to move again.

"Yes, I'm afraid it's north of Burnley and under the circumstances I can understand if you weren't very happy about the changes. With you being betrothed, that is, and your fiancee beginning her new job at the hospital in Bolton."

He had to think quickly. More lodgings perhaps? Somewhere nearer Colne, where he could rest his head until Friday night, then visit Ada at the weekend. Jesus, Mary and Joseph, what a mess. She wouldn't be pleased, he was sure of it.

"I have an aunt who lives in Burnley, if you have to look for new digs, Mr. McAuley." Freda looked pleased at the prospect. "She's a good cook and keeps a clean house and I go to visit her once a week."

"Thank you, Freda. It's a lot to think about. I take it you'll want me to drive over to the brewery now, Mr. Fletcher and introduce meself."

"So, Ada Moscrop, a newly married woman. Never thought I'd see the day." Matron Chandler sounded sarcastic, as Ada sat in the woman's office waiting for her superior's instructions.

"So your husband was able to get back from Ireland in time for the wedding. That was a bit of luck, wasn't it?"

She had definitely been the talk of the hospital whilst she'd been away, thought Ada resentfully. Probably the flames had been fanned by Alf, the porter, who had looked distinctly uncomfortable when she had passed his lodge earlier.

"Yes, it was right up to the wire. All dressed up and nowhere to go if he hadn't appeared." She made her voice sound jocular, whilst inside she was seething at all the nosiness. She'd wear her ring for always now and make them eat their words.

"Have you found a replacement, Matron Chandler, or do you

wish me to continue as a Ward Sister on Men's Surgical? I am quite willing to present myself for duty as long as you wish."

"Or until the pitter patter of tiny feet restricts your intention."

"Yes, I understand that if under the circumstances a suitable person applies, you will want me, as a married woman to submit my resignation. So shall I go and take up my nursing duties now?"

It was early that evening when Daniel, first to come into the cottage and finding nothing for him to eat, no Ada to cook for him nor even a bed to lay himself on, decided irritably to venture again to the local hostelry. The Dunscar Arms this time, as he remembered Ada telling him that the wife had obliged her with a sandwich one lunch hour. Perhaps if he gave her a pathetic tale, something about his wife not being home and she hadn't left a meal, she'd take pity on him and he didn't mind a pint or three whilst he was there.

He stroked a wing lovingly as he passed his car, parked across the lane where he could keep an eye on it. He had missed the little vehicle whilst he'd been away and wondered, jealously, if anyone else had driven it from the brewery in his absence.

"So the wanderer returns," said Reggie Thornton, who was propping up the crowded bar when Daniel entered the fuggy room and found it to be full of workers on their way home. "What can I get yer, my treat?"

"I'll have a bottle of stout," he replied, seeing that there was still no shiny pump proclaiming that they served Guinness there. "On yer way home, are yer? Does it get crowded like this every day?"

"Usually. Some come in off the six six shift and are desperate for a drink. Those two over there are from the bleach works. You can smell them from over here and Ronnie and Pete work at Eagley Mill. They're standing alongside John who's a tackler and Tim's a moulder. The other men work up at the quarry. I don't see them much as they usually drink in The Flag. Settled in have yer?

"Yes and no, we haven't got a bed yet and we've nothing to eat until she visits the grocers. I'll have to ask the landlord if his wife'll make me a sandwich. Still, I'm sure my wife has got it all in hand, she's a great organiser."

"Most of them are. Yer never said what yer do for a livin, mate. What did yer do fer a livin' back in Ireland?"

"Ah, could yer just excuse me for a minute, Reggie, I need to get to the lavatory. Back in a mo'."

He waited until Reggie, a talkative soul, had been caught up in another conversation with some men who were propping up the bar. Then spying the landlord's wife, who was walking from the kitchen with a tray of glasses in her hands, asked if she could oblige him with a sandwich.

"I don't cook, never have cooked, " said Ada in explanation, when Daniel came back to the cottage later and wanted to know why there wasn't any food. "I've never had to as I've always eaten in the hospital canteen and my mother, God Bless her, only showed me how to fry an egg, make a decent loaf of bread or make a batter for a Yorkshire pudding. I can cook you one now if you like. Not a Yorkshire pudding, but a fried egg."

"No, don't bother yerself." Daniel stood on the back door step smoking a last cigarette before he got on his makeshift bed. "I had a cheese sandwich at the Dunscar."

And plenty to drink as well, thought Ada, as she finished off the bottle of lemonade that she had bought on her way to the train station. "Anyroad, I've a bed, a wardrobe and a chest of drawers being delivered tomorrow and I've arranged with Hetty to let them in, as I have to be away early."

Chapter Fifteen

It was a few weeks later when Daniel was greeted by his office door by Freda, who was looking quite concerned as she hovered there.

"I've put a letter on your desk, Mr. McAuley," she said, gently. "The postmark is all blurred, so I couldn't see if it was from your father over there in Ireland. I hope it isn't bad news about your granny again."

"Thank you, Freda," Daniel replied, feeling suddenly irritated and wanting to call her a nosy cow, but he knew she was only concerned for his welfare. She had appeared quite put out when he had told her that he would be staying on at his lodgings. Thank heavens she didn't know that he and Ada were cohabiting, or she would become a woman scorned, he had no doubt.

Not that this cohabiting business was much to his advantage. With Ada travelling each morning on the train before cockcrow, then working a twelve hour shift before returning, whilst he was driving hither and thither in the northern parts of Lancashire, there had only been a Saturday or a Sunday, whichever was her day off, when they could really be together.

The newly purchased double bed wasn't seeing much action. She was always bloody tired, so coupling had been put on the back burner and she had told him that if he wasn't happy with his diet of eggs and bread, then he should cater for himself. So now he had a daily meal in what ever cafe was handy. It was usually a substantial one with a pudding for afters. He was finding that it was costing him a lot from his wages though and he was glad that she hadn't asked him for any house-keeping.

Daniel opened the letter gingerly, whilst praying that it wasn't his father giving him more bad news about the Black and Tans and that someone had found out where he was living. Perhaps it was something to say that hostilities towards the dissidents were over and if he wanted, he could go back home. The words on the page leapt out as he scanned them. It was from Millicent Pearson, the girl he had met at Bowness, at the Lakeside Manor Hotel.

My Dear Daniel, she had written. He held his breath.
I have been giving a lot of thought to your proposal of marriage and have decided to accept if you are still willing to have me as your wife. I realise that I may have hurt your feelings in this matter, but I have news that I would like to share with you. I hope it will be in order to visit you this Saturday in Blackburn. I had intended to visit my family this weekend anyway, as it is my 21st birthday. If I don't hear from you, I will meet you at the train station at a quarter past eleven on Saturday.
Love Milly.

Fecking Hell! What was he to do? Write back saying that he had found another love and he had been so hurt by her rejection that he didn't want to see her again? Tell her that he was having to go back to Ireland and would no longer be at the address he had given her? It was a good job he hadn't given her Mrs. Dewsbury's address, his previous lodgings, as he wouldn't have received the letter and then where would that have left him? She could have easily turned up here at the brewery and he wouldn't have been in. Anyone from the brewery could have told her the true story. And what was this, she had some news that she wanted to share with him?

He put his head in his hands and rued the fact that he couldn't keep his willy in his trousers. If what he thought was true, he'd be trapped again!

Ada looked tired when he wandered in that evening and as he watched her washing one of his shirts, then taking it to the mangle in the outhouse, he felt sorry that his feelings towards her didn't go beyond the admiration of her character. He liked her feistiness, her independence, her brisk no nonsense personality, but he couldn't, hand on heart, say that she was the woman of his dreams. Milly was that person. The thoughts of making love to Milly, could make his cock grow. Whilst with Ada, the sharing of the bed had only compensations. They were fast asleep as soon as their heads touched the pillow most nights.

"Would you like me to make you a cup of tea?" he asked, after he came in from smoking a cigarette in the back yard and reflecting on his situation. "You look tired. Is all this getting up early and travelling gettin' too much for yer?"

"Something like that," Ada said, sitting on the sofa, then kicking her shoes off. "It doesn't help that I'm six weeks pregnant neither."

"What!" Daniel thought his heart was going to jump out of his chest and he could hardly get his breath as it was. Pregnant? Expecting a baby? Jesus, Mary and Joseph, what was going to happen next?

"Well, that's what usually happens when a man and woman get together to make a baby, doesn't it?" Ada said with a flash of humour. "That's probably why I feel the way I do."

"Have yer been sick? Have yer gone off food that yer used to eat before?" Daniel remembered that Connie had those problems when she was expecting.

"Yes, and I've also seen the doctor at the Infirmary. He confirms that a little Moscrop will appear early on next year."

Shite.

"You don't look too pleased about it Daniel, I thought you would be cock a' hoop that you were helping to fulfill a dream of mine. You don't have to stick around if you don't want to, I can easily bring it up on my own."

She could too, thought Daniel, as he stood there dithering on what he should say to her. *She had the cottage in her name and money in the bank and he had what? A car belonging to the brewery, a stressful job, no savings and nowhere to run if anyone came looking for him. He'd be a fool to give her up, especially as he knew for certain that this expected baby was the fruit of his loins and no one else's. He'd make a good father. Given the opportunity, he knew he would.*

"I know you could, but you're not going to. We'll raise this child together, Ada, me love."

The flowers he bought Milly cost him one and sixpence. A great big bunch from the market and the lady on the stall bound them in a pink satin ribbon with a big bow.

"There yer are love. She's a lucky girl to have someone like you as her husband. Not many blokes buy flowers for their wife."

He supposed, as he walked down the street towards the station, that he did look old enough to have a wife. He had grown his moustache again, thick and bushy as he liked it, even though Ada had remarked that it felt as if she was being kissed by a bristly hair brush. He was wearing his best suit, the one he liked to wear on special occasions and he had polished his shoes until he could see his face in them.

Ada, good old Ada, was still working, even though she had promised him she would give her notice into Matron, now she knew for certain she was expecting his child. Knowing her, she would cover up, hide herself under her big white apron. She was thin enough, as there still wasn't a pick on her. He had all day now to sort out this new situation he might find himself in and perhaps the rest of his life to rue it.

Milly was standing outside the main entrance, all dressed up in a lemon calf length dress with a matching jacket. She wasn't wearing a hat and her short brown hair looked shiny after much brushing. Her pretty face broke into a smile when she saw him saunter around the corner and she left her suitcase and handbag for a moment, whilst she ran to embrace him.

"Oh are those for me?" she cried, snatching the flowers and planting a big kiss on on his cheek, then standing back to look at him critically. "Look at you all dressed up in a suit and shiny shoes and what about that moustache you've grown? You look like a manager, not a brewery worker."

Daniel's heart began to beat that bit faster and he could feel the blood rushing through his veins, as he remembered those times when she had let him have his way with her. He remembered the feel of her warm flesh, plump and rounded under her cami-knickers, as he lay upon her body and showed her his love. It was love that he was feeling, wasn't it? Not just an urgent need to satisfy his desire.

"I think we need to talk so," he said, taking her hand, then her suitcase, as she carried the flowers. "I know a little cafe where we can talk things over and I'll buy yer some dinner as well."

They found a vacant table easily, as the morning shoppers still enthralled with the variety of products on display upon the market stalls and in the many small shops that abounded, didn't yet have the pangs of hunger to draw them in at that time.

"What can I get fer yer?" he asked, drinking in the sight of this nubile young girl who appeared to want him in her life. There was six years in age between them and he knew he looked older with growing a moustache.

"I only want to nibble on something," she said, smiling at him suggestively, making his knees turn to jelly. "I had a full breakfast before I came away this morning."

"A chicken barm cake then?" he asked, then suddenly began to feel deceitful when he remembered that he and Ada had a chicken balm cake each, last time they were in the cafe.

"Perhaps a piece of cake," Milly answered. "They looked delicious on the counter. Yes, I'll have a piece of cake."

"And I'll have a ham barm," he said to the waitress who was hovering, glad he was banishing those thoughts by eating a ham one. The waitress looked familiar and he wondered why he thought that. He didn't usually take notice of waitresses.

119

"So the news, Millicent Pearson," he said, trying to make his voice sound light hearted, although it might be that he was facing his doom.

"Well, do you remember that you asked me to marry you and I said no, because I wanted to remain a receptionist?" Millicent lowered her voice conspiratorially and Daniel nodded. "I'm expecting your baby." She watched his face, as his mind began to war with itself within and wondered if he would accept her news with a sense of responsibility or tell her to go to Hell. "Daniel, you did ask me to marry you. Have you changed your mind since we saw each other, or do I have to bear this child alone?" She looked so downcast that he thought she was about to cry.

"No, Milly, me darlin'," he quickly made his mind up. "You don't have to do this on your own. I was just a bit shaken by your news, that's all. One minute I'm a single man with me heart near broken and the next I hear I'm to be married to my dearest love."

It was strange how life could present its predicaments, but with a little careful planning and a bit of the luck of the Irish, a solution to it all would overcome.

"I was hoping to be married in our local church," Millicent said, as they wended their way back to the railway station, because she had persuaded him to accompany her, as her family had organised a birthday party. "It's in a little village and the church is called St. Saviours. I haven't asked, but I presumed that you were a Protestant, although I know that there are a lot of Catholics in Ireland."

A Proddy wedding was just the job, thought Daniel, after he had paid their fares and they sat waiting for the train on a bench together. He wouldn't be committing a sin by marrying Millicent, as the Protestant religion wasn't recognised by the Roman Catholic church. It had been because of some horny old English king, who had become tired of his wives and wanted to divorce them which the Catholic church wouldn't allow, that the Protestant church had been created. It didn't cross his mind at all that there might be similarities with that king in his own life.

"So tell me," Millicent said, after she had thanked him again for the flowers and told him that she couldn't believe that she was twenty one, as the years after the war had flown so fast. "How come you're wearing this rather smart suit and have grown a moustache? I thought you told me you worked for a brewery."

"I do work fer a brewery, but as an Area Manager and I have to tell yer now, I'm away a lot with me job. When I came to Lakeside Manor, it was to rest me mind, as the work gets stressful and so I wanted a couple of weeks away to get meself sorted. As yer can tell from me accent, I'm from the Emerald Isle and me father has a small brewery just outside Dublin. I'm over here to learn from a bigger company, as one day the brewery will be mine."

"Is that so?" Milly was intrigued. Wait until she told her snobby sister.

Stoneclough, a small village at the bottom of a hill, with a couple of pubs, a sweet shop, a grocers and a butchers, was situated near the River Irwell and home to members of the Pearson family. Across the bridge, in a place called Prestolee, were large mills that provided work for those in the community. There was the Kearsley Paper Mill, just across from the Pack Horse Bridge and two others called the Irwell Bank Spinning Mill and the Irwell Valley Mill. Both were situated on the banks of the river and on land close to the churchyard of Holy Trinity.

Some of the extended Pearson family worked as spinners, but Bunty, Milly's elder sister, had inherited her parents' clogger firm, which involved making and repairing clogs for the mill workers. Bunty employed five men and was a stern taskmaster and the family lived in a nice two storey white washed house near Ringley Lock.

It was just after two in the afternoon, when Milly and Daniel arrived at the family home. It had appeared to Daniel to be a long walk from the train station to the place called Ringley, especially as he was carrying Milly's suitcase. She carried her handbag and flowers and the temperature on that day in August, for once, was rather warm. Milly, being her usual effusive self, pointed out the bridge that spanned the River Irwell, where the village of Prestolee sat in splendid isolation surrounded by the river and the Manchester, Bolton and Bury Canal. Daniel felt concerned that he hadn't a clue where he was headed to and hoped that he would be able to find his way back home.

What the hell was he going to tell Ada? he fretted, as they passed the long rows of terraced houses which lined the street and accommodated those who worked at the mills in the area. By his calculations, these babies, both which he had fathered, would be born only a couple of weeks apart! Should he tell Ada the truth, or maybe part of it, or think of something entirely different to explain his disappearances?

Bunty Pearson was built like an Amazon. If Fate had decreed it different, she would have been born a man. She didn't suffer fools gladly, had been known to stand her ground against any bullies in the area and could do the job of making clogs as well as any of her workers. Had Daniel known of her existence, he would never have made love to Bunty's younger sister, because as soon as he met her, he knew he was going to regret his action for the rest of his life.

Chapter Sixteen

It was late when Daniel stumbled along the unlit road from the train station, as he tried to find his way back to the cottage and when he did so, it was to find Ada darning a pair of his socks and a pile of ironing sitting on the kitchen table.

"I wondered where you'd got to," she said, putting the kettle on top of the range to boil again. "I got in about eight. Gosh it was busy on our ward today. There was an accident on Preston Road and we got three of the casualties. Have you eaten? I've not got much in, I've been feeling a bit queasy."

"You should be resting, not about to tackle a load of ironing at this time of night. I'll make yer a brew, as yer call it. Now sit."

Daniel shook his head. Was he dreaming? Had he really spent the last few hours with the Pearson family, celebrating Milly's twenty first birthday and their engagement with a cake and plenty of beer, when he should have been sitting here quietly reading a newspaper or nudging a bottle or two at the Dunscar Arms.

"I found a letter on the mat from my brother in Australia," Ada continued. "He said congratulations and he said he hopes he'll get to meet you one day. Him and Sara keep promising themselves they'll come over and visit England, but he likes it there in Melbourne. I told him in my last letter that I'd gone up to Gaitsrigg to find my family and he was surprised I'd done that, but I needed to do something while you were away."

"Yes, I'm sorry about that me darlin'." Daniel felt a pang of guilt as he thought of his deceitfulness, both today and when he was supposed to be in Ireland. "Perhaps one day we can take a train ride up to see them all and you can introduce me. It must be nice fer you to suddenly have a family, when there was always just you two. Come on now, it's time for bed. You go up and I'll bring yer a nice cup of tea."

It was later when he lay at the side of Ada, after kissing her cheek and patting her shoulder until she slept, he reflected on the truth of what he had done. It would surely come back one day in the future and bite him on the bum.

By the time he and Milly had arrived at this place called Ringley, where the River Irwell flowed under a narrow stone built bridge, across from a clock tower and a church called St. Saviour, Milly's 21st birthday party was already in full swing. The house was situated down a narrow lane and set at the top of a path in a large garden. It was full of anyone who belonged to the extended Pearson family. There were spouses, children, cousins and neighbours, all helping themselves to food from the groaning table. Pies and sandwiches of every variety, cakes, biscuits, jellies and blancmanges sat in a glorious assortment.

A little child, who had been given the job of keeping his eye out for the arrival of the birthday girl, signaled them all of Milly's arrival and then as she and Daniel stepped into the living room, everyone began to sing. Milly was swamped, as everyone rushed to kiss her cheek, hug her to them, hand over presents and wish her well, whilst Daniel stood in the doorway, looking on.

"Ah, you must be the gallant Daniel McAuley," commented a tall and bulky lady nearby, with her long brown hair swept into a bun and her ankle length dress covered with a voluminous pinafore. "Come through here with me, I think we've got a lot of talking to do me laddo, don't you?" She pushed her way through the crowd, with Daniel hastening to follow, until they were in a large cluttered kitchen, where another young woman who looked a bit like Milly was buttering some slices of bread.

"You can leave us Nelly," the woman commanded. "As yer can

hear your sister's arrived and I need a moment to speak with this one. Do sit." She pointed to a kitchen chair and Daniel, surprised that he was being treated as if he was a small boy being given a talking to by his headmaster, did so.

"Right then, I'm Bunty, Milly's elder sister. I've been responsible for my sisters since our parents died of influenza just after the war and so I feel it is my duty to ask you of your intentions towards Millicent. She told me in her last letter that she is expecting a child and you're the father." She waited for him to say something and when he only nodded, she continued with her diatribe.

"So I take it that I can make all the arrangements with the rector of our local church, call the banns, organise the catering and you'll be there with your friends and family on the day." Then suddenly her rounded face split into a grin and putting out her hand, shook his with the force of a monkey wrench, then walked to the living room door to make an announcement.

He felt momentarily terrified as he listened to Bunty telling the guests that beside the party being to celebrate Millicent's birthday, it was also to celebrate her engagement. His bowels felt as if they had turned to water, when everyone began to shake his hand and tell him what a lucky man he was. He just wanted to run away; run away from this dreadful situation he was finding himself in. How was he going to cope with two pregnant women and a wife in Ireland and the stressful job he had committed himself to? It was a punishment. A punishment from God, for all the sins he'd been committing.

It had been hard to get away, he thought, going over the events of the day, whilst he lay next to Ada, breathing in the smell of the rose petal soap she had washed her hands and face in. And he only did so, after he had told Milly that if he didn't catch the last train and be back at his lodgings by ten thirty, the front door would be locked against him by his landlady.

Before he had left, Bunty guided him through the kitchen and led him to a long whitewashed building at the bottom of the yard, where she showed him all the hammers, cutting tools, lathes, lasts, bundles of leather strips and boxes of studs, which were all used in the making of the clogs. She was proud of the fact that she was a woman and ran the business with a steady hand and she was most impressed to hear that Daniel was an Area Manager instead of a worker at the brewery. "I thought you were a cut above," she said. "As soon as I saw you all dressed up in that there suit, with your shiny shoes and Homburg hat, I knew you were more than just a brewery worker, like Millicent said. Tell me, will yer be taking her to Ireland, when all the unrest over there settles?"

"I don't think so" he replied truthfully. "At least not until me Dada passes on and I'm left to run the brewery."

"Then welcome to the Pearson family, Daniel." Bunty took him to her ample breast and hugged him.

He had been advised by Bunty, that until after the wedding when he and Milly would be moving into the family home and sharing Milly's old room where a double bed was to be installed, he was to continue living at his lodgings. She was having no hanky panky under her roof and when Milly returned to Ringley after serving out her notice at Lakeside Manor, he would be allowed to visit when he could. That suited Daniel, he would be able to live with Ada until his double life began.

All ran surprisingly well, until one evening when Ada was around nine weeks pregnant and Milly was due back from the Lakes at the end of August, Ada greeted him with a nicely cooked roast dinner, which Daniel had the feeling that Hetty might have had a hand in. Ada's cooking hadn't improved since they started to live together, so he was quite surprised to see her dishing up meat and vegetables on a couple of porcelain plates, she had treated herself to.

"To what do I owe the pleasure," he asked, after having driven back from Clitheroe as early as he could, because it was Ada's day off and he thought perhaps they could take a nice walk though Egerton village to the reservoir and back again. He had eaten a sandwich at a little cafe in the fortified town and was expecting a fried egg on toast from Ada.

"I think we need to talk," she said mysteriously, as she handed him his plate of food, then sat down at the table to eat her own. "Hetty and I had a walk to the butchers and she said she would show me how to cook a sirloin. I promised her some slices later on."

"And?"

"Someone at the hospital said they'd seen you in the Springfield Cafe with a young woman."

"Ah." Daniel played for time by getting up and walking to the sink to get a cup of water. Was this the time to tell her? Was this the time to tell her a partial truth? It must be, as he wasn't going to get another opportunity. "Ah, well it seems that I am now going to have to tell yer about the dilemma I am finding meself in, Ada, me love."

Her face didn't show any emotion as she listened to his tale. Perhaps she had known that one day he would come to her with the truth of the matter. She ate her food slowly, chewing mechanically, until he'd finished.

"Well, it's like this. Yer know when I went back ter see me sick granny? God bless her and keep her. It was then that Connie, that's me real wife, asked me if she could come across with Winnie and live with me. I told her no, because at that time you and me were goin' to live together and it would 'ave been a complication. Truth be told, she turned up with her suitcase. It was that day I came home late without the car... perhaps yer don't remember. But that was the day of her arrival and I had to put her up in the Cumbria Hotel. No, only for the night," he said quickly, as Ada's eyebrows rose as she thought of the expense of it. "I felt I owed it to her. Me conscience was prickin' and so I tried to talk her inter going back home. I have ter tell yer Ada, I didn't succeed. Yes, she did go back home, but only to collect Winnie and their belongings. She'll be arriving in September sometime."

"So where's she going to live? I suppose you'll have to find a place together. So will that mean you won't be helping me to bring up our baby?" Daniel stood up, suddenly feeling agitated and so he went towards her, wanting to hold her in his arms and show her that it was she he loved.

"Give over, Daniel, don't you worry about me," she said firmly, backing away then walking quickly to the kitchen. "I can manage. I've known all along that it might come to this and that ours wouldn't be a life long relationship. Now you sit back and finish that dinner. It would be a shame to waste it and I'll make us a nice cup of tea."

The first Banns of Marriage mentioning the names of Millicent Pearson (Spinster) and Daniel McAuley (Bachelor) were read out to the church congregation on the last Sunday in August. Providing no one had just cause or impediment to stop their marriage from going ahead, the couple were to wed on the 30th of September. There was only one slight hitch in the scheme of things, Daniel couldn't produce a birth certificate. According to Daniel it had been burnt in the Dublin Records Office during the Easter Risings. The Reverend, a naïve man of the cloth, was willing to overlook this.

It was a fine morning, when Daniel, who had stayed the night before at the home of Peter Jones, a man related to the family and who had been chosen to be his witness, walked down the path at St. Saviours. He was dressed in his best suit, a light brown pin striped and had purchased a light brown Homburg hat to go with it. He had kept his black moustache, though thinner, aware that Milly had remarked she wasn't too keen on it. Much like Ada, she thought it was like kissing a hair brush.

Poor Ada, Daniel thought, as he walked slowly towards his destiny. It should have been her he was meeting at the altar today. It should have been her all dressed up in white, with a big bouquet and a couple of little bridesmaids. Instead she was working her last shift at the Infirmary. It had been bound to happen. She was just over three months pregnant now and Matron had found her replacement.

He knew that he was going to miss her. She hadn't insisted he leave, after he had told the story of his marriage complication. In fact she appeared to welcome his presence in her bed that night, as if she was filling herself with memories for the future and he had been allowed to stay at the cottage for as long as he wanted.

Chapter Seventeen

He had been there at the cottage when Ada, an "elderly primate" in midwifery speak, decided to pack her bag with her nightdress, slippers and wash bag in readiness and had made up the little wooden cot that Daniel had brought, with a feather filled pillow and little blankets. She had already packed the terry towelling nappies, the muslin squares and the multi-coloured shawl that she had crafted from left over wool into knitted squares. Along with a white hat, mittens and bootees that she had so lovingly made and the little white dress and matching cardigan, a present from Mrs. Thornton, the previous owner of Daisy Nook, she felt she was fully prepared. Now recuperating from her injury, Mrs Thornton, occasionally shuffled along from her son's house to pass an hour or so with Ada.

Ada's pregnancy, full term plus one week, had been without drama, but on that evening when Daniel had come to visit, something he had been doing since early in the New Year on a regular basis, she was beginning to feel that the birth might be imminent.

Daniel, already a father to a son, as Milly had given birth in the Bolton Royal Infirmary on Chorley Street three weeks before, now felt duty bound to take Ada there too. This was going to be his new son or daughter and he was prepared to take full responsibility, even if the nurses in the maternity ward raised their eyebrows when they saw him again. Indeed, he had even persuaded Ada to allow him to register the birth in the town hall at Bolton, just like he had offered to register his and Millicent's son. But that pleasure had gone to Bunty.

It had been a hard few months living in Bunty's household. She had standards. That was what she told him, after she found he hadn't put the lavatory seat down after using it. If it was meant to be permanently in the upward position, they would have been made that way. And Milly, now back in the family home and suffering a little with the "baby blues", had her younger sister, Nelly, in constant attendance and behaved as if she was related to royalty with each passing day. He found it hard to live in such a situation, being treated as if he was a lodger at the house in Ringley and an incomer by the local community, as no one seemed to want to engage him in conversation, when he propped up the bar in the Lord Nelson.

If it hadn't been for his little son, whom they had named Arthur John McAuley and was the apple of everyone's eye, he would have done a bunk, as he called it. Milly didn't need him, now that her baby had been born "in wedlock". Bunty didn't need him as she was used to doing everything her way and "she didn't need a man to tell her what to do". And so he found it peaceful living in the cottage in Dunscar with Ada when he could. For the moment anyway.

It was around nine o'clock in the second week of April that Ada decided it was time to go. She had just finished washing up the dishes from the evening meal, when she felt something trickling and advised Daniel, who was sitting at the kitchen table writing up some notes from two of the hostelries he had visited that day, that she could do with a lift to the hospital. There was no time to spare, she had felt a niggling all day, but had put it down to the baby getting itself prepared by wriggling.

Daniel, feeling quite composed as he drove her down the road towards the hospital was unprepared, when out of the blue, Ada asked him how his wife and child were settling in?

"You told me that they were staying in lodgings in a place called

Kearsley, last time we spoke about them. Do they have relations there? Only you don't seem to be spending a lot of time with them."

She winced as the birth pains became more urgent, but as she knew his explanation was going to take her mind off them, she listened, with a grim look on her face, to his reply.

"So her brother lives there and the little girl is going to a school in Prestolee. Funny that. There was no mention of these people or places when I saw a photograph of Mr. Daniel McAuley and a Miss. Millicent Pearson being married in St. Saviours Church in Ringley. Hetty gave me a few old editions of the Bolton Evening News, to cover the mattress. Just in case I needed to have the baby at home. Sometimes I think that you must be either suffering from amnesia, Daniel, or you've forgotten which lies you've told me in the past."

His hands trembled on the steering wheel, as her words, calmly said in her usual unflappable fashion, made him wonder whether he should tell her the truth and admit his bigamy. Tell her that he was tricked into it and frog marched to the church by the older dominant sister, or come up quickly with another story.

"Daniel," Ada tapped him softly on his arm, as he blustered his way through another explanation which he thought might please her, saying how this woman called Millicent had tricked him, just like Connie had before. "Are you so spineless that when these things happen, you just have to go along with them? We've just won a war by standing up to a group of tyrants, for heaven's sake. Well, when I've had this baby we'll have a long talk about where we stand in the future. I take it you'll be staying at the cottage whilst I'm away."

It was after they'd said goodbye and Ada had been booked in and was ready to be wheeled to the birthing room, that she found out the truth of the matter. One of the midwives called Agnes, whom Ada had got to know during her hospital appointments and found that they had a lot in common having been nurses in the

First World War, told Ada that it was strange to see Mr. McAuley bringing her in the car.

"Isn't your name Moscrop? Only the man who has just brought you in was called McAuley and his wife gave birth to a little boy about three weeks ago."

"Oh, Daniel, he's a neighbour. My husband's away on business unfortunately," said Ada, with her fingers crossed behind her back, as she hated lying.

The birth was long and arduous, not helped by the fact that Ada's pelvis was narrow and the contractions, after a while, began to slow. It was a bruised and sore Ada that waited to expel the placenta, after giving birth to a little girl thirty seven hours later and vowing that there would never be another one.

"Tell me when you'll be back here next year," her friendly midwife said chuckling, as she handed over the baby to be suckled at the breast. "I'll book me holidays."

It was ten days later after he had received Ada's short note, when a sheepish looking Daniel stood at the door of the maternity ward, nervously waiting for her to be discharged. It was like waiting for his death warrant to be signed, as he hadn't a clue of how she was going to treat him. He had kept away in case of rejection. Only once had he called into the hospital to inquire how Mrs. Moscrop and the new baby was and been told that Mrs. Moscrop and her baby daughter were doing well.

He had been ecstatic! Another little daughter. Not a replacement for Winnie of course, but a daughter of his own flesh and blood. He wondered, fleetingly, what Ada had called her. Would she choose a name like Dora or a modern one like Marion?

The moment came when he met the little person, who was going to mean so much in his shallow life. Ada, looking pale and sallow, walking slowly as she had been recommended total bed rest after she had returned home, appeared holding her shawl wrapped bundle, whilst her friend the midwife, carried her bags.

"This is very kind of you, Mr. McAuley," she said, tongue in cheek, knowing that her words would scotch any rumour, other than he was her neighbour. "Would you like to hold little Gracie, whilst I take my things from Agnes. How is your wife, Mr. McAuley? Is she and your baby boy doing well?"

Gracie was beautiful. Her dark brown eyes gazed back into his and he felt as if he was looking into the eyes of his paternal grandmother. He had always loved his granny. She had taken him on long walks into the countryside, telling him tales of the Republican martyrs who had died whilst fighting for an independent Ireland. She had bought him toffees from the little village shop and sang him songs that she had learnt in *her* childhood and sometimes she would dance a little jig to the tune of *The Kerry Dancers*. Now Gracie would have that abiding love, which he'd had for his precious granny.

"She looks like you," was Ada's only comment, as he passed little Gracie over, before opening the car and putting the bags onto the bucket seat. "She does so," Daniel said happily.

It was a picture of domestic bliss. The fire in the range was glowing nicely, the kettle steamed drowsily on the hob, whilst Daniel poured two large portions of a vegetable broth into porcelain bowls and placed them on the table.

"My, my, you have been busy," Ada remarked, as she came down from settling Grace into her cot upstairs, after giving her a feed from her breast. "I didn't know you could cook, Daniel. And I have to say that you have kept the cottage looking nice."

"With the help of Hetty, I have to admit. Though the broth has been made with me own fair hand, after remembering watching me granny making it. And yer not to bother yourself fer at least a week, because I've taken time off from the brewery."

"But what about your other family, surely they'll be wondering where you are? And your little boy, what did you call him, surely he'll be missing you as well?"

"Ada." Daniel leant over the table and took her hand in his. "They couldn't care less whether I come or go and little Arthur wouldn't even notice. I am surplus to requirements, now that I have made an honest woman of Millicent."

"But she isn't an honest woman, is she, Daniel?" Ada got up from the table and put the empty bowls into the sink. "She's like me. Living over the brush, as they say. Cohabiting and whatever else people are called when they are not properly married. All I can say is, thank heavens you didn't go through that farce of a wedding with me."

"So, yer not cross then?" He felt his spirits soar as he said it. "Yer not going to throw me out and never let me see Gracie? Because that is what Bunty, Milly's sister would do if she finds out what I've done. I'd never get to see Arthur again, the poor little chap."

"Why should I?" Ada spoke flatly. "All this is what I ever wanted." She gestured around the inside of the cottage and included Daniel. "I wanted to live in the country and in a happy home with a man who would give me babies. The only thing I'm missing is a garden to grow my vegetables in, but getting three out of four of my wishes isn't bad."

In 1923 and into the following year was one of contentment for Daniel. His children thrived, although Arthur was put on a bottle because Milly had neither milk nor the inclination to suckle him and Grace grew plump and pretty with each passing day. Ada, enjoying her new found freedom from the regimentation of a hospital, wrote long letters to her brother Charles and his wife Sara, who now had a child of their own whom they had called Chadwick. She also tried her hand at simple cooking and took her baby daughter in the large, black perambulator for country walks.

There had only been a couple of clouds on Daniel's horizon. Bunty had insisted that Arthur was baptised in the Protestant church, although Daniel had hidden the fact he was Catholic anyway and Ada wasn't bothered whether Grace was baptised at all. In the end Ada complied with convention and had Grace christened in the church at Walmsley, especially when she found she was expecting another baby, which was due in the early summer of 1924.

Life was lived by a regular pattern. Monday to Thursday nights were spent in the cottage, whilst Daniel gave Ada respite from an energetic Gracie, who entertained them with her babbling and her lively ways. Weekends were spent with a happy-go-lucky Arthur, who loved to be tickled and hugged by his doting father and an indolent Milly, who kept him at arm's length in their bed.

Daniel's highlight of the year, besides the birth of his beloved babies, was watching Bolton win the F.A cup against West Ham with Reggie Thornton at Burnden Park and getting completely stocious later in the Dunscar Arms.

It was the beginning of January 1924, the year that Malcolm Campbell set a world auto speed record on Pendine Sands, Ramsey MacDonald formed the first Labour government in Britain and George Gershwin introduced his composition of Rhapsody in Blue. Freda, still with a pash for Daniel, even though she knew he was now married with a child, although not altogether clear who he was married to as Daniel never talked about his family, put a letter on his desk. This one was clearly postmarked and she wondered if perhaps his granny had died this time and he would be rushing back to the Emerald Isle. She waited, with bated breath as he opened it.

> *Son, how are you. I am thinking that you can come back home now. The danger has gone and I need your help with the brewery.*
> *Dada.*

Freda watched, as Daniel, ashen faced at first and with hands trembling, placed the letter back into the envelope and exhaled his breath.

"Shite", he said, suddenly feeling annoyed at this unexpected turn of events, just when life had come good again. "Oh sorry Freda, excuse me language. A bit of bad news from home."

Chapter Eighteen

She was there waiting in the doorway, as he parked his car across the lane from the cottage. With Gracie cradled in her arms, Ada smiled in welcome, then watched as Daniel walked up the path as if he was carrying the weight of the world on his shoulders.

"Don't ask," he said, as he took the wriggling Gracie into his arms and kissed her plump little cheek. "It could be Armageddon all over again for me."

"You've lost me," Ada remarked, as she pushed the kettle back onto the hob and stirred something in a saucepan. "Wait until you've had your tea, then I'll settle this one and then we can talk about it. We had a lovely walk today, didn't we Gracie? We had a look at the new war memorial and then as far as the park in Egerton, then up the hill where we bought some eggs from the farmer's wife, then across the tops and back down again. I was fair worn out pushing you up that steep hill in the perambulator, wasn't I Gracie? No wonder I've not an ounce of flesh on me now."

Gracie smiled and giggled. At ten months she was alert and active and beginning to try out a couple of words, one of which was Dada. He realised, with a heavy heart, that she'd be the first to miss him.

"So tell me," Ada said, after they'd eaten her best efforts at an Irish stew and Gracie had been fed from her little bowl, then washed and put to bed. "What's brought that hangdog look upon your handsome face? Trouble at mill?" She tried to make light of whatever was troubling him. It couldn't be that bad, surely?

"I had a letter from me father." Daniel took her hand as they sat together on the sofa. "He wants me to go back to Ireland."

"What, permanently?"

"It seems so. I suppose with him getting old and me two brothers both away in the Americas, he wants me back. That's why I came to Blackburn. (He didn't admit to Ada that he'd been a member of the I.R.B) I came to learn the ways of a bigger brewery, so that I could pass on a few tips to me Dada."

"So it looks as if you've got yourself into another fine pickle, Daniel McAuley. One wife in Stoneclough, another back in Ireland and Gracie and me. What have you decided you're going to do?" Her face looked concerned as she asked him her worrying question, so wandering to the back doorstep to think on his reply, he lit a cigarette.

"This is it, Ada, I don't know what I'm going to do. How can I leave you and Gracie and another little baby on the way? Then there's Arthur…oh no, I'm not goin' to even think of Milly. She's fine as she is with Bunty, she'll never miss me."

"And your wife in Ireland and your father, who'll probably need you to run the place now he's getting older?"

"Well, I was forced into marrying Connie, because she were expectin' and there's no love lost between her and me. I won't be missed."

"So another poor lass who lost her honour, because you couldn't keep control over where you put your willy."

"No Ada, that isn't the truth of it at all and I'll tell you why one day. But all this thinkin' is givin' me a bit of a headache, so it is. Will yer oblige me with an aspirin and a nice cup of tea."

He knew if he could, he would dodge going back to his homeland. He liked this old cottage in Dunscar, living with his little family and driving his shiny car. He liked his job at the brewery and his visits to the Dutton hostelries, where he had got to know each of the landlords and many of their staff. He loved the freedom and the fact he had no one else to answer to, other than Mr. Fletcher who let him get on with it. Now it looked like

138

the bubble he had lived in for the past couple of years, wasn't going to last much longer.

It was a few days later, after Daniel had lain awake at night contemplating his future, bitterly remembering that his father liked his own way in all things, when Mr. Fletcher called him into his office for a chat. Freda had told her boss, confidentially, that on receipt of a letter which she had presumed was from his family in Ireland, his area manager had seemed rather shocked. So shocked, she intimated, that he had used a word that should never be heard by a lady's ears. She'd been quite put out and had to make herself a strong cup of tea, she was so shaken.

"So Daniel," Mr. Fletcher gestured him to sit, then looked at him with concern. "Any problems? Freda seemed to think that you may have had bad news from home again."

He appeared uncomfortable, as if he realised that he was breaking his secretary's trust by approaching Daniel, but something needed to be said. His area manager was well liked by all who met him, because of his amiable personality, charm and handsome looks and he didn't want to lose him.

"Is it your family? Your Uncle Dickie seemed to think that all was well there, last time we spoke on the telephone."

Daniel dithered. Should he come clean and tell his boss that his father wanted him to go back to Ireland? That the experience of him working at Duttons over the past few years, would be to his father's advantage? Or should he use his granny's illness one more time? Though Mr. Fletcher's next words put a totally different view of his future.

"I shouldn't really be telling you this yet, Daniel, but as things stand I'll tell you now, but you must keep the knowledge a secret. As you know, since you joined us in 1919 we've been rather busy acquiring smaller breweries. So much so that the Board has decided to appoint a Facilities Manager. It would involve the person appointed in arranging the maintenance of buildings and their upkeep; the services supplied to meet the needs of the people who work for us and would also be responsible for arranging the cleaning and the heating of our hostelries. A big job Daniel, but your name was put forward as the one person who could do it standing on their head. What do you think to that then? Happier?"

He sat back and watched the different emotions flitting across Daniel's face. Contemplation, indecision, hopefulness and then eventually a smile which said it all. "I certainly am, Mr. Fletcher. Although I'll need to get a message to me father."

Dada, how are you? I like it here in Blackburn. I like my job, I like my life and I have many friends over here so. Could you not get a Manager in to help you? What about promoting one of the workers, like Jimmy? As for Connie and little Winnie, I won't shirk my responsibility towards them.
From Daniel, your Son.

"And that's all you wrote to him?" Ada said, after Daniel had come home elated with his change of fortune. The deed was done, the letter sent and he was happily telling Ada of what he'd done.

"Don't you think that there might be consequences? I mean if he asked you to go back to Ireland, there must be a reason why."

"Aye, he'll want all the knowledge that I've gained over the past five years. He'll want a list of all the improvements to be made. He'll want me to make my peace with Connie and give him lots of grand babies and live under his jurisdiction again. Why should I, when I've everything here to keep me happy *and* a new job on the horizon?"

"Duty? Conscience?"

"You're sounding to me as if yer want me out of yer life." Daniel's tone was surly, as he listened to her try to point out the pit falls in his decision. "Don't yer want me here? Is it that you've got what you've wanted and it doesn't include me?" He lit a cigarette, then got up from the table where they had been eating another of Ada's stews and opened the back door impatiently.

"I'm just trying to play Devil's Advocate, Daniel." Ada followed and put her arms around his waist and cuddled him. "Whatever your decision, then that's fine by me."

It was a different story when he mentioned that his Dada wanted him back to run the brewery, as the family sat down to dinner on Friday evening at Milly's home. Little Arthur was sitting in his wooden high chair at the table being fed from a bowl by Nelly, his adoring slave, and the rest of the family ate a meal of fish and boiled potatoes, a dish that they always ate on Friday.

He had been a fool to mention it, he realised later, because as soon as he had done, both Milly and Bunty's ears pricked up.

"Oh, that would be great," Milly's normally jaded features perked up at the thought of getting out of Bunty's way. "Would we have our own house in Ireland and little Arthur would have a garden to play in?" She always bemoaned the fact that Bunty's workshop took up most of the yard.

"Well…"

"Just think," Bunty said proudly. "A brother-in-law with his own brewery. I can see all the male members of the Pearson family booking their tickets on the ferry boat."

"Well, it isn't set in stone yet," Daniel blustered. "There's a lot to consider beforehand. Especially as I've been offered promotion over here that I'm thinking of taking."

He realised then that he'd dug himself in even deeper, when Milly started talking about moving to a nice new house nearby instead.

Retribution from his father came quickly in the next week's post.

Son, I am lepping. You better get your backside over here or we'll be finished. You'll be no son of mine.
Dada.

"Short and to the point, Daniel." Ada remarked after he had shown her his father's letter and pointed out that " lepping" meant his father was leaping with anger. "So what's next? What about your wife and your little daughter? Surely you'll have to consider their welfare."

"There you go again, Ada, making me feel as if I'm not wanted here." Daniel got up from the sofa and paced the floor angrily. His Irish accent was considerable with emotion as he talked.

"Well, I'll tell yer about Connie, shall I? She tricked me inter marrying her, so she did. She was already up the duff when I walked her up the aisle. Some married man accordin' to the gossips. I did me duty. I shielded 'er in marriage, when I could 'ave walked away and let 'er face the consequences on her own. The same goes fer me Dada. It was 'im who wanted me to come over to Blackburn. Learn the ropes of runnin' a bigger brewery and passing on what I learnt to 'im. It's all done fer other people. When do I get a say in runnin' me own life, Ada?"

"You're not doing a bad job so far, Daniel." Ada's tone was soothing, especially as she had been holding a sleeping Gracie in her arms whilst Daniel was being cranky and the child was beginning to stir. "You've got a good job, a nice car, two children if we include Arthur and one on the way."

"And promotion, Ada." He was soon appeased by her words and glad he had something else to share. "That's what I was going to tell yer, if I hadn't got the damn letter from Dada today. I'm going to become a Facilities Manager for all the breweries' hostelries."

Chapter Nineteen

Ada would have said, had she been asked, that giving birth to Florence on that July day when the 8th Olympic Games closed in Paris, was just like shelling peas, compared to the thirty seven hours she had spent in labour with Gracie. She felt as if *she* had been awarded a Gold Medal when she looked down upon her fair haired baby. As Florence, named after Florence Nightingale in a tribute to the nursing profession, had easily latched onto Ada's breast and began to suck hungrily.

Daniel had been ecstatic. With the help of Hetty and a couple of weeks away from his exhausting new job with the brewery, he was able to devote his time to his lovely little girl. Gracie, now aged fourteen months, with dark curls and a Spanish look about her, a throwback to Daniel's ancestry, had begun to toddle a few weeks before and was very proud of herself. She chatted constantly. Not that Daniel could make out many of her words, as a lot of it was babbling. She knew though, how to call him Dada and when he heard her, he thought his heart would burst with pride.

It had been arranged, once the pains had begun and Daniel had taken Ada into hospital, that he wouldn't come back until it was time for Ada to be discharged. Conscious of the need to employ a little propriety, should Agnes, the midwife, put two and two together to make five, Daniel waited at the cottage for her note to arrive.

His short visits to Milly, just a few hours or so to play with little Arthur, whilst Hetty held the fort, was blamed on pressure of work and the brewery insisting on him attending meetings in different cities in the North. Milly, after the first flush of joy when she thought she would be moving house and away from the clutches of her elder sister, had retreated into her shell once more.

So, it was all the more of a shock when one weekend after Ada had returned to the cottage with little Florrie and so he was able to return to Ringley, that he found that Milly had flown the nest, leaving little Arthur in the care of Nelly and Bunty.

"It were the fact you didn't buy her a house that swung her," Bunty said, when Daniel arrived with his small suitcase filled with dirty washing, so it looked as if he had been staying in a hotel somewhere. "She thought with you having a new job at the brewery, there might be a bit of extra money going spare and she's always wanted to live in one of them big houses on the road to Whitefield. She even got excited at the thought of you and her starting a new life back to Ireland, but her dreams became ashes when you said you wanted to stay here in Ringley and didn't want to move."

"But we got to keep little Arthur," Nelly said complacently, happy that she now had the full care of her nephew, as Bunty was in the workshop during the day. "Come up to Auntie Nelly, there's a love." She took him from Daniel, who had been giving his son a cuddle whilst they were speaking.

"So where's she gone?" Daniel thought it only polite to ask, although he was happy that Arthur would be in the two women's care and not in Millicent's.

"Back to the Lakeland Manor Hotel, as far as I'm aware. She said to give you a message. She said that she would be coming over once a month and she doesn't want to see you here. And if you would do the necessary, she'd like a divorce as well."

"A divorce?" Daniel looked bewildered. "What have I done that makes her think a divorce is up fer discussion? I've been a good father to Arthur, he's wanted for nothing. I bought him his cot and perambulator and I gave her money for his food and clothing. It's not my fault if the brewery wants me to stay wherever it is they send me to. She knew all this before we got married, so what brought this on?"

"Nelly, take little Arthur into the yard and perhaps you could play a game with him. Daniel, sit there and I'll make you a cup of tea. I can see from the suitcase that you're staying."

"Now Daniel," Bunty said confidentially, when Nelly was out of earshot. "Do you remember when you first asked Milly to marry you and she said no? She said it was because she wanted to continue working in Windermere."

Daniel nodded.

"And then she found she was expecting little Arthur, so what choice did she have?"

"You mean to say she only married me because she was expecting?" Daniel knew this to be true, but decided to act the innocent, as what would Bunty know?

"It appears so. But now she's realised she was never cut out for motherhood and would like a divorce so that she can be free."

"Well, I'm afraid I'll have to think on it, Bunty. I mean, I married her in good faith and marriage is fer life, yer know. But I'll move me things and I'll find another place to hang me hat, as they say and I'll be back every weekend to see my son."

If Ada noticed that she now appeared to have a full time "husband" she didn't comment, as both Gracie and Florrie were becoming a handful and so any help that came her way was gratefully received. On the nights that Daniel stayed away, his job as a Facilities Manager stretching his mind and the area he was covering, Hetty, her neighbour, would step into the breach and help bathe the children at bedtime. Florrie, a fair haired version of her elder sister, though blue eyed, was rather boisterous, noisy and full of mischief and the once calm, unflappable Ada, was bone weary most of the time. So, it was with a sense of relief when Daniel suggested that they go away for a few days, especially as the new Austin Tourer that had come with the job was bigger.

It was April 1925. The weather was cold and there had been

gales and heavy rain. Ada was thankful that she had got Reggie Thornton to erect an overhead clothes drier in the kitchen, as the girls went through a multitude of terry toweling napkins every day.

"Well, where do you suggest?" Ada asked, as Daniel helped her by folding some of the children's clothes to air in the warming compartment of the oven. "It would be horrid in Blackpool in this weather and I don't fancy going up north to Gaitsgill to introduce you to my family. It would be even worse up there. Anyway, when do you ever get time off? This new job you've got should be done by two of you, not one."

"I suppose once I've managed to visit all the pubs and they've all got what they're needin', it should get easier." Daniel was proud of his position as a Facilities Manager, as many of the landlords had welcomed him. He had saved them all from pestering the brewery for all things necessary and the man who had taken over as the Area Manager, was a great help as well. "Perhaps the beginning of June then, if yer don't want to go over the Easter holidays, Yes, June would be nice in Blackpool and it's a sort of an anniversary."

"For you and Millicent maybe," Ada said, a trifle sourly. "I suppose she'll be expecting you to take her and little Arthur away on holiday too."

"Ah." Daniel thought that this might just be the time to come clean about his bigamous marriage.

"The thing is me darlin', Millicent has left the boy with his sisters and gone away. She's asked me ter divorce her." He watched Ada's face that went from a blank look to incredulity.

"You mean after all that messing around trying to make an honest woman of her, at least on paper anyway, she's gone and left you? Words fail me, Daniel, other than what are you going to do?"

"I suppose I'll divorce her eventually, but it's little Arthur I worry about now. I'm allowed to see him every weekend, bar one, when she comes down to see him on the train. But what if she meets another bloke and my son is taken from me?"

"I don't know how she could leave him anyway, poor little

chap," Ada said, still reeling from his revelation. "I mean, those two upstairs drive me to distraction, but I'd never leave them. You said just then that she comes down on the train. So do you know where she's living?"

"Yes, she has a job in a hotel in the Lake District...Ada, I've something else I need to tell you too."

"Whatever it is, I've enough to think on at the moment. If it's a matter of life and death and I need to know, just tell me. But in the words of something I heard at a wedding I once went to, if not, *forever hold your peace.*"

Thank God, he thought later, after they had put the children to bed and Ada nestled against him on the sofa and she told him a bit more about Nana Moscrop and her family in Gaitsgill. And how her cousin Moira was in regular contact by letter, especially since Ada had given birth to Nana's great grandchildren. *What if he had gone ahead and told her that he hadn't gone to Ireland to visit his sick granny, but gone for a little holiday in the Lake District instead? He knew that he wouldn't be sitting at Ada's side, stroking her hair and breathing in the goodness of her. He would probably be nursing a broken jaw in the car, with his suitcase in the boot!*

It was left to Ada to make arrangements for their forthcoming holiday and after consulting Hetty, who had been a regular visitor to Blackpool when her husband had been alive, she had sent a letter of inquiry to a Mrs. Jones, who ran a small hotel in Raglan Road. Hetty had assured her that the place was clean, Mrs. Jones welcomed well behaved children and the food, although perhaps a little basic, was adequate. She also had a Family room and would provide a couple of cots if necessary.

Ada sighed, as she listened to the children squabbling inside the tent she had made from her wooden clothes horse with a blanket over it. What wouldn't she give for some time alone. Some peace and quiet where she could let her mind go blank, or even read a book for an hour. Something she hadn't done since reading *Women In Love by D.H. Lawrence*, before Gracie had been born.

She loved the girls. She loved both girls right down to their little fingers, but sometimes she wished herself back on the wards. There had been a certain peace, a regimented level of discipline, a structured day where everyone knew their place in the scheme of things. Here, depending on the weather, her only recourse to something approaching peaceful, was to take the girls on long walks, hefting the perambulator containing her two precious burdens along bumpy cart tracks, whilst hoping that at some point in the journey, they would fall asleep for a couple of hours.

It was a sunny Saturday morning in the first week of June. Ada having risen early in order to make egg sandwiches for the journey and fill a couple of bottles with cold tea for her and Daniel and one with the home made lemonade that Hetty had donated for the girls, began to lay out the clothes for the journey. Two pretty floral dresses with white pinafores and black patent shoes for Gracie and Florence, a light blue linen knee length dress for herself with a matching jacket and white strappy sandals and a clean striped shirt, light brown trousers and a short black jerkin for Daniel.

The suitcases, one large and one small had been packed the day before and a holdall carrying a dozen napkins and muslin squares, lay waiting with various family toiletries by the front door. It was with a sense of relief that Gracie, a quick minded two year old, with a keen sense of perception, had been clean and dry for the last couple of months. It had made the family washing so much easier now that she could wear bloomers.

The small hotel, a ten bedroom dwelling just off the promenade and in one of the streets at the North Pier end, had been a bit more expensive than Ada would have liked to have paid, when she received the confirmation letter from Mrs. Jones, the landlady. At twelve shillings per person for a family room and then the cost of food, because only breakfast was included, Ada began to despair when she reckoned up her savings which were dwindling. Daniel, with a well paid job since he'd become the Facilities Manager, was a little bit stingy when it came to tipping up some of his pay and she was loathe to start an argument.

He still sent a bank draft to his family in Ireland and he still had the support of little Arthur to pay, but he liked to present a neat and businesslike appearance to the people he met on a day to day basis and the cost of his barber, suits, shoes and other men's apparel didn't come cheap. Much as she disliked the idea of returning to some sort of job in the nursing profession when the girls were old enough to go to school, she might not have a choice.

So, it had come as something of a surprise when Daniel had appeared the previous evening with a small bouquet of red roses and an envelope bearing a five pound note, which he said she must treat herself with. On the outside of the envelope he had written her a little message of his love.

To my darling Ada on our 3rd anniversary together. Thank you for making me a happy man.

Chapter Twenty

The town of Blackpool was heaving. The trains at Central Station spewed out its passengers at regular intervals, as the happy masses from towns and cities released from the drudgery of everyday servitude, looked forward to spending a weekend there.

Most headed to the back streets of the fun time capital, where landlady's waited with bated breath for the influx of lodgers, who were only in the town to enjoy themselves. Notices put up in their hallways, declared that a fine would be levied for careless use of the amenities, especially if bedrooms were left in a dirty, untidy state. Most landlady's were strict and stern, charging extra for a bath or use of the salt and pepper pots, but some were kind and hospitable and soon became a family friend.

Mrs. Jones was one of the latter and Ada could see from the welcome that they received and the fuss that was made of Gracie and Florrie, the reason why Hetty and her husband had visited each year. The room they were shown was clean, large and spacious, with a small truckle bed for Gracie, a cot for Florrie and a double bed. Breakfast was served between eight and nine each morning and if they wanted the use of the bathroom, it was free.

She also said she could recommend a variety of eating places, some cheap, wholesome and good value for the family and to beware of buying food from the wooden carts on the sea front, as not everybody washed their hands.

The newly opened Stanley Park was a must whilst they were in Blackpool, as was the Tower that they had seen on the horizon when Daniel drove the tourer along the Preston Road. A man called Reginald Dixon, played a Wurlitzer, a type of organ that rose up from beneath the floor, in the Tower Ballroom, or for the children there was a trip to Pleasure land. It was a pity that they hadn't come in the Autumn, as the first ever Illuminations were to be shown along the promenade.

The sun was warm and the air was still, as they wandered along the street towards the promenade later. Daniel carried Florrie and Gracie toddled along beside a laden Ada, who carried a blanket and buckets and spades. The perambulator, too big to be carried in the tourer, had been left behind at the cottage.

It was as they entered the garden near the sea front, where an ornate fountain sploshed, much to the girls' glee and a sundial made of granite attracted Ada's attention, that a voice which came out of nowhere, suddenly gave Daniel a fright.

"Hey you! Daniel. Commere!" A thin man with a sparse covering of hair on his head and an Irish accent stood near the entrance to the pier, his face splitting into a grin after he had shouted.

"Do you know him?" asked Ada curiously, wondering who it could be, as she didn't think Daniel would know anyone in Blackpool.

"Aye, take Florrie from me and look after the girls if yer will while I see to the fella. Get the girls an ice cream from that cart across the way."

He sauntered over, his face trying hard not to show that he was feeling uneasy and his legs felt all wobbly.

"Fergal," he said, holding out his hand and shaking his brother-in-law's with a firm grip. "What are yer doin' here in Blackpool?"

"I could ask yer the same meself. Especially as I see yer've got family in tow." Fergal's eyes took on a hard look, as if he wanted to punch Daniel on the jaw.

"Oh them." Daniel shrugged nonchalantly. "They're me mate's girls. We work together at the brewery and he promised them a day out, but at the last minute he had to let them down. I offered. They'd been so lookin' forward to it."

"Very kind of yer," Fergal replied morosely. "There's yer missis and little Winnie back in Ireland who'd quite like a day out in Blackpool, so they would."

"Ah."

"Yes, ah. The last time I was over, I'm workin' in Manchester by the way, there was talk of you goin' back and taking over the brewery. Connie was as pleased as punch and was goin' to have a big party for yer return. Then she tells me yer'd written to yer Dada and told him yer were stoppin' instead in Blackburn. Not anythin' to do with yon family then?"

"Of course not. As I told yer, they belong to me mate. Look Fergal, I've got ter go…" He had suddenly seen Gracie waving from across the road and to his horror he could hear her shouting "Daddy". It would only be a matter of minutes before Fergal heard her, put two and two together and then himself would be lying out cold on the floor. He was saved by a couple of men who had already paid to go onto the pier, shouting to Fergal to hurry the feckin' well up or they'd go without him.

"Look mate, here's me card from the brewery." Daniel snatched a business card from his wallet and thrust it at his brother-in-law, hoping that the man couldn't see that his hand was shaking.

"We'll go out for a beer one night and have a catch up, so we will. Just tell the man on the gate and he'll come to the office and get me."

"Aye I will, no doubt about it. Though last time I did, the fella didn't know you worked there."

His senses were reeling as he lurched along like a drunken man, back to where Ada was sitting on a wooden bench with the children. To her consternation, he collapsed!

"A momentary loss of balance," she said to the gawping crowd, who had rushed over to see what had beset the poor man, who had seemed to be having difficulty getting air as he staggered. "He'll be fine soon. No, he doesn't need an ambulance. Here, Daniel, put your head down between your knees, you'll feel better soon. It's the heat," she said to another concerned passerby. "We're not used to it. I don't remember it being so warm for years."

"Daddy." Gracie stood at his side and patted his back like she would her teddy bear. "Daddy, are you better now, because me and Florrie want to ride on the donkeys. Can we go now?"

"So what on earth was that all about?" Ada asked, after the girls had been walked up and down the beach on the back of a donkey and then settled down to dig in the sand. "You gave me such a fright."

"I gave meself a fright, Ada," Daniel said, putting his arm around her shoulders, so that he could feel the goodness of her. "I suppose I'm goin' to have ter tell yer one day. When I was younger..."

He went onto to tell her of how he had copied his older brothers and enlisted in the ranks of the Irish Republican Brotherhood and his obvious fear of reprisal from the British government. "Being sent to Blackburn by my father was two fold. First to learn the rudiments of a bigger business, so that I could pass on my knowledge to him on my return, but also to get me away from the danger, which was his main concern. The man you saw me with was Fergal. He's me wife's brother and a bigger thug you'd be hard put to meet, so he is. If it hadn't have been for his mates calling him over, I'd be dead meat."

"Phew." Ada blew out her cheeks and looked at Daniel worriedly. "No wonder you were in the state you were in, I thought you were having a heart attack. So what will you do? Will you go back to Ireland and face the music or stay here and bluff it out, as you usually do?"

"You know me so well me darlin'," Daniel said and kissed her on the cheek.

The rest of the week passed quickly, although Daniel was mindful of Fergal and kept looking over his shoulder, in case his brother-in law hadn't been just on a day trip, which he had presumed. He felt so uncertain of what the future might hold, that he lurked around the gypsy tents, wondering whether in case he was in danger, he should have his fortune told. But his Catholic upbringing came to the fore, when he realised it would be a be a bit of sin if he consulted a gypsy.

They took the girls on rides along the promenade in horse drawn landaus and watched the merry crowds on the carousels. They saw the Witching Waves wicker cars and the roller coaster in the Pleasure land and they giggled their way through the Noah's Ark attraction themselves. At night, whilst Mrs. Jones kept an ear out for the girls while they slept in the bedroom, for an extra charge of course, Daniel and Ada drank draught champagne at Yate's Wine Lodge and ate seafood in the Oyster Bar. They watched a summer show on the Victoria Pier, danced a couple of waltzes in the Tower Ballroom and all in all had a happy family holiday. Except for the threat of another appearance from Fergal of course.

Back in Dunscar, life resumed its familiar pattern, Daniel headed off each morning in his dark blue tourer and Ada, mindful that time could fly in a blink of an eye, tried to spend more time with her little ones.

It was on the following Saturday morning, when Daniel drew up outside the Pearson dwelling along the Ringley Road, that he found Bunty standing on the doorstep smoking a cigarette. It was unusual to say the least, as on most mornings Bunty could be found in the workshop and it was Nelly who got Arthur ready for his father's visit. Daniel joined her, lighting his cigarette with his newly purchased petrol lighter that he had bought for himself in Blackpool.

"Nice day for a walk along the riverside with Arthur," he remarked, noting that she looked annoyed and disgruntled about something. "Everything all right, only I don't usually see yer much at this time of the morning?"

"It's our Millicent, the little cow. She's only got herself entangled with that fellow up there in Windermere. You know... that manager who give her the job back?"

Daniel nodded. "Yer mean Mr. Greenwood, yes I know him."

"Well, she sent me a letter. I got it yesterday in the post. It seems that his parents have died and he's come into money and he wants her and him to open a hotel together."

"And she wants a divorce from me?"

"Yeah, it looks like it. Although she'd probably be quite happy to live over the brush, but it'll be him that'll want it done proper."

"Where do I sign? As yer know or put two and two together, it was Milly that pushed this marriage onto me. If it hadn't have been fer little Arthur, I wouldn't be standing here now. Tell her when you write that I'll be quite happy to get shut of her. Although where will that leave me and Arthur, do yer know?"

"The same as always. As far as I'm concerned she's not fit to be his mother and I'd take her to court to get his custody if I was you."

"Well, let's sleep on it. Let's not be hasty. Arthur's a happy little chappie while he lives with you and Nelly."

And what would Ada say? he pondered, as he wandered across the Ringley Bridge with his son toddling beside him. She wouldn't be happy if he suddenly foisted little Arthur upon her and the cottage wasn't big enough for another person anyway.

As early as 1926 there were signs of a financial crisis looming in the civilized world. There were too many goods being made and not enough people to buy them; farmers were producing too much food and so the price of what they could get for their products were lower. And many people found themselves out of work, as employers began to draw their horns in.

That wasn't the case in the brewing industry. Men still drank in their local, whilst wives and children did without, relying on the goodwill of family and friends or the pitiful sum given out by the unions for the support of them. Daniel, secure in the knowledge that his job was for life should he want it, continued his rounds of the hostelries each day.

It was one Friday afternoon in September, just as he was relaxing in his office chair after writing up his notes for Mr. Fletcher, that Freda came to tell him that the gate man had sent a message to say that he had a visitor. Daniel's spirits plummeted as he realised that his visitor could only be Fergal, who had probably come to give him more grief about Connie, his sister. He dithered. Should he pretend he was out? Send a message back to say that he was tied up and would see him later, or beard the devil in his den and meet him?

His thoughts flew to Ada. He had promised to be home early, as Hetty had said she would keep an eye on the children if they would like to spend some time together at the Dunscar Arms. It was Daniel's thirty first birthday that day and Ada would have made him a cake. She was becoming a dab hand at baking, now she'd got the hang of the oven and had a few tips on her culinary skills from her neighbour. And his lovely girls would be waiting to make a fuss of him as usual.

He'd chance it. Take the fellow to the nearest pub and stand him a glass or two of the Guinness. That should surely satisfy the fecker and then he'd send him on his way.

It was the red hair that caught his eye first, as he ambled slowly across the yard and towards the gate house. A lorry, laden with wooden barrels, its engine throbbing loudly as its driver showed Wilf, the gate house keeper his documents, momentarily caught his attention, before he focussed on the red hair again. The child looked familiar, but became lost in his view as Fergal strode towards him.

"Happy Birthday, Happy Birthday," he sang with a sneering tone. "Look who's come to share it with you... Connie and Winnie!"

He made it sound as if he was a magician taking a rabbit out of a hat and to Daniel's dismay, there was no doubt that walking towards him was little Winnie and his wife.

Chapter Twenty One

The girls had gone to bed by the time Daniel arrived at the cottage. Ada wasn't best pleased and after a frosty welcome, placed a plate of sandwiches, a bowl of trifle and a slice of birthday cake on the kitchen table, after he had smoked a cigarette.

"What was it this time?" she asked sarcastically. "A herd of cows on the road? A fallen tree trunk or some barmaid baring her bosoms again?" She suddenly smiled and patted him on the shoulder affectionately. "I still can't get over that barmaid at the White Horse doing that to you."

"Well, Ada, it was none of those things. I'm sorry that I missed me birthday tea, I just couldn't get away. I'll make it up to them, I promise."

"Did you pop in to see Arthur?"

"No, I'll have to do that tomorrow. I've still got to sort a few things out with Bunty over the divorce, as you know."

"I don't know why your bothering. You weren't married to Millicent in the first place, so getting a divorce won't change anything."

"No, but I'm still married to Connie, aren't I?"

"Come on, out with it Daniel, I can see you're dying to tell me. I'll make us a brew while you're telling me, or would you like a drop of home made cider instead?"

"No, I'll have a cup of tea. I think after I've told you what happened to me today, we'll both be drinking the cider later."

Ada never uttered a word, as at first haltingly, he told her the truth without embellishment. Occasionally her eyebrows would raise, sometimes she'd shrug, but he was quite unprepared for her reaction.

"I think that this time you should pack your bags and set up home with your real wife, Daniel. You can see the girls, just like you do with little Arthur, but it's got to the stage of enough is enough, as far as I'm concerned. I turned a blind eye when you and Millicent had to get married, as at the time I was desperate to have some babies of my own. But I've got them now, I don't need you to get me pregnant Daniel, so what's the point of you hanging around?"

"Because I love you Ada," and as he said it, he felt that he meant it. "And I want to be here to help you rear the girls. I want to share your life and be here with you until we're old and totterin'." He took her unyielding body into his arms and kissed her passionately on the lips.

"Give over, Daniel." She pulled herself away from his embrace and went to make the tea as the kettle was whistling.

"Look, she and the girl have come all this way to start a new life with you in Blackburn. What did you expect? Once your father had decided to walk away from the brewery, why should they be his concern? From what you've told me, the child isn't even related to the McAuleys."

"I know and I've always made it clear to her that our marriage was over and I wasn't going back to live in Ireland."

"Did you Daniel? Well if that's the case, why is she here?"

He asked himself the same question the next morning, after a fraught night lying at the side of Ada, knowing that this might be the last time he did so. Why had Connie suddenly decided to join him over here? It had to be that Fergal. Her brother would have talked her into it, though why he should he didn't know.

Connie was waiting with Winnie at the railway station where Daniel had arranged to meet them, with it being a well known landmark in the town. She looked tired and he realised with a pang that his little Winnie, taller now that she was nine years old, looked thin and scrawny in her green knee length dress and a grubby white smock to cover it. Her bright red hair had been woven into two plaits and she had a lot of freckles on her nose and forehead.

Connie had an unhealthy look about her. Her auburn shoulder length hair, once her pride and glory, was streaked with grey and the clothes she wore, an ankle length dark brown dress and horror of horrors a black knitted shawl that had seen better days, was her only outfit. Her shoes, black lace ups, were battered and worn and he wondered, momentarily, what she had spent the money he sent her on.

"Did yer sleep well?" he asked inanely, as they settled on the same bench that he had with Millicent, a few years before. "Have yer had breakfast?" The New Inn that he had hurriedly rushed them to, in his dazed attempt to put them somewhere before he could escape his nightmare, had promised bed and breakfast.

Connie nodded, but Winnie stared ahead and said nothing.

"She doesn't remember me, does she?" For some reason he felt sad as he looked at this solitary figure, who should have been running up and down the platform in excitement, like his own little daughters would have done. Winnie had taken up a big part of his heart after she'd been born.

"No, she doesn't and she doesn't know why she's 'ere either. When I told 'er that she was going to see her Dada, she said she 'adn't got one."

"Well, I suppose she's right, I've not been a father to 'er. Although that is something we'll have to talk about Connie, if you and Winnie want a future over here with me."

Connie nodded again, but this time there was tears in her eyes, which looked as if they could begin to engulf her.

"I'm sorry, Daniel and when I'm feeling a bit stronger, I'll tell yer about what happened with Winnie's father. It was our Fergal who persuaded me to get on the ferry with him. We went up to Dublin once your father threw us out."

"He did? Jesus, Joseph and Mary, what kind of man does that to his family? And this a supposedly God fearing man."

"But we're not family, Daniel. He knew from the start that you didn't want to marry me and that it was the Catholic priest and all the gossips in the village that forced you to. He was kind fer a while when he thought you were coming back and helping him to run the brewery, but when he got your note he was lepping. He told me to take Winnie and throw meself on the mercy of me family, but Mammy is ill and Dada can't afford to keep us."

"But I sent yer a bank draft every month. That should have kept yer both in food and clothing."

"I never saw it. Yer father took it and cashed it in up in Dublin when he visited his bank. We ate with your parents and any clothes we had were given to us by the Parish. Yer Dada said the money yer sent was fer our bed and board, so 'e did. Eventually I managed ter get a lift with Paddy and we went ter see if yer Uncle Dickie would help us out, because it were 'im that sent yer over to Blackburn in the first place."

"And did he? Did he help yer out?"

"Yes, he let us stay fer a few days, while he got a note to our Fergal and then himself came over ter collect us. Poor Winnie was as sick as a dog when we got on the ferry and I wasn't much better."

"And now yer here and I'm not sure what I'm goin' ter do with the pair of youse." Daniel said, feeling a bit bewildered.

The shop assistant in the local department store was amazed at the transformation. A woman and a young child had entered the portals of the establishment an hour or so ago and she could have sworn that the pair of them were paupers. Not so now. The woman, still scraggy haired and looking as if she should make an appointment at the Barbara Elizabeth Hair Salon, was wearing a smart dark green tailored jacket over a floral hanky hem dress and a pair of cream patent leather open toed sandals. In her hand she carried a large leather holdall and the assistant, having seen the woman disappear into the underwear department earlier, assumed that it was what the bag contained.

The little girl beside the woman had also had a transformation, or so it seemed. Gone was the grubby smock over the knee length rag she'd been wearing. Instead she too wore a floral dress with a green tailored jacket and a pair of open toed shoes. Though her shoes were flat and didn't have a Cuban heel like the mother's sandals had. She presumed that the woman was the child's mother, until just as they were about to disappear into the mass of passersby on the high street, a man, who she recognised as Mr. McAuley from the brewery, began to walk along besides them. My, my, it was something to tell her friend Freda, next time they met.

He couldn't tell from Ada's face whether he was welcome, when that evening he let himself into the cottage and was besieged by Gracie, who wrapped herself around his knees and Florrie burbled her hello. The table was set for three though, whilst Florrie's high chair was set up nearby.

"Shall I throw me hat in? Am I welcome, Ada?" he asked, as she looked across from where she was spooning mashed potatoes into an earthenware tureen.

"Depends on who's asking. Is it Mr. Moscrop, come home for his tea and then help to put his little daughters into bed? Or is it Mr. McAuley, who has to get back to his family from Ireland later on?"

"It's the first one, Mrs. Moscrop and whatever you've been cooking smells wonderful."

"You should have seen them, Ada, they looked terrible," Daniel explained, as later when all was quiet after he had spent a little time cuddling his children, then laying them down to sleep, he sat downstairs with Ada. "The pair of them looked like they'd fled from the potato famine, they were so thin and tatty looking. Connie said that she never saw a penny of the money I sent over.

Dada took it fer her bed and board and never give her any of it. And little Winnie...would yer believe it? She never even went ter school. Eight years, nearly nine years old and can't even write her name, never mind read a sentence. I mean, how the hell has it come ter this, I thought he was looking after them?"

"But what about your mother or Connie's family? Surely they could have done something about their plight?"

"Mammy wouldn't. She always looked ter Dada and Connie's mammy is ill. Her Dada couldn't afford to keep them, as he's hardly nothing comin' in. If it hadn't been fer Paddy Devereux who took her and Winnie up ter Dublin, I don't know what she would have done."

"And what did she do when she got to the city? Surely she couldn't have got a job with the little girl to look out for."

"Well, it appears that Uncle Dickie, he's some sort of a relative of us McAuley's, took pity on her. He helped me Dada get a start with the brewery, so he's not short of money and he lives in a big house in Dollymount. She and Winnie stayed there, until her brother Fergal went over from Manchester to collect her."

"And the rest, as they say is history. Because being the good Catholic man that you are, you won't be able to shirk your responsibilities.""Something like that. Oh Ada, what am I going to do? I don't love Connie. There's still the sin of her fornication between us and I've got so used to livin' here with you and the girls and being a proper family. And what will I do about little Arthur or even so, what am I going to do with Connie now she's here? What a mess. I don't know how I got meself in this fix in the first place. One minute I'm a young man, with the whole world at me feet if me Dada's brewery had become as big as Duttons and next minute, excuse me blasphemy, but I'm up to me neck in shite."

It was what he had always admired about the woman he once knew as Sister Moscrop, Daniel thought, as he stood outside smoking a cigarette, after they had finished off the remains of the cider and made love together quietly on the sofa. He admired her calmness under duress. Not only was Ada willing to help him find somewhere that he could rent for his Irish family, she had come up with an artful plan that would mean he could share his life with both his families, without the compromise to either of them.

Connie, once she and Winnie had settled in, would have to be told of the existence of Daniel's second family and whether she liked it or lumped it, that was up to her. Arthur's being though, would have to be explained a long time in the future. There was only so much that Connie could be expected to cope with, after all.

Chapter Twenty Two

It was a few days later when Ada, mindful of the fact that Daniel couldn't keep paying for the room at the New Inn, presented him with a rent book for a terraced house in Astley Bridge.

"I knocked on every door in Old Road, asking if anyone knew of a place to rent and one old dear told me that the family next door had moved in with his parents in Halliwell and so it's empty. She said that the house belongs to the people who own the Holden Mill, so on my way back to the cottage, I went into the office and inquired about renting it. I suppose with all these lay offs, they were glad to get it off their hands again. So here you are, here's the rent book and you owe me seven and sixpence. They can move in on Monday if you want them to and there's a Catholic church nearby called Holy Infants and they've got a little school."

"Was there any furniture?" Daniel's spirits plummeted, when it hit him that the tourer would only be able to carry a couple of suitcases in the boot.

"An old bed and a couple of raffia chairs, but I believe there's a furniture shop in Bolton that will make deliveries."

Daniel shook his head. "Jesus, Mary and Joseph, it's going to cost me a fortune. It's a good job that you don't take much for me bed and board. What with this and paying out for little Arthur, I'm going to be constantly broke."

"Ah well, Daniel, you and I are going to have to talk about that."

It transpired that Ada, who had always been careful with her wages and her nest egg in the District Bank, had found that after the purchase of Daisy Nook, the cost of having the wall taken down to make the back bedroom bigger and all the things she had to buy to make the cottage more comfortable, her savings were depleted somewhat. She was frugal in her every day expenditure, but the girls, now they were older, quickly wore out their shoes and dresses and ate like gannets most of the time. Gracie especially, a plump little madam, with an inquiring mind and a tendency to argue, loved to wander in the field and copse behind the cottage, coming back with grubby clothes and grass stains. Gone were the goats that used to live there, as the farmer had sold the land. It was rumoured that a row of semi-detached houses were planned to be built in the future.

"I was thinking about going back to nursing," Ada announced, after Daniel had sat down with a scowl on his face, thinking that he probably wouldn't even be able to afford a couple of pints at the Dunscar Arms with Reggie Thornton anymore. "I can put Gracie's name down at that school in Walmsley and Hetty said she'd keep an eye on Florrie if I wanted to work a couple of days a week. It won't be for a year or so, but the money I have in the bank won't last for ever."

"What and travel all that way to Blackburn?" Daniel said, trying to assert his authority. "You'd 'ave ter go on the train and yer might not be back in time to pick up Gracie from school. No, I won't allow it. Their welfare is far more important than you rushing off becomin' Florence Nightingale once more."

"And who's going to stop me, Daniel?" Ada's eyes narrowed and she bunched her fingers, as if she was ready to pop him one if he insisted. "I make the rules in this place and don't you forget it and you'll be too busy playing house with your real wife, anyway. And anyroad, I won't be working back at the Royal Infirmary, I've got an interview with the Matron at Blairs."

Ada was waiting there, with the perambulator full to the brim with cleaning stuff, a packet of tea, milk and biscuits, along with a spare kettle and her little daughters, when the motor bus let down its passengers at the bus stop on Blackburn Road. She couldn't help but recognise poor Connie and her little girl. They both looked pale and sickly and Ada, summoning up all her training and the empathy that she had practiced over the years, vowed to assist them all she could over the following days.

"Good morning, are you Mrs. McAuley?" she asked politely, as Daniel's wife and the little girl, dressed in their brand new outfits, stood in bewilderment on the pavement. "I'm Mrs. Moscrop and these are my children, Grace and Florence. Daniel asked me to meet you, as he has to be in Clitheroe this morning. I hope he mentioned me…I'm his landlady."

"Aye, 'e said you'd be waitin'. Said you'd got the key and we 'ad to be 'ere by ten o' clock, 'cos they're comin' with some furniture."

"Yes, that's right. I believe he telephoned the furniture shop at some point last Thursday. Shall we go? It's just across the road, opposite that public house called The Lamb. Gracie, hold the handle of the 'pram, I don't want you getting run over by those drays."

They were just in time, as chugging up the hill on its way from Bolton, came two flat bed lorries, their loads covered against the elements with old black tarpulin. They were hopefully bearing Connie's bits of furniture, but it was difficult to see.

"Mrs. McAuley?" The driver of the first lorry came to a halt and his mate climbed down the vehicle's steps and called out cheerfully. Ada nearly answered, but stopped herself just in time when Connie nodded at her side. "Got yer furniture." She stepped back, as Connie taking the key from her, rushed forward to open the door of the house that Ada had brought them to. This would be the first time either woman had seen inside.

Ada noticed the smell immediately. It was an odour of mustiness and a mouldy smell, perhaps from a lack of cleaniness by the previous occupants she was inclined to think. She opened the casement window, just as the delivery men carried two wooden ends and a base for a double bed into the living room. Its presence caused a pang, as Daniel no doubt, would be sharing it with Connie. His real wife, the wife that he had made his vows to in a Roman Catholic church, not the woman he cohabited with and who had bore him two children. But that wasn't going to stop her carrying out her duty to another human being. It was what she had been trained for, after all.

It was a weary and exhausted Ada, who pushed the pram' along the road and back to the cottage later. Winnie, at first reluctant to play with Gracie and Florrie, as she had never been given any responsibility before, had sat on a blanket in the back yard and told them tales of her home in Ireland. Not that either of them understood a word she was saying, as Winnie had an Irish brogue which made her hard to understand. Florrie soon got sleepy and was laid down in her pram whilst Winnie rocked it and Gracie, wandered in and out, whining she was hungry.

Daniel hadn't been stingy, although it was probably going to be his permanent home in the future, Ada thought. Beside the wooden bed, two bedside tables and a large mirrored wardrobe, he had bought a single bed and a bedside table for Winnie's room. The steep wooden stairs, which ran up from the tiled floored kitchen, were similar to those in Daisy Nook. And there was a large third bedroom in the middle, which could accommodate another double bed.

Downstairs, along with a colourful patterned rug, which was laid onto the dark brown linoleum, sat a dark green two seater moquette sofa and two matching armchairs placed in front of the fireplace. The kitchen had a modern freestanding gas cooker in a grey colour and a white stone sink. Along with a small mesh fronted larder and a wooden table with four chairs, they had all been carried on the back of the second lorry.

Before long the whole house and the outside lavatory, began to smell of Jeyes Fluid, furniture polish and Lysol, as the two women had worked side by side without a break until dinnertime. Then Ada, mindful that the poor woman wouldn't have a penny piece to her name, treated them all to fish and chips at a little cafe in a group of shops nearby. She had done her duty, even down to showing Connie where to shop, with the one pound note that she had given her.

For the next few years life, once again, settled into a pattern. Daniel, his guilt manifesting itself now that he was expected to attend Mass each Sunday morning, as Winnie had started school at Holy Infants, stayed mostly in the McAuley home, but managed to snatch a couple of nights away at Dunscar. It had been hard for him, when on that first evening, he had insisted that if they were to spend the rest of their lives together, Connie was to tell him the truth. But he was sorry when he heard that she'd been taken advantage of. The clue of who Winnie's father was, could be had in the bright red hair belonging to a member of the minor gentry that Connie had worked for at his residence. Connie forgiven, she had to be as she was not the only sinner in the marriage, found her feet once she had been given the role of Daniel's wife again and made sure that his life was comfortable. Whilst Ada, once the girls were old enough for school, worked a few hours when needed at the convalescent home.

The only person to miss out on Daniel's further plunge into domesticity was Arthur. If he saw his father once a month he was lucky. Milly, after a long wait and a host of legalities, married Mr. Greenwood, but didn't take her boy. It was better that he be looked after by his Aunty Nelly and attend the little school across the river.

It was in the October of 1929 that the Wall Street Crash, occurring in the U.S.A, but causing the sharp fall in prices on the London Stock Exchange, plunged the Western world into the beginning of the Great Depression. As usual it was the masses that were affected. Mostly it was those employed in the creation of cotton goods, clothing manufacturing and factories connected in the supply of the food chain. Banks were forced to call in loans and many speculators lost their fortunes. It was a grim time for many, but this time there was help at hand. People were able to get a handout from the government, the birth of the social services had arrived.

One evening at the beginning of April the following year, just as Ada was reading *The Squirrel, The Hare and The Little Grey Rabbit*, by Alison Uttley, to the girls before settling them, Daniel arrived at the cottage in his car. It was unusual for him to arrive on a Friday evening, as weekends were reserved for Connie and a trip if possible to Stoneclough to see Arthur, so the girls, excited as little puppies, danced around with glee.

"Don't ask," he said, after Ada had inquired what had brought him there and he had put the girls to bed with a promise that he would still be there in the morning. "I've told Connie that I'm staying overnight at a conference in Blackpool, so that I could be here with you." He took her in his arms and nestled into her gently, then drew her onto the sofa beside him.

"I've lost me job. Well, when I say I've lost me job, I've got ter the end of the month to find another. That's when the car goes back and it'll be Shank's pony for me."

"Phew! I thought it was a job for life you had and the brewery would never be rid of you. What's brought this on? Is it something to do with that merger you told me about?"

Daniel nodded. "Something like that. Only Mr. Fletcher's retirin' and they're closing his department down. The yard will be used for storage in the future and the plant is being moved to the brewery on the other side of town. Poor Freda's lost her job as well, although I'm sure she'll get employment as a secretary elsewhere."

"Let's hope so. According to one of the newspapers, there's a Lancashire Cotton Association being set up by the Bank of England to rescue the spinning industry, so that's a start. Perhaps the banks will follow suit and shore up any other of the manufacturers and businesses that are having financial difficulties, meanwhile. I hope they do, I'm fed up with walking through all that mud and slutch on Darwen Road, whilst the builders find the money to continue. Those houses along the front and at the back of us, should have been finished months ago."

With the luck of the Irish, it wasn't long before Daniel had found another job, this time in the building industry. The 1930's economic recovery relied partly on a house building boom, so short term interest rates were reduced close to zero by the government and brought down the numbers of the million unemployed. Daniel was given the job of a "snagger", a term used for the man employed to oversee the quality of work at a finished house, before it was put on the market.

With the job came a small Bedford van. It was big enough to carry a few tools if necessary, but Daniel still wore his suit each day and still travelled far and wide if the developer, called Blakes that he now worked for, needed him to. His job as a Facilities Manager had prepared him for any eventuality and he became known as a precise and careful inspector of a family's future home.

In 1931, Winnie had left school and taken up a job as an apprentice in the nearby Holden Mill. She was still a quiet girl, hadn't made friends easily and had often wondered whether she should take up religious orders and become a nun. The thought of marrying, after she had heard the going's on between her mother and the man she was supposed to call Dada in the adjacent bedroom, had made her think twice about becoming wed. The parish priest, a kind young man from Galway, who had recently arrived in Bolton, was mentoring her.

Gracie and Florrie, now aged eight and six and half respectively, attended the little school at Walmsley, where they were taught reading, written English, arithmetic, history and geography. The teaching staff, under the guidance of the long serving headmaster, were attentive to the needs of all the pupils. Many children blossomed and went onto greater things.

It was not so with Arthur John McAuley, who petted by his Aunt Nelly and disciplined by his Aunty Bunty, who privately called him a 'rum 'un', only attended St. Saviour's school if he was forced to. He much preferred running wild to sitting in a stuffy school room, listening to the teacher droning on about nothing of interest to an eight and a half year old boy. Unknown to all, he was suffering from dyslexia and couldn't read the written word at all. So to all intents and purposes, he was un-teachable, so he stayed away from school as often as he could.

At various times of the year, a letter would arrive at the Ringley household, asking if Arthur was still a member of the school, or had he gone away? It was followed by a couple of slaps on the bottom with a slipper from Aunty Bunty, whilst Aunty Nelly cried in a corner and then a dose of the cane from the headmaster, when he was escorted to the school by Aunty Bunty the next day.

No wonder the dark haired Arthur with his slender frame, preferred to roam the countryside, especially the area that surrounded the village of Prestolee. With a fast flowing river and a canal above, where narrow barges transported goods for local businesses; deep dark forests that hardly ever saw the light of day, fields full of cattle and inquisitive looking sheep, the place was an education in itself for the inquiring young mind that Arthur had.

Chapter Twenty Three

In 1933, when the Nazi Party was gaining momentum in Germany and a Federal Election was being planned that July, Ada started to work full time as a Staff nurse in Blairs Convalescent Hospital. Built in 1887 from part of the proceeds of money left in his Will by a man called Stephen Blair, to be used for the sick people in the area, it was a three winged property, that looked as if it might have been a former gentleman's residence. The middle part of the building was for the sole use of the Matron, accommodation for her nurses, with offices and a dining room. One wing had been used for female patients and the other for the the treatment of males before World War 1, but when Ada, taken on as a Staff nurse, as there was already a Sister working there, the place was exclusively for the recuperation of men. She supposed that she was well suited, given her experience on Men's Surgical at Blackburn Royal Infirmary.

By this time, Gracie was well able to keep an eye on Florrie and continued to do so until it was time for her to leave school in April 1937. A quick-witted, talkative girl, had she applied her mind to her studies, she could have become a nurse like her mother, or gone to a ladies college and become a teacher one day. But although Gracie had the intelligence, she lacked the discipline and chose to be an apprentice weaver in Eagley Mill, as money and a good time was more important.

Arthur, three months older, had started work at the Kearsley Paper Mill, which belonged to a family called Fletcher, where cigarette paper and toilet rolls were made. He still couldn't read, nor write his name, but he knew how to count up the coins in his wage packet.

It was in June 1937 that Ada had to take some time off work and travel up to Gaitsgill. Nana Moscrop, mother of Wilfred, Ada's father had, at the grand old age of 97, gone to meet her Maker. Her daughter, Moira, who had kept in touch with an annual Christmas card and the occasional letter, had kindly let her know.

The funeral had been arranged for Friday, which coincided with the start of Bolton Wakes Week at the end of June. An event where each mill town in the area chose a week when their employees could have an annual holiday. Gracie and Florrie travelled up to Carlisle on the train with her too, as there was no way Ada would have allowed her daughters to stay alone at home. Even though Gracie wailed that Hetty next door could keep an eye on them, Hetty could be wound around Gracie's little finger, Ada knew. The girl, already, had a following of smitten young men from the mill, who would have fainted with delight if she as much as looked their way. Gracie dressed a little too fashionably for Ada's tastes, but of course it was her fault, that she knew. She never took a penny off Gracie for her bed and board and so her weekly wage was spent at the shops in Bolton every Saturday afternoon.

There were many changes in Great Britain at that time. King George V1 had his coronation in May, as his brother King Edward V111 had chosen to abdicate so that he could marry Wallis Simpson, an American divorcee. Neville Chamberlain, he who told the country that there was "Peace in our Time" became the Prime Minister, little knowing that Britain would be at war with Germany in 1939!

There was much discussion in the canteens, workshops and alehouses across the land, after hearing on the news that Adolph Hitler, the man who had become the German Chancellor, was creating mayhem throughout Europe because of his treatment of the Jews. Boatloads of frightened German residents, fleeing from the anti-semitic hate crimes in their homeland, after Hitler had ordered that all Jews must be herded into ghettos, landed on British shores. It was a time of foreboding for many, as they recalled the millions of deaths, only twenty years earlier, because of the Great War.

It was a sunny morning when the three of them gazed out of the compartment windows at the passing countryside. Sheep munched on green grass in the lowlands and the blue sky above the hills and valleys, heralded another warm day. Ada, dressed in a black calf length dress, a long matching jacket and a black saucer shaped hat, had a momentary twinge of resentment, as she recalled that it was around about this time fifteen years ago that she had been looking forward to beginning married life with Daniel. Her hopes had been dashed when she learnt that Daniel had gone back to Ireland, ostensibly to visit his sick Grandma, but in reality hiding the fact he already had a wife. That had been when the urge from within to belong to someone, somewhere, Ada had travelled on the train to find her father's estranged family in Carlisle.

It was strange how life could change in the blink of an eye, she thought as she looked at Daniel's daughters, one dark, one fair, who she wouldn't be without, but she had lost her friend Betty because of it. And didn't gain the husband, whom the upset with Betty had been all about. Daniel McAuley had a lot to answer for when he met his Maker, just like Nana Moscrop had the other day, but at least he'd fulfilled the dream that she'd had and she was very grateful for it.

The last time she'd seen him was a couple of weeks before, when all dressed up in a smart three piece woollen suit, with a single breasted three button jacket, a white striped shirt and the obligatory moustache, he had called to see the girls after taking Winnie to the railway station. According to Daniel, the girl was travelling over to Dublin to stay in a convent.

His daughters however, had accepted the fact that their father didn't live with them anymore. His story, literally made up on the hop, when Gracie had asked him a couple of years earlier why he didn't live them with them at Dunscar, was that his sister, who had come over to live in Astley Bridge from Ireland, was poorly. It was his duty to help her, he had told his elder daughter and he knew that their mother could look after them, without him.

He had smiled sadly at Ada over the top of Gracie's head and for a moment she missed having him about the cottage, remembering how, sometimes, she yearned for his body to be cuddled close to hers in the double bed upstairs. Then she dismissed it as a foolish notion. He had done his job and she wouldn't want another child for love or money. Now that she was forty five, she knew it might destroy her.

Gracie, dressed in the latest fashion which showed off her already curvaceous form due to the wearing of an emphasizing brassiere, wore a pretty knee length chiffon brown flecked frock, a light brown duster coat and a pair of white round framed sunglasses. Her white patent leather shoes with the tiny hour glass heel had been fought for. Ada had drawn the line at her fourteen year old daughter wearing shoes that were far too adult for her, preferring her to wear a pair of lace up shoes instead. It wasn't until they were standing on the platform at their local station that she noticed the brand new shoes, but didn't want a scene in front of all the other passengers. The little minx was also wearing, horror of horrors, a dab of face powder and a smear of red lipstick and looked far much older than her fourteen years. Especially with the "updo" hairstyle that someone at the mill had shown her how to do.

Florrie, on the other hand, was Ada's double. White haired, slender and just about growing a couple of buds on her chest, she wore a plain calf length navy skirt, a white short sleeved blouse and a navy blue cardigan. It was a similar outfit to the one she normally wore to school. She was a quiet girl, studious and a credit to her family according to her teacher, who had great ambitions for her star pupil. She liked to read and often tucked herself away upstairs in the room she shared with Gracie, as Ada had decided to have the wall of the third bedroom knocked down, when the girls were small. Sometimes she was forced to succumb to Gracie practising different hairstyles on her shoulder length hair or her face being smothered in makeup.

Slow to anger, calm if faced with anxious situations and could have possibly followed in Ada's footsteps, if that was what Florrie had wanted of course. But she dreamt of travel, studied atlases and geography books avidly and wrote and received many letters from her cousin Chadwick, in Australia.

It was early afternoon, when stepping down from the train at Dalston, they found that Jed, Moira's brother, was waiting for them on the platform. Ada barely recognised him, as the only time she had met him was briefly on the evening before she had left Gaitsgill for Colbrook. That had been fifteen years ago and of course he looked much older now.

"Ah, you must be Jed, Moira's brother," she said, crossing over to where he stood under the station clock and smiling at him sadly. "I'm sorry about Nana Moscrop. I didn't know her well, but I know she had a loving family."

"Aye, she were a good mother," the man replied, sniffing a little, as if it had only just hit him that he wouldn't be seeing the old lady again. "Good of yer to come. Are these yer bairns?"

"Oh yes, this is Grace, my elder daughter and this is Florence." She beckoned the girls to stand at the side of her, so that she could introduce them.

"Fine lookin' girls, " he said, as if he was inspecting a couple of heifers and Ada remembered that he used to work on the family farm until his father died. "Your young 'un takes after the Moscrop family. Anyroad, I've the motor outside. It'll save yer travellin' on the motor bus and the funeral's at three." He picked up their suitcases. One for each of them, although Gracie's weighed a ton. They followed as he strode outside to where a brand new shooting brake stood.

"She were a good mother," Moira said, as her brother had said to Ada earlier. "We never did without, unlike some of the raggedy arses that were in the same class as us. She were kind and carin'. Never raised her hand unless we needed it. What can I say, we'll miss 'er, won't we Jenny? She were a good nan to you as well."

"And a nice great nana to us," a boy, called Des, who looked to be about eighteen said, with his mouth full of cheese cake, who was standing next to Gracie, who had also been tucking into the food that Moira had provided for the funeral tea. "Gran, this stuff's delicious. Did yer mek it yerself or did yer get it from Dalston?"

"Cheeky monkey," Moira replied affectionately. "You've been eating this since yer were nay high, but today I added yer nana's secret ingredient, but I'm not allowed to tell yer what it is."

"I don't think I've ever eaten this before," Ada said. "It tastes more like a pudding. Even when I lived in Colbrook, I don't remember seeing it."

"Well, it's made from curd. I'm surprised your Dad didn't get your Mum to make it for 'im. I'll get yer some from the bakers before you go back home, as I haven't time to make any more at the moment. Which reminds me we need to sort yer beds."

The following morning the girls set off for a walk around the area. They were accompanied by Des, short for Desmond, who had lived and played around the area of Gaitsgill since he was born and had been taken on as an apprentice at a local cotton mill.

Gracie and Florrie had both stayed the night in the house belonging to Jed and his wife and Ada had stayed at Moira's home. It felt strange for both girls to suddenly have a family. They had always been told that their mother's relations lived near Carlisle and Melbourne, in Australia respectively. Their father's family remained an enigma. They knew he was from Ireland, but he had never taken them to meet his sister, their aunty, who lived in Astley Bridge.

It was a bright sunny morning and the two girls wore dresses without a cardigan or jacket, whilst Desmond, their cousin, wore a

Fair Isle jersey over a pair of light coloured trousers. Their cousin was a stocky lad, with brown hair and blue eyes and must have been fairly handsome, because Florrie could hear that Gracie was using her silly girly voice when she spoke. It was her way of letting a boy know that she liked him.

They walked along a narrow footpath, where through the trees they could see a sparkling river, as it splashed and gurgled on its way to Dalston.

"It's a good place to catch salmon in the Spring" Des remarked, when after listening to Gracie telling him all about her new friends at the mill and how they were all hoping to see a film with Bette Davis and Spencer Tracy in, he decided to change the subject. "Dad and I caught a couple of big ones last time and everyone was fed up with eating it after a while. I miss Nana Moscrop. She was the best maker of Toad-in-the-Hole." "Toad-in-the Hole, what's that when it's at home?" Florrie asked curiously, having only been used to the basic culinary skills of Ada's.

"Oh, it's sausages in Yorkshire pudding. Nana used to make it in a big dish and she made tons of onion gravy." Desmond paused for a moment as if he was thinking. "I wonder why we've never seen you two before in Gaitsgill?"

"Something to do with family secrets, I believe," Gracie said, pausing to throw a couple of stones into the river, whilst they stood on the grassy bank. "Mum won't tell us. She said that Nana Moscrop took her secret to the grave."

A similar conversation was being had between Ada and Moira, as they sat eating cheese sandwiches and left over cake for their lunch, on the day after Nana Moscrop's funeral. It had been a morning of clearing and cleaning, after many thereabouts had visited the home for what was called "the Wake". It was a time for many to pay their respects and condolences to the deceased person's family.

"You know, I never understood why our Dad always favoured us young un's over Wilfred," Moira confided, as she sipped her tea. "He were a lovely lad. Well behaved, kind to us younger ones and worked his guts off on the farm, but it never seemed good enough. Dad would sometimes shout at him, slap him, pick on him for nothin' that I could see. I remember once, when we all came in covered in mud because we used to like sliding on a piece of wood down the river bank. Dad was so angry, because we made a mess all over the floor when we went charging into the kitchen without taking our wellies off and he blamed our Wilfred for allowin' it. Wilf was only eighteen months older than me and I should have known better, as I was around about ten at the time. But, before we knew it Dad had punched Wilf in the chest, knocked 'im to the ground and then started kicking 'im. Wilf was screaming and shouting for Mum to help 'im, but she stood there in shock and never raised a finger to help 'im. We were horrified, even Jed was cryin' and Franny had run to hide in the scullery. Then Dad picked him up and threw him on the sofa, as if he was a bit of rag. He walked off and it was up to Mum to help Wilfred up the stairs to bed and put some arnica on his bruises. He couldn't go to school for a couple of weeks and I once heard Mum saying that if Dad did it again, she'd get Harry Croft to put us on his cart and take us all to the Workhouse in Whitehaven. Whether she would have done, I don't know, but he never raised a fist again to any of us."

Ada listened to her cousin's story with growing horror, then revulsion for the man, who to his mates in the pub and his fellow farmers who he met at the cattle auctions, was a quiet, amiable kind of person, according to Nana Moscrop. Little did they know that Ted Moscrop had harboured a bitter grudge against the boy, who was ostensibly, his son. Poor Wilfred was the bastard child of William Tomkinson, the owner of the farm that Ted had tenanted and Ted must have carried that resentment of his landlord to his grave.

Ada made no comment and only patted Moira's arm sympathetically, whilst keeping her own counsel. Some things were better left unsaid and be consigned to the hidden veils of time.

Chapter Twenty Four

It was in the April of 1939, three weeks after Germany had occupied Czechoslovakia and 7,000 Jews had fled Lithuania, that Grace Moscrop celebrated her sixteenth birthday, unaware that by her 17th birthday, Great Britain would be at war. Daniel, having not been seen for a week or so, turned up to celebrate the event with her.

"You're so grownup now, so you are," he said, passing over a brown paper parcel to his excited daughter. "Where's the time gone since me and yer mother got together and made you, our little Gracie? No, let me finish, Ada, it has to be said. If it wasn't fer me having a barrel rollin' on me foot, Gracie nor Florrie would be here today. Has yer mother ever told yer that story?"

Both girls quickly shook their heads, although they were mindful of the fact that once their father started telling a story, it could be a while before Gracie could open her parcel. His love of Irish history, told with relish and the woes of his ancestors blamed on the actions of British landowners or some king from way back in time that had caused the misery, could go on for a while.

"Let her open her parcel," Ada said, noting the flush on Gracie's face, be it from excitement or annoyance at the delay. "Then we'll have our tea. I had the cake made especially at a bakery in Bolton. I've been so busy lately with this new department they've opened at the hospital."

"Look Mam, a handbag!" Gracie fell upon her present with delight. She had long since wanted a white patent leather handbag, that would match the heeled shoes which had caused so much controversy. "It's got a zip inside and two pockets. Oh, thank you Daddy, you couldn't have chosen better!" She kissed him briefly on the cheek, then ran upstairs to find her purse, which she usually carried in her coat pocket.

"That was very nice of you," said Ada, thinking what a shame that Daniel couldn't spend more time with her and the girls, instead of spending all his time with Connie. He was still a handsome man, even if he had put a bit of weight around his belly. The product, she supposed of his liking for Guinness and his lack of exercise.

"And I've got something for you as well, my little princess," Daniel said next, pulling Florrie onto his knee, as he was sitting on the sofa. "Go on, open it. It'll help with your studies when you get to go to night school."

"Oh, it's wonderful." Florrie sounded delighted, when opening the long flat parcel, she found a fountain pen nestling in a piece of tissue paper. "Just the thing I'll be needing Daddy. Although Miss Slater said that if there isn't a war I might get to go to the Charlotte Mason College in the Lake District, but I'll be just as pleased to go to night school if I have to."

"Let's have our tea." Ada didn't want to talk about the possible war with Germany, which seemed to be the talk wherever you went. Especially the story of how someone had built an Anderson shelter in their garden already. "Gracie, come downstairs and you can blow your candles out."

It seemed that Daniel wanted to talk about the war though. After their daughters had gone for a walk, professing to be visiting a couple of friends who lived in the new houses just along the Darwen Road, he lit a cigarette and stood in the flagged stone yard.

"Commere, Ada," he beckoned, as she stood at the sink later, washing the crockery they had used at tea time. " Come and sit on the sofa with me, 'cause I've something to tell yer. I might be goin' away."

Ada spirits sank as she heard him. She was fond of her irascible Irishman. Never knowing what his mood would be, or what tales he was about to tell her and he was usually stretching the truth.

"Connie wants to go back to Ireland now that war is looming its ugly head. She says she'd feel safer there and of course there's Winnie. She hasn't seen her since she became a postulant."

"A postulant?"

"She went to live in a convent up in Dublin and hopes to become a nun one day. Connie's never felt accepted over here, even though she joined the congregation at Holy Infants."

"But why do *you* have to go back with Connie?" Ada insisted, knowing that if she didn't see Daniel again, it might cause her and the girls a lot of heartache. "Doesn't she have family that she could go to? Didn't you mention a brother?"

"Aye, it were Fergal that came up with the suggestion. He doesn't want to be caught up in another British war, just like I don't. I managed to escape the last one and now, thank God, I'm probably too old if there was a "Call up" anyway. But there is one thing that I've been mulling over, so I have. If war is declared with the Germans, the building company I'm workin' for, is thinkin' of gettin' into demolition. There's talk of me being made into what they call an Assessor. Someone who would assess a building, say in the city and decide whether it was worth doing up again or demolish it. My boss said it would be a reserved occupation, so even if they decided that forty four was still young enough to be recruited into the British Army, I'd get away with it."

"And what do you think, Daniel? Would Connie be happy to go back to Ireland, leaving you behind and possibly not seeing you again for another few years, just like what happened before?" Ada held her breath as she waited for his answer. For some reason it was important to her suddenly that he should stay.

"I'd miss the girls and Arthur, although the poor fellow hardly sees me nowadays with all the travellin' I'm doin'. And of course I'd miss you Ada. I'm the father of your children and no doubt that's where I am in your peckin' order, but you and I have known each other for a lot of years."

He pulled her close and before they both knew it, Daniel was lying on top of Ada, kissing her ear and her neck. "Oh Ada, yer don't know what it's been like, trying to be the dutiful husband to the woman that I'm married to, but don't really love," he said sorrowfully, whilst his willy began to grow and she could feel it nudging against her hip. "It's you I let into my dreams. You who I'm hugging and laying me body next to when I'm sleepin' at night and if only I'd met you before I had met Connie, you'd be Mrs. McAuley instead." He drew up her skirt and began to make love to her hungrily, only pausing to find a way into her cami- knickers, conscious that at any time the girls may walk in and spoil their intimacy. Ada just felt thankful that she hadn't thrown away her douche.

It was a little while later, once Ada had made a pot of tea and Daniel had stirred a couple of drops of whisky into each cup from the silver flask he carried in his overcoat, that the conversation returned to Daniel and the situation that needed careful thought. Ada, her senses stirred by his lovemaking, knew that his answer had to be a positive one. Otherwise life for her, would be just one long round of working and motherhood.

"Have you given any thought to the house and furniture, if you got it into your head that Ireland would be a great deal safer?" Ada asked, hoping to start him thinking of the why's and wherefore which Daniel didn't usually do. "I mean if you were to give that all up, went to Dublin, then found you'd made the wrong decision, you'd be stuck. And what would you do for a job? Didn't you tell me that your father closed the brewery and sold off some of the land to someone? Unless of course you asked that uncle, the one who got you the job with Duttons to help you."

"Aye, Uncle Dickie. He's some relation to me Dada, although I've never found out what. He must have made his money in the brewery trade, because it was him who helped set me Dada up.

I think Connie's hoping that he'll find her a job, or maybe he'll need someone to work at his home in Dollymount. But if Fergal goes back and I decide not to, they'll probably get a place together anyway."

"Leaving you to move back into the cottage with me." said Ada, wondering illogically if she wanted to give up her freedom for a man again. "Leavin' me to move back into the cottage with you, if you'd 'ave me." Daniel said, caressing the back of her hand lovingly.

It was a few evenings later, when once again Daniel turned up on Ada's doorstep, again bearing gifts. "I thought you might like these," he said to his delighted daughters, when they saw he had brought a Cadbury's chocolate box, with a country cottage scene on the lid. "Seems if Hitler gets his way, we'll not be seein' many of these again."

"Why's that, Daddy?" asked Florrie, even though she was stick thin, she loved to eat chocolate if it came her way. "Oh, they'll probably be shortages," he blustered, not wanting to frighten his children if he could help it. "Look what else I've brought yer, a bunch of bananas!"

"Beware of Greeks bearing gifts," said Ada rather inanely, aware that Daniel had come to tell her of his decision and was trying to lighten the atmosphere. " Or should I say Irish...it was something to do with the Trojan horse...Oh, it doesn't matter. Now you two, I don't want you being sick, so take it easy with the chocolate."

"Connie says the war will be over by Christmas, if there is one," Daniel said later, after he had made a fuss of his daughters before they went to bed. "So she reckons we should keep the house on in Astley Bridge. She'll travel across with Fergal and I'll continue working for Blakes. That's as far as we got with the discussion, as she got angry when I said that I didn't want to pack it in and go back with her. I suppose that it was me and you the other night that swung it fer me."

He smiled at her wickedly and she gave him a slap on the shoulder.

"So how's that going to work?" Ada asked, wondering if she would have to cook for him and wash his clothes, once his wife had done a bunk back to Ireland. She had already been told that if a war started, she would be expected to work long hours, as the hospital might be on standby to accept war casualties. A different role to the one she worked at currently, as she was in charge of a private ward, for the recuperation of a company's sick male employees. "You'll have to muck in and help me with the cooking and housework now that I'm working at the hospital."

"What ever yer willin' fer me to do, Ada, me darlin'," he said, snuggling in to her, whilst running his hand across her buttocks.

Over in Stoneclough, a few miles away, Arthur was sitting in the Stoneclough Reform Club watching his mate whilst he took his turn at the billiard table. Too young at aged 16 to be drinking alcohol in the many public houses around the area, he was spending his evening playing billiards with Johnny, who he worked alongside in the factory. Johnny Francis, a reckless kind of lad with ginger hair, would sometimes buy him a glass of beer when no one was looking.

It was an anxious time for many there that night, as the talk of an imminent war was the topic of everyone's conversation. Johnny, who would be eighteen that summer couldn't wait for it to start and had joined the Reserves at Fletcher Street Barracks, just so he could be in it from the beginning.

"You'll regret it" a chap who had managed to escape being killed in the Great War commented, as he listened to Johnny getting braver with every empty glass. "Got through it by the skin of me teeth and good mates who I depended on. But besides that, those bloody Germans are as tough as old boots and won't be happy 'til they rule the world."

"Well, I'll take me chances," Johnny insisted. "We beat them last time and we'll do it again."

"Let's change the subject, Johnny," Arthur said, as he listened to some angry mutterings about young pups and babies still in napkins coming from the older men, who were playing cards at a nearby table. "What do yer fancy are *my* chances with Gertie Millward? I believe she let Harry put his hand up her skirt."

War indeed was declared a few months later, after Florrie had celebrated her fifteenth birthday and a decision had to be made about her education. By that time the government had decided to raise the school leaving age to fifteen, so although Florrie had her thoughts firmly fixed on future travelling, she decided that after being given a glowing school report and her Leaving certificate, for now it was best to stay at home and find work in an office. She duly got a job at the head office of the Pelham Clothing Company on Bradshawgate and with secretarial tuition three times a week at night school, Florrie was quite happy to bide her time.

Gracie though was relishing in the new found freedom that she was finding, now that her mother was hardly home and her father spent a lot of his time travelling. She began to visit the Palais de Danse on the corner of St. George's Road. Principally to learn to dance if at any time she was questioned, but the amount of eligible men who went there was also a draw. She found she was in great demand at the Saturday afternoon tea dances. With her swirly satin frocks that she saved up every penny of her wages to buy, or persuaded a friend who worked as a machinist at Burton's Clothing Factory to make for her, she learnt to fox trot and quick step with the best of them and loved every exciting minute of her life. Even her work at Eagley Mill became eventful, when the management, mindful of being responsible for their employees if a bomb should drop on their factory, ordered that a shelter underneath the building should be built and there was plenty of nice looking workmen for her and her pals to goggle at.

It was coming up to Christmas and most people had begun to call the threat of a German invasion, the *Phoney War*. There had been no major hostilities, other than Hitler marching into Poland in September and it was another eight months before any major fighting started in France. It was due mostly to the atrocious winter which affected most parts of Europe and the effect of Britain and France gathering intelligence on their common enemy.

Gracie meanwhile, was having a wonderful time. She loved clothes, latest hairstyles and makeup, going on dates and sitting on the back row with various fellows she'd met up with. There was no shortage of partners at the Palais de Danse, as many young men, having enlisted in a local battalion, were allowed a measure of freedom before their training had begun.

One particular evening, as Gracie sat with a group of girls, listening to the band and waiting to be chosen by a handsome partner, the M.C announced a waltz. A young dark haired man with brown eyes, along with a tall ginger haired mate, came across to their table and asked Gracie and Marion, a girl who worked in the weaving room, to dance. The young man looked familiar and after taking Gracie in his arms and whirling her around the floor a couple of times, he introduced himself as A.J. "Short for Arthur John," he said. "But Arthur sounds old fashioned, so my mate Johnny calls me A.J. Do you come here often?"

"I've been coming here for a while now. Mostly to the tea dances before the war." Gracie said, wondering if she had seen him before somewhere, as she suddenly felt as if she had known him forever and perhaps that was a sign of instantly falling in love. Other lads had only one thing on their mind when they stepped out with Gracie, but up to now she'd only allowed a bit of petting and was still a virgin. Not that she wasn't anxious to be *deflowered* by the man that she could possibly marry in the future, but there hadn't been anyone she would give up her virginity to. But was there someone now, she wondered?

Chapter Twenty Five

They met as often as they could, but by now Gracie and her friend Marion, had started work at the munitions factory in Euxton. Naturally it was the extra wages that attracted Gracie, not the uniform, which was a dark brown turban and a matching boiler suit and had to be worn for protection. It was dangerous work filling shells with dynamite which was combustible. All in readiness for an invasion that could happen any day.

There'd been a few false alarms by then, when newly appointed Air Raid Wardens decided to try out their equipment and their authority, sending most of the populus into sheer panic. And an incursion by a fleet of German Heinkel Bombers had been driven back by coastal batteries on the East coast in the summer. To many people though, the war was real. It was especially real to the people on the Channel Islands, who were invaded at the end of June in 1940 and lived out the war under the heel of the Nazi jackboot. Then British airfields and aircraft factories began to be targeted, mainly on the outskirts of London and Portsmouth.

Gracie and Marion chose to ignore the inconvenience, which up to now hadn't affected their lives very much, except for having to remember to carry the dreaded gas mask around, which was an annoyance. They heard the terrible news of death and destruction on the wireless, but somehow all this was happening to other people, not them. They were doing their bit at the munition factory, even if it did mean rising at cock crow for the seven to two shift and trundling sleepily on the bus which picked the workforce up at convenient points each morning. It wasn't until the shortages in the shops began to invade their personal lives; food, makeup and clothes being suddenly in short supply, because of convoys in the Atlantic bringing in imports being attacked on their way to England, that the nuisance of it all sank in.

The newly created Ministry of Food, who had secretly been stock piling food in depots in case of a German invasion since 1936, gave out ration books to the populus which had been printed as early as 1938. Little had been told to the public of the threat to their freedom.

Meantime, Gracie and A.J, when they were able, did a spot of courting. Not too much at first, as A.J lived on the Manchester side of Bolton and they both travelled to their respective homes on the last trains. Their favourite places to visit was the Theatre Royal or the Grand on Churchgate, where after watching a variety show, they would buy a couple of pasties at the Olde Pastie Shoppe, to eat on the way to the railway station.

In April 1941, when Gracie turned eighteen and A.J, already eighteen, had enlisted in the Lancashire Fusiliers but not started his training yet, they decided that it was time that they met each others family. A.J had explained that he had been brought up by two aunties and lived in a place called Ringley, next to the River Irwell. Gracie had said that she lived in a small cottage with her parents and her sister in a place called Dunscar, although they didn't see so much of their Dad.

"I don't see mine at all nowadays," A.J said, as they waited on the station platform one evening, after watching a film starring Laurel and Hardy, a couple of comedians that made them laugh. "He went off to Ireland, just as soon as the war was declared. Aunt Bunty said he was a coward. He dodged the first world war and then took off again this time. Mind you, I didn't see so much of him anyway, when I was growing up. He was always away working."

"Same with mine. If we saw him twice a week we were lucky.

Mum said he had a job that involved a lot of travelling. Strange that, my father was Irish too but he's still here. He volunteered to be an Air Raid Warden. Anyway, what about we go to mine on your next leave weekend and then we'll go to see your aunties another time."

Florrie, by this time, had settled into her job as a junior secretary in the head office of a clothing company. To her mind, it would do until the end of the war was declared, which according to the newly appointed prime minister, Winston Churchill, would, if everyone did their bit for the war effort, not be far away. She dreamed of travelling to Australia, once the conflict was over and people were allowed free movement, which at that time was very restricted in case you were a spy. Perhaps visit her Uncle Charles and cousin Chadwick, in Melbourne, see Ayers Rock and the bridge over Sydney Harbour. The world would be her oyster, as they say.

Not for her, this business of courting, which her elder sister appeared to be doing with a boy called A.J. Nor visiting the dance hall, theatres or cinemas, when every penny she could save, after she had paid bus fares, board and bought a few bits of clothing, went into her bank account in town.

At aged fifty, Ada was ashamed to admit, that even though there was a war on and everywhere was doom and gloom, everything was good in her own little world. She had her cottage, her lovely daughters, Daniel, still with his handsome looks, though growing a lot more grey in his hair and moustache, stayed more at her home now than the house he had kept on in Astley Bridge. Besides his assessor job with Blakes, he was a volunteer Air Raid Warden and now she had been asked to transfer to the Bolton Royal Infirmary, seeing as she had nursed the wounded during the first world war. Manchester had been bombed in the previous December and Liverpool in the August before, so there were plenty of casualties for her to nurse during this war too.

She hardly saw Daniel and for this reason she had a telephone put in the cottage, so that if he wasn't coming home he could let her know. If he wasn't out inspecting a bomb site somewhere or patrolling up and down Darwen Road, making sure that there were no chinks in the locals' blackout curtains, he was catching up on his sleep throughout the day.

Then one weekend Gracie announced that she was bringing her boyfriend A.J to meet them. He was about to start his training in the Army and she wouldn't be seeing him again for the next three months. Strangely enough, Ada's shifts that week coincided with Daniel catching up on all his paperwork and it was arranged that this young man, whom Gracie claimed to have fallen in love with, could come to tea that Saturday.

"I don't know what I'll do without him," she said to Florrie, the night before his visit, when she was going through her skirts and blouses deciding what to wear. "He makes me go all weak at the knees when he kisses me and he's so handsome. Mum and Dad will love him, the moment they set their eyes on him."

It was just before three o'clock, when Gracie, who had waited at the station for the two thirty train, arrived through the front door of the cottage with a young man in tow. Daniel was in the back yard having a smoke and listened to the sound of excited girly voices and Ada was filling the kettle with water from the sink. They were having a proper Sunday tea even though it was Saturday, according to Florrie, who had helped her mother prepare the egg and cress sandwiches on freshly baked bread, a lemon meringue pie with the egg whites all golden brown on top of it and a Victoria sponge cake that Florrie had made. It didn't matter that rationing was beginning to bite into the purchases of most households and most people had to make do and mend. This was a welcome guest who was coming home with Gracie. She might even marry him one day.

To say that Daniel felt jealous before the event was an under statement. It would be another man who would be holding his eldest daughter in their arms and doing things that he didn't want to think about. Out of all his children, Gracie was his favourite. She looked like him and she was a bit of a mad cap at times and tried not to be serious for long. But she was a decent loving daughter and he hoped that this young man would treat her well.

A.J had his back turned to Daniel, when his father walked into the room. He was looking at a women's magazine that Gracie had laughingly brought his attention to and Florrie and Ada were chatting nearby. Daniel thought he looked familiar. His height, his weight and of course his dark, handsome looks, so similar.

"So, this is your young man, our Gracie," he said, whilst his heart was hammering in his chest and sweat was beginning to appear on his brow. They'd know now. His daughters would know about this extra child that he'd kept a secret for eighteen years. His mind went into overdrive. He tried to remember what he had said to Ada on that day when she had told him that she had seen his bigamous marriage in the newspaper. He'd been truthful and she'd accepted his explanation, but his daughters… what were they going to say?

"Dad?" Arthur looked puzzled, as he turned to see the man whom he thought had fled to Ireland, standing in his girlfriend's living room, as large as life. "I didn't know you knew the Moscrops…you never said."

"Ah." For a moment he was speechless, as Ada stood there with a look of despair on her face and the girls momentarily stunned.

Chickens coming home to roost. It was a calm and collected Ada who made the a move towards their visitor.

"Arthur, it's very nice to meet you," she said. "Gracie told us that you met at the dance hall. Such a coincidence, what a small world."

"You knew about A.J, Mother?" Gracie was shaken and her voice sounded hoarse as she spoke. Was it true what she was hearing? She and her boyfriend had the same Dad? Didn't that mean that there was no chance of them having a relationship? No courtship, no marriage? He was her brother, for pity's sake. She turned and fled upstairs to her bedroom, beginning to sob as she realised the implications.

"Chickens coming home to roost, Daniel" said Ada solemnly, shaking a finger at him, as he stood there with his face white and looking all wobbly. " Florrie, nip up stairs and see to your sister. Arthur, would you like a cup of tea?"

Florrie found Gracie sitting on the stool in front of her dressing table mirror, dabbing her eyes and sighing dramatically. "It's not the end of the world," Florrie said, patting her sister embarrassedly, as they didn't go in for outward signs of affection. "Just think, we've got an older brother. A handsome older brother that you can show off to your friends."

"He was supposed to be my handsome fiance. We were going to announce our engagement on his next leave," Gracie wailed. "What fools we've been. Surely we could have seen that we were related. We look alike, have an Irish father and like A.J, we didn't get to see our father very often either."

"It would be interesting to find out how we got this older brother and how he was a secret which we knew nothing about." Florrie passed another handkerchief, knowing that if she could rally her sister by invoking the inquisitive side of her nature, she had won.

"Yes your right." Gracie stood up resolute. "Let's go and see what Dad has got to say for himself."

But upon descending the stairs and finding Ada busying herself in the kitchen, they found that the men had flown the coop. So it was up to Ada to give her girls some sort of explanation that would satisfy.

"Your Dad, God love him, was always easily led," she said, after they had sat down and she had passed around the sandwiches. "I believe it was a one off and the young woman found she was expecting Arthur. Your Dad stood by her, but she ran away, leaving her sisters to bring up the poor little soul. I believe she is married to a man who has a hotel in the Lake District."

"So really, poor Arthur was just like an orphan. No Mam, no

Dad, just his aunties." Gracie felt an overwhelming pity for the man she knew as A.J. "Well, we were lucky, weren't we Florrie? We've got an understanding Mam, who could forgive our father getting another woman pregnant like he did." *Her mother might be a saint,* she thought to herself, *but she would never forgive her father for his deceit.*

"You know, thinking about it, I was wondering what your van was doing outside when I got here," said Arthur bitterly, as father and son walked along the lane to the Dunscar Arms. "You told me you were going back to Ireland at the beginning of the war. We all said you were a conchie and Aunt Bunty said you were a coward."

"Well I'm neither, Son. Things just got complicated and I decided to live with Gracie's Mum."

"Instead of me."

"Arthur, your mother beggared off with her fancy man. What was I supposed to do? I was never welcome at Ringley. Your Aunt Nellie wanted you all to herself and your Aunt Bunty hates men anyway."

"And how do you know Mrs. Moscrop and tell me the truth this time, Dad?"

"Ah, well that's another story. Let's settle ourselves in The Dunscar and I'll buy you a beer."

"So what did you tell him? The truth or a lie? He seemed to be friendly enough when Gracie and Florrie offered to walk him back to the station." Ada continued washing the dishes at the sink, whilst Daniel helped himself to left over cake.

"I told him the truth, well the partial truth. I haven't told him about Connie or the fact that Winnie wasn't mine. No, I just said that you had a grand career and you wanted to keep the name Moscrop because of it. The girls were the product of the love between us and he seemed to accept that. It was like he had to be the one that was legitimate, he didn't want to be my bastard son."

"Well, let's hope he doesn't mention any of this to our

daughters. I don't want them putting two and two together and making five."

Strangely enough the girls never did broach the subject of Arthur to their parents. Perhaps it was because they didn't want to know the whole truth of the matter anyway. Whatever it was, talking about it would have caused embarrassment and being the respectful daughters that they were, they kept their opinions to themselves.

Chapter Twenty Six

A few months later, just before the British Expeditionary Force left for foreign shores, Gracie announced to Ada that she was marrying Johnny Francis, A.J's friend. Johnny was home on leave and had been advised by his sergeant, along with other members of his platoon, that if they had a loved one, it would be a good idea to marry her and then they could leave their wife an army pension if they died. Each man was given a five day pass to carry out this duty, before embarkation.

Johnny wasn't much of a catch in Ada's opinion once she had met him. He was a few years older than Gracie, rather plain and didn't seem to have a lot of brains in that devil-may-care ginger head of his. But he seemed a kind enough young man and still reeling from the revelation that Gracie could have hurtled into marriage with her half brother, if she hadn't brought Arthur home to visit the family, she gave her daughter her permission willingly and even offered to make her a cake. After a low key wedding at the Register Office in Howell Croft, when only close family attended and A.J decided he couldn't face them at all, Gracie and Johnny honeymooned in Blackpool. Well, an overnight stay really, just to get the nuptials out of the way.

Life didn't change much for Gracie, once she had said goodbye to her new husband at Bolton Station, where many people stood on the platform to wave their loved ones off to God knows where. She still lived at Daisy Nook, was still going to work at the munitions factory; the only things that were different was she now received an allocated Army payment and she wore a wedding ring. The marriage didn't stop her and best friend Marion, from visiting the Palais de Danse on a Saturday afternoon.

One Monday morning in October, when Ada having been on a night shift, after being asked to work longer because a bomb had dropped on Punch Street in Tonge Moor, returned home to find the cottage empty. It wasn't unusual, as Gracie was up with the lark every day, with it being a one and a half hour journey to Euxton and it was assumed that Florrie had gone to work. But Daniel had promised to help Hetty with one of her black out curtains that was sagging a bit and hadn't returned as promised. Ada was so tired from her fourteen hour non stop shift that she collapsed into bed and thought nothing more of it.

Daniel still hadn't made an appearance, when feeling revived after an all over strip wash, she wandered next door to see Hetty. Her neighbour, in her late sixties now, was preparing her dinner. A cabbage soup, made from some of her vegetables that she grew in her small garden. After the government had declared that the populus should "Dig for Victory", Daniel had taken up both Ada's and Hetty's flags in the back yard.

"No, last I heard he was on his way to somewhere because a bomb had dropped on a row of terraces. See he fixed the curtain for me before he went. Then we had a cup of tea and he said he was going to the ARP station to see if anyone was there who might want a lift in his van. Hasn't he telephoned you on that fancy instrument you had put in?"

"Not this time, Hetty. If he's been told to go to Manchester or one of the other cities he does, but not if it's local. Though having said that, Tonge Moor Road is a bit close."

"Oh, he's bound to be back soon. Stay and have a bit of soup with me and tell me how the girls are getting on with their jobs."

Daniel had indeed been to the bomb site where most of the terraced houses hung precariously, with a sagging roof, or no roof, or just two walls or cellar showing that a house had been there. Most of the residents had been put into the back of ambulances or taken to the nearby community hall to be treated for shock by the volunteers from St. John's. A couple of chaps from the bomb squad hung around in case they were called upon to dismantle any unexploded bombs lurking in the crater.

"I'll get off, Lenny," Daniel shouted to one of the wardens he knew, who had appeared on the scene, as he had. "Got some paperwork for Blakes to catch up on."

He walked to where his van was parked a few streets away. His suit smelt of smoke, his shirt had black marks down the front and his shoes were covered in a fine dust from the footings he had walked through. With this in mind he decided to go to his house in Astley Bridge and change into a pair of corduroy trousers and one of his jumpers. It would give Ada some time with the girls if she went to work on the night shift and he hated her seeing him when he wasn't looking his best. He whistled as he strolled along, feeling grateful that Bolton hadn't been too badly affected by the air raids, which seemed to have been attacking the North west of England a lot recently. Not yet anyway, but after the evacuation of the British Expeditionary Force from the beaches of Dunkirk a few months before, Hitler seemed determined to bomb the whole country into oblivion.

The house in Old Street was quiet, when Daniel turned the key in the front door lock and walked into the living room. At that time of the evening most people were indoors, eating their supper or getting their children ready for bed. He was reminded that he hadn't eaten since that morning, when he had helped himself to some of the porridge that Gracie had made before leaving for work. Then he'd eaten a biscuit at Hetty's when she had made him a cup of tea. Of course the fire in the grate was out. It had been a couple of days since he had used the place to sleep in, when he'd been on his way back from Manchester in the early hours.

It was with a bit of a shock, after having visited the lavatory, then giving himself a good wash in the kitchen sink, that as he was busying himself slicing a piece of ham from a small hock he kept in the meat safe for just this purpose, he heard the sound of a floorboard creaking above. The noise caused him to stop the preparation of his ham sandwich. Perhaps it was a rat. He had to admit that the place was a bit of a tip, not having a woman's hand in keeping it clean or tidying. It hadn't seen a sweeping brush since Connie had gone back to Ireland. He clutched the knife in his hand and trembling slightly, wandered slowly to the bottom of the stairs.

"Fergal?" The noise had been made by his brother-in-law, who was standing upstairs on the landing, staring back at him sleepily.

"Aye, how are yer, Danny? I wondered when yer'd be back again, so I took a rest on yer bed, whilst I were waitin'." His thin frame began to amble down, tucking his collar less shirt into his black shiny trousers, with his sparse hair standing on end in wisps.

"Our Connie give me the key. She said yer wouldn't mind me stayin'. Oh, were yer makin' a sandwich?"

"I was so." Daniel couldn't believe his eyes. The last time he'd seen Fergal was when he'd brought Connie over from Ireland. He wondered briefly what the man was doing there, before he turned his attention to slicing some bread.

"Connie all right?" He felt he should ask after the welfare of his wife. "And Winnie? Do yer ever hear about Winnie?" He wandered over to Fergal with a plate of sandwiches, then turned back to make a pot of tea.

"Aye, Connie's fine. Seems happy enough working fer Uncle Dickie, although she hopes you and her will get back together again after this lot's over. He's give her a nice little cottage at Dollyer, which overlooks Bull Island. You'd love it. When I'm not over here, I stay in one of the bedrooms and I must admit it's a very nice view."

"And Winnie?"

"Not seen or heard from her since she went up to Dublin. I think once they're in there, they get cloistered." He took a bite from his sandwich and chewed it hungrily, then began to slurp from the cup that Daniel had handed him. "Anyway, Uncle Dickie said that next time I saw yer I was to remind yer who yer friends are. He's not keen to hear that yer not workin' fer the brewery anymore."

"Eh? What's that supposed to mean? I had to leave when there was a takeover."

"Aye, that was so, but he was expectin' you to go back with Connie. He looked cross when Connie told him yer'd got a job with a building firm and was stoppin'."

"I don't understand, Fergal. What's Uncle Dickie got to do with you and me?"

"Know who yer friends are Danny." He tapped the side of his nose. " That's all I'm sayin.'"

It was a couple of hours later, after a trip to the local pub where both Daniel and Fergal downed a great deal of Guinness then stumbled back home, when it was made clear what Fergal had been on about.

"Commere, Danny, look what I've got to show yer," he said, producing a small brown leather suitcase that had been hiding behind the sofa. "Know what this is?" Daniel shook his head and continued on to the lavatory, whilst Fergal kept opening and shutting the lid of the thing. "It's fer keeping in touch with Uncle Dickie," he said proudly, when Daniel returned. "I suppose you could say it's somethin' like a typewriter, but I had to learn how to do this Morse code thing."

"So what's wrong with using a telephone? There's one on nearly every corner now."

"Ah, but you wouldn't want an operator listening into what I'd have to say to Uncle Dickie."

"Like what?" Daniel dismissed it all as a load of bunkum. Fergal was a boaster, he had always made a lot out of nothing.

"Like where the ammunition factories are. Where the docks are or the ship builders or the bomb makers. I'm like a spy. I ferret out the information and pass it on, so I do. Danny, surely you know what I'm getting' at? We Irish have no love for the British. They've kept us down like dogs over the centuries. Forced us off the land by the starving of us. Puttin' up the rents which we couldn't afford and making us take the King's shilling to help fight their wars that we wanted no part of. Well, this time our allegiance is with their enemy. Germany stood by us when it looked as if the Home Rule Bill was going through and sent us guns and ammunition, so now it's our turn. We can turn this war around and make us the victors."

"So you're willin' to kill thousands of innocent people just so another foreign power can tell us what to do instead of the British. Listen to yourself Fergal, yer not a murderer."

He turned away angrily, as he thought of his daughter Gracie and others like her, who were in danger of death every time they walked through the doors of the ammunition factory. Not only from the affects of ingesting the yellow powder that was used to fill the bomb shells or a careless worker causing an explosion unintentionally, but now there was a threat of espionage. And Fergal's next words put the chills up him.

"Is it true that there's a place nearby called Euxton?" Fergal pronounced the word Euston, but Daniel knew the place he was on about. It was where his daughter was doing her bit for her country, by the filling of the bomb shells.

Florrie was in a state of great excitement. She couldn't eat, she couldn't sleep and it was all because she'd had a letter from Chadwick, her cousin from Australia. He was journeying up to Bolton just to see her and his Aunt Ada at the weekend. He had a three day pass from the base where he was stationed with the Royal Australian Air Force and couldn't wait to meet his English family.

Of course there were restrictions on the words that he could put in print on the writing paper, as usual censored by an unknown hand, but Florrie knew that Chadwick had been part of the Empire Air Training Scheme and was a Flying Officer now, flying the Beaufighters.

She was extremely proud of this Australian cousin, who since they were in their teens had been communicating by letter and couldn't wait for Friday to see him. Mr. Pelham, God Bless him, who was the managing director of the firm she worked for, had granted her a day's leave.

"Well, all I can say is don't get too close to him like I did with Arthur." Gracie had said bitterly, when Florrie had told her the news. "You'll get your heart broke, like I did and I wouldn't mind, but I've never seen A.J since. I thought once he knew he had family, he'd keep in touch with us. You know, come for Sunday tea and suchlike. Johnny says he's never set eyes on him since the night before the wedding, when they all went out for a drink."

"Oh, Gracie, he was probably embarrassed. Can't look us in the eyes, can't bear to be close to you. Anyroad, didn't he join up when he was old enough to?"

"Well, I don't know that, do I? It would look odd if I suddenly turned up at his Aunty Bunty's house and asked to speak to him and I've never liked to ask Johnny."

"Ah well. Let's look forward to seeing Chadwick at the weekend. I'm going to meet him on Bolton Station."

It was just as Ada was hanging the washing out around eleven thirty on Tuesday morning when Daniel appeared on the back doorstep, smoking a cigarette and looking as if he had seen a ghost, he was so pale and shaken.

"God, you look rough," she said, finishing pegging the last sheet onto the line, then looking at the grey clouds above critically. "It's a good job I've got the overhead pulley or I'll never have clean sheets for our visitor.""Visitor?" Daniel looked alarmed for the moment, then regaining his composure, he asked again.

"Oh yes, we've got Chadwick, my brother's child, coming to stay. You know, my brother who lives in Australia. It appears that Chadwick, who's stationed down south on one of the R.A.F bases has some leave due, so he's coming here to make our acquaintance. Hetty said he could stay at hers, but she hasn't got any sheets for the spare bed, so I've washed some of mine. Will you be around this weekend to meet him or you off on one of your jobs?"

"Well, actually I wanted to talk to you about something, Ada. I'm thinkin' of givin' the house up and movin' in with you. That's if you'll have me," he finished hastily, when he saw the look of surprise on her face at his suggestion. "I know I said I'd keep it on for Connie in case she wanted to come back one day and live in it, but that's something I wanted to talk to you about. I need your help to vanish, before someone gets me."

Chapter Twenty Seven

He was a delight to be with. Tall, blonde haired, blue eyed and sporting a tan that told of many days spent on Victorian beaches. Chadwick had the family captivated with his tales of golden sands and lapping waves, where children paddled and families spent their weekends cooking food on their "barbies" and meeting up with friends. Florrie fell instantly in love and had to be reminded that Chadwick was her cousin, by both Ada and Gracie.

"It's the uniform," Gracie advised, whilst the girls busied themselves in the kitchen, laying the table, slicing bread, opening up a tin of Spam and putting out a bowl of tinned peaches. Rationing had now begun to bite in most households, unless you were not adverse to purchasing luxury goods on the black market. Eggs, bought from an opportunist farmer were plentiful, as was cheese and butter, late crops of potatoes and apples from the orchards in the autumn and everyone had a ration book issued to them to be used at their local shops.

"It matches the colour of his eyes. All the girls I know fall in love with a fellow once they start wearing a uniform. It's what's underneath that's more important, you know."

"Gracie!" Florrie looked embarrassed.

"Oh, I didn't mean… I meant his character, his personality, not that." She flicked her sister playfully with a tea towel, causing the others sitting in the living room to wonder what their laughter was all about.

"So how are your father and mother?" Ada asked, as she and Daniel sat together getting to know their visitor.

"Oh, you know. Dad's always busy at work and Mum loves her garden and now that we've got a small shack at Geelong, many of our weekends are spent away."

"Geelong?" Daniel queried, feeling awed by this relation of Ada's who spoke with an accent he had never heard before. "Yeah, it's a place by the beach and overlooks the Southern Ocean. The family home though is at Footscray on the outskirts of Melbourne. Hey, you should all come over one day!"

"We'd love to, Chad," said Ada, thinking it would be a big adventure travelling to the other side of the world to visit her brother. "As soon as this war is over we'll get our tickets…won't we Daniel?"

She had said that tongue in cheek, remembering back to Daniel's stumbling confession after he had arrived on Tuesday morning asking if he could stay. He'd been ashen faced and trembling and she had rushed to find his hip flask that he kept in the cupboard in the bedroom. She assumed that he had witnessed a terrible scene when he had gone to check the security of the bomb site, but all he could say was that he wanted to disappear.

"Calm down, Daniel," she had said later, as she had watched him slurp the contents of the flask, whilst he sat looking into space, as if he was reliving whatever it was that had affected his mind and body. "It can't be that bad if you've managed to drive here from wherever. What was it? Tell me, I get to see casualties every day."

"I need to hide away. I'm being followed. Ada, I need to tell yer something. Something that I've been keeping from yer for years.""Not another child of yours about to come to my attention, Daniel?" Ada said it despairingly, whilst watching his face closely for a reaction.

"No, worse than that. I used to be a member of the I.R.B and they're after me."

"You've lost me Daniel. Who's after you and why should they want to find you anyway?"

"Well, when I was a youngster, I used to follow me elder brothers around and they belonged to this organization called the Irish Republic Brotherhood. I suppose to me it was like being part of a youth club, although we did a lot of marching, pretending we were soldiers. And it was nothing to do with the church, it was political. Anyway, the weekend that I was to marry Connie, was during the time that the Easter Rising took place in Dublin. We should have been there to support the dissidents, but we wasn't and sometime later, Uncle Dickie, who's somethin' big over there in the city, persuaded me Dada to let me come to Britain. As yer know, I was given a job with the brewery, but it all must have been part of a scheme of things. Because do yer remember that time when we were supposed to be gettin' married and I went off somewhere? It was because a fella had been looking fer me. Then, do yer remember when we were in Blackpool with the girls and yer saw me talkin' to that fella by the Pier? That fella was after me too, but I managed to dodge him. Then last night, just when I had decided to stay the night at the house, because I was in a bit of state after being at the bomb site, I found that someone had been in there. Someone had slept in the bed, eaten from me meat safe and finished off me bread. It put the shits up me, beggin' yer pardon Ada, so I'm thinkin' of giving back the key and goin' into hidin'."

She had looked at him open mouthed. She couldn't believe her ears at what he was telling her. Talk about being unworldly, this man of hers took the biscuit.

"And is that it?" she had said in her usual to the point manner. "Once you've gone into hiding, there'll be no more skeletons?"

"Skeletons?" Daniel suddenly shivered. "No, but I need yer to write a letter to me family."

Florrie was everything that Chadwick thought she would be, although the photograph she had sent him didn't do her justice. She looked like an angel with her light, almost white hair that she wore in the latest roll up fashion and her creamy skin and pretty pale blue eyes. Chadwick was smitten. From the moment he saw her waiting for him on the platform at the station, smartly dressed in a dark green matching dress and jacket, a pair of beige Cuban heeled shoes and a little cream coloured saucer shaped hat on her head, he knew that she was the only girl for him, even if they were supposedly related. He would marry her when this shout was over and take her away to live in happiness in Australia. They'd have children. A boy and a girl, who would make him proud, just like his parents were proud of him.

Oh, he knew that there was a war to fight. Not only here in Europe, but now the Japanese had begun an offensive against the Americans as well. The world had gone mad, with tyrants everywhere wanting domination and battles in places that people had never heard of. But in the end good would triumph over evil and that was what kept Chadwick strong in his belief.

It was another cold winter that following year, especially in Eastern Europe, where war between the Germans and the Russians raged on relentlessly and 800,000 citizens of Leningrad had to be evacuated along the frozen wastes to safety. Frost lay heavily on the ground each morning in the northwest of England and many lakes and ponds were frozen over for days. Children, released from the confines of home and schools, took the risk of perilously skating on the thin ice, much to their mothers' alarm.

One evening, Hetty, an avid reader of the Bolton Evening News, noticed the report of a body that had been found in Clough Lodge, a pond that existed near Old Road. A young boy, having fallen in the water once the ice had begun to thaw, had unwittingly dislodged a leg that had been weighted down by a large lump of concrete and his action had freed the cadaver from its watery grave. Nothing was known about the identity of the unfortunate man and he was written off as just another statistic in the ongoing war.

There was much to read in the papers nowadays. Singapore

had fallen to the Japanese, whilst Royal Navy cruisers had been sunk by Japanese aircraft and it had been heard that one million German soldiers had been killed in action since the war began. The report of a body found in a small northern village, quickly became yesterday's news.

One evening, as the family listened to the wireless, when reports of the Japanese offensive against the Americans was beginning to gain momentum, Gracie brought up the subject of her moving out.

"It's not that I don't like living here," she said hastily, when her mother looked at her in disbelief and her father looked at her sternly. "But when all this is over, me and Johnny will need somewhere to live and now that Dad is living back home, it would be rather crowded." *And it was because her father was getting on her nerves with the way he spoke to her. She wasn't a little girl anymore. If she wanted to go to the pictures, or the Palais de Danse or stay at a friend's house, she didn't need his permission or be told what time she had to be home before the door was locked. And if truth was told, she still held him responsible for A.J disappearing from her life. She often wondered where he was. Was he dead or had he come home safely when the men at Dunkirk had been evacuated? Or was he being held a prisoner by the Germans in one of their prison camps? He could be anywhere and apart from that bond of him being her brother, she knew she secretly loved him and thought about him every day.*

"Well, your Dad's not given his key back to Holden's if you wanted to live in Astley Bridge and there's all that nice furniture. Isn't there Daniel." Ada looked at Danny meaningfully, as she had already sent off the letter to his father in Ireland, as he had requested, but he didn't seem in a hurry to clear the house or give back the key.

"No, I don't want 'er livin' there," he said hastily, before getting up and disappearing through the back door for a smoke.

"What's up with him? I thought you said he'd done it up and the furniture's a lot more modern than ours is. Astley Bridge would be a great place to live, as the bus for Euxton stops near The Lamb."

"Oh, leave him to me, Gracie, I'll talk him round. I'll go and put the kettle on and I'll put some whisky in his tea."

"So, what was that all about?" Ada asked, when the girls had gone to bed and Daniel had settled on the sofa knocking back a couple of whiskies.

"Yer know what's up," he replied, looking a little glassy eyed, as if he was suffering some inner torment. "It would only need somebody who knew me to knock on the door and Gracie or her husband could tell them where I live. What would have been the point of you writing that letter to Dada telling him that I was fatally injured in a bomb blast? It would all start up again. Next time it could be Fergal or Connie who comes looking for me."

"I doubt it," Ada said patting his hand reassuringly. "Why would they bother to come all that way from Ireland to see for themselves that you were dead? Anyroad, I'll take the key back and if you want I'll see if we can put the furniture into storage. There's a place under the arches at the bottom of Tonge Moor that stores stuff for people."

"If yer like," he said, realising that he couldn't turn up in person if he was supposed to be dead. The woman next door always had her curtain twitching and might see him using his key. "But if Gracie finds a place to rent somewhere else, I'll let her have the furniture. As long as she arranges a removal van."

The nightmare came when he least expected it. The body floating, its arms outstretched in anguish, its hollow eyes in the yellow skull pleading for mercy, whilst all the time Daniel stood warily. He hadn't meant to kill Fergal. It was an accident brought on by the booze and the thought that the man who was walking down the steep stairs ahead of him, might play a part in the murder of so many innocent souls. Pictures of Gracie, her body shattered into pieces and her short life ended at the hands of this monster, caused him to stumble against his brother-in-law, who in turn had lost his footing and fallen in a heap at the bottom of the stairs. The tiled floor of the kitchen had come up to meet him and within a few seconds Fergal McKenzie was no more.

It was at the end of May that year, when a letter came for Florrie from cousin Chadwick. As usual it was heavily censored by the powers at be, but it asked if Florrie would meet him at their usual place and named the date, which was the following weekend. Florrie walked on air that week and couldn't wait to call around to Gracie's house to tell her.

Gracie hadn't moved far from the family home. There had been a place to rent in nearby Clay Street. A terraced dwelling with a living room, kitchen and three bedrooms above and Daniel's furniture fitted perfectly.

She often blessed the day when she had married Johnny Francis. Not because she was in love with him, but their marriage had given her some freedom since he was away in the army and the nice little allowance, that was paid without fail into a post office account.

"I don't know why you're getting so excited, our Florrie," Gracie said, when her sister came flying through the front door, desperate to tell her the news. "He's our cousin, get over it. Go and find one of those handsome Yanks that have started coming to the Palais de Danse at the weekend."

"I don't want a date with one of the handsome Yanks," Florrie said soberly. "I want to go to Australia when the war is over and Chadwick will be able to show me the ropes when I get there. Although, I must say it's a pity we're related, I'm sure he'd make a very nice husband. Anyroad, how are you settling in? Does it feel strange having your own bedroom and not sharing it with me?" Gracie shook her head. " No, I've got the whole of a wardrobe and dressing table all to myself now, but I'll tell you what is strange. You know how Dad said I had to get a removal van to shift his furniture, now that he's given the Blakes' van back to the building firm? Well, when me and Mam turned up outside the house last Saturday, he was hovering around the pub' on the corner. As soon as Mam had opened up and we stood in the living room waiting, he shot in, raced upstairs and came downstairs carrying a holdall and a small suitcase. He said he'd been looking after somebody's stuff because they'd been bombed out and had nowhere to store it, but the man had telephoned that afternoon and asked him to meet him in town. Then he asked if Mam would return the wheelbarrow to number 17, then off he went and the last we saw of him was at the bus stop. Mam said, when he got back home later he was what he calls stocious and spent most of the next day in bed."

"It's all right for some," Florrie said, wondering why suddenly her father was without a job, when he had always been in employment. "Though Mam did say all this visiting bomb sites has been getting to him."

"Pfft," Gracie's snort was derisive. "I'd like to see him doing Mam's job then. This is the second war when she's had to treat casualties."

On the 7th May 1942, the Japanese had called off their planned attack of Port Moresby on the eastern coast of the Territory of Papua, due to being defeated in the Battle of the Coral Bay by the Allies. Papua, Timor and the Dutch East Islands which had been occupied by the Japanese, were not far away from Australia's northern coastline and naturally the people of Australia had began to feel rather vulnerable. The bombing of Darwin Harbour earlier in the year and the capture of Singapore in February by the enemy, had caused deep despair, and fearing that the Japanese may make another attempt, some of the squadrons that were seeing action in the air above Europe were recalled. Chadwick Moscrop's squadron was one of them and as he set off for Bolton from the air base at R.A.F Lakenheath early one Friday morning to say goodbye to his British family, he knew that he must share a secret with Florrie, his love.

It was a long journey, made difficult by recent attacks on the larger cities that Chadwick had to travel through and the trains were full of forces personnel who had been given much welcomed leave. By the time he had got to Bolton, he was worn out, but Florrie was there waiting, even though she'd spent most of her time sitting in the station cafe after work. Her joyous smile as her eyes alighted upon him, made his journey worthwhile.

She'd had time to think over Gracie's recent words whilst she made her cup of weak war time tea last in the cafe. It was all hot water and sweepings from the tea factory floor, as proper tea leaves were like gold at that time. Then the woman behind the counter tutted meaningfully, so she treated herself to a cup of coffee made from roasted chicory.

The two sisters had enjoyed some time together in Gracie's home on one of her rare days off from the munitions factory, as at the moment they were working flat out. Chadwick, of course had come up in conversation, because Florrie mentioned that he had sent a telegram to her office, telling her on what day he would arrive.

Gracie was of the opinion that there would be tears before bedtime. Her sister had all the signs of having fallen in love with their cousin, even if she denied it when challenged. "You don't want to fall into the same trap as I did, Florrie. A.J is the nearest I will ever come to being in love with anyone and look what happened there."

Gracie had said those words bitterly. Before she had found out that A.J was her half brother, she'd had such plans. Marriage, babies and all the things that would make their life long union full of happiness.

"But this is a bit different, Gracie," Florrie had said, determined that she wasn't going to end up like her sister had. Married to a man who gave her a weekly allotment from the army. No chance to really get to know each other, as Johnny had virtually gone away after the wedding. One night spent together on their honeymoon, was not really ideal to guarantee a life time of wedded bliss.

"Chadwick knows that I want to emigrate to Australia after the war. I can get a job there now that I'm a qualified secretary, or maybe they'll have a teacher training college in Melbourne that I can attend. Either way, Chadwick says that that Australia will welcome people who want to live there after the war. You and Johnny should think about emigrating too."

"But you won't be able to marry him," Gracie insisted. "He's your first cousin and you wouldn't be allowed to get wed."

"Who said anything about marrying him, Gracie?" Florrie knew she would like a shot if they were not so closely related.

"Ah, but you would if you could." Gracie was not for changing her mind about the situation, no matter what her sister said.

Chapter Twenty Eight

Hetty from next door had seen to it that Chadwick had eaten the best breakfast she could provide, considering there was a war on and had made a few egg sandwiches for his journey as well. She felt sad to see him go, as he was a nice young man and she knew she would probably never see him again, now that he was returning to his homeland.

Florrie had managed to have some time off work, after she had explained to kindly Mr. Pelham that her cousin was returning to Australia with his squadron in a few days time. The British nation was very grateful for the help coming from their allies in the Commonwealth, although the entry of the Americans into the fray after Pearl Harbour had been bombed by the Japanese, was regarded by many with suspicion. The U.S had helped Britain defeat the Germans twenty one years before and so the thinking man must have wondered why they had been reluctant to help them win again. Not many knew that 60,000 U.S soldiers had died in combat in the earlier conflict and the nation wasn't happy to send anymore of their boys back for more.

It was a sunny day. Ada had gone off to work sadly, after giving Chadwick a big hug and promising that after the war they would all come over for a holiday. Daniel was still in bed, sleeping off the beers that he had shared with Chadwick the night before.

The young couple decided to have a walk in the countryside before Chadwick had to catch the train at 12.30. Florrie wore long black trousers, which had become popular once there were material shortages. A smart blue jacket over a light jumper and a pair of walking shoes completed her outfit. She was unaware that she had chosen a similar coloured jacket to Chadwick's uniform and so they made a fine looking pair as they wandered together up Hospital Road.

"I wish this war wouldn't keep rumbling on," Florrie remarked, as they walked past Blair Hospital, then the entrance to a whitewashed farm and a couple of fields where the farmer and two land girls were busy with the harvesting. "Surely Hitler knows that he's going to be beaten one day, now that their V1th army has been defeated in Russia and our allies are making inroads across Europe. I can't wait to start my new life in Australia."

Chadwick nodded in agreement. "It won't be long before we'll be together again Florrie. Once I'm back in Melbourne, I can see what needs to be done to get you over. I have to ask you something first though. What say we walk up the hill? Let me admire that panoramic view over Bolton for the last time and I'll breathe in the fresh air before I'm stuck on a train again." He smiled at her when she looked back at him inquiringly. "I'm sure you'll like what I've got to say as much as I will."

His thoughts went back to the evening before he was supposed to report for duty in Melbourne. His parents had seemed all jumpy for days and he put it down to their concern for his well being. Neither of them thought he should enlist if he didn't have to, but it was an exciting adventure for a young man. It was his father who asked him to share a bottle of Jack Daniels in the lounge room after dinner, whilst his mother washed the dishes in the kitchen. And then his mother, his gentle mother, had sat beside him on the sofa knitting a pair of thick woollen socks.

Her face was expressionless as she knitted, whilst hoping that the last sock would be finished that evening, as she didn't want her precious son with chilblains on his toes if he had to fly at high altitudes.

"Now son, " his father said, throwing an anxious look at his wife before continuing. "We've something that we never dreamt we'd have to tell you, but with you going off to war, we need to tell you now." He looked sad, then it all came tumbling out.

"Your poor mother had a lot of trouble bearing babies and at one time I thought I was going to lose her when she became so ill. I decided that enough was enough, but your mother was adamant. She wanted us to have a child together, didn't you Sara?" His mother had nodded and Chadwick saw a glimmer of tears in her troubled eyes. "So, I took it upon myself to…er…avoid… er… husbandly duties, but it made us very sad. Then one day, I was talking to someone at work who suggested we should go to the Mother and Baby Home in Melbourne and give one of the unfortunate children there the chance of a better life. As soon as we saw you lying there in your little cot, staring at us so seriously, we knew that we wanted to bring you home. So that's what we did and we named you Chadwick after your mother's uncle, who was a fine young man."

Chadwick stopped walking for a moment, then drew Florrie to stand beside him against a nearby wall. " You know what me being adopted means, Florrie. We could marry. I'm not your cousin, we're not related. I know that we could make each other happy. Do you feel the same way as I do?"

Florrie nodded, still dumbfounded. She hadn't believed what she was hearing last night when Chadwick had announced to her mother that he had been adopted by Uncle Charles and Aunty Sara. So they weren't related at all and as she had gone to bed with her thoughts in a whirl, she wondered if he felt the same way as she did. They could marry and be together for ever…

And there and then, just when her heart began thudding in her chest at the thought of it all, he took her hand and kissed the back of it tenderly.

"I knew you did." Chadwick drew her to him and not caring that they might have an audience in the field beyond watching them kissing, he locked her in an embrace that had her trembling. "So now you know that I'm not your cousin, Florrie, it's time to tell your family that we'll marry. I know that my parents won't mind and I'm sure Aunt Ada will be delighted." They began to walk towards the cover of a nearby copse, so the grinning farmer couldn't see their passion.

"What's ailing yer lad?" Ada asked, when she came home from a long and exhausting day at the hospital, to find Daniel sitting on the sofa, with his mind gone to heavens' knows where. "Have you had something to eat today, or have you been staring into space?"

"I had a sandwich. Hetty had made a load for Chadwick's journey, so he left some behind for me and Florrie's lunch."

"Ah, that was nice of him. Did he get off okay and where's Florrie?"

"She's gone round to Gracie's. She went with him to the station and saw him off."

"Well, I can't get over the fact our Charles adopted him. You'd think that me own brother would have let me know about it. Wouldn't it have been dreadful if Florrie had fallen in love with him and they'd ended up like Arthur and Gracie?"

"Well, she has. I mean Florrie has fallen in love with him, as yer put it. She made me get out of bed to tell me before he went. Now he knows he's not 'er cousin, they're going to marry."

"Young un's eh. It'll probably peter out with all the miles between them. Anyroad, do yer fancy a dippy egg and some toast? That's all we have in at the moment."

It was later as Ada rinsed out a few clothes to hang outside overnight, as it promised to be a warm one, when after smoking a cigarette, Daniel collapsed back onto the sofa. She worried if he was ever going to pull himself together and get on with life. She knew very well about the trauma he must be dwelling on, after he had seen the devastation of bombed out houses, the ambulances ferrying the injured to the hospitals and the dead being carried away in a hearse.

She saw the results of Hitler's ambition to bring the nation to its knees on a daily basis, but she knew she was strong and Daniel was weak. Always had been since she had got to know him all those years ago. He'd always been a proud man; took care with his appearance, wore a smart business suit and a Homburg hat and was treated with respect by everyone he met.

But no one would recognize this Mr. Daniel McAuley if they met him now and why would they? He'd only made the effort to shave when Chadwick was expected, but before, he'd grown a stubbly beard that made him look like a tramp. He wore a pair of corduroy trousers and a tatty collar-less shirt that had both seen better days and a down heel pair of worn out tartan slippers, which Ada would have thrown into the bin, if it hadn't have been for the war.

Since she had sent a letter to Blake's, informing them that Mr. McAuley was in no fit state to work for them due to an accident on the bomb site and then a telephone call to the boss of the A.R.P headquarters, who had said that Danny was welcome back when he felt up to it, he had walked around as if he had lost his mind. Deep down she knew, that long term and for his own sense of worth, whatever it was that was causing his night sweats and restlessness, wouldn't be cured by his alcohol consumption and idling away his days. She was sympathetic and tried her best to understand what he must be going through, but when she thought of all the shocking sights that the soldiers on the Front would have to see, it was difficult.

"Yer know Ada," he said, when she had come back in after hanging out her washing and he had opened another bottle of beer. "I was thinkin' about what it would be like to start afresh in a far off country."

"You mean like Australia, Daniel?" Ada was tongue in cheek as she said it. "Because you already started afresh in this country."

"Aye. After listening to Chadwick, listening to his tales of kangaroos and koala bears and beautiful white sands on the beaches, it reminded me of when we once went to a place called Derrynane. Me mammy had family in Kenmare and they took us to Derrynane one day and it was wonderful to run along the long wide beaches, looking out to sea at the little islands. Did yer know that the next stop across the Atlantic Sea is America?"

"No, I didn't. A lot of people emigrate to America too. When were you thinking of going?"

It must have appeared to an onlooker that the world had gone mad in 1943. Battles raged from the Atlantic to the Pacific and along the Mediterranean coastline. In Italy, Mussolini was imprisoned and the Italians who had fought with Germany now became Allies. It was here on the island of Sicily during *Operation Husky* that Johnny Francis took a bullet in his leg. After having the bullet removed at the Field hospital, he was returned to Blighty to convalesce.

It was all a bit of a shock to Gracie, who to all intents and purposes was a single woman, or an outsider would think she was, judging by the various men who walked her to the bus stop from the Palais. It was also a bind to have to visit the hospital on a daily basis, as the factory had been busy in the creation of the Bouncing Bombs that were used in the Dambuster Raids in the Ruhr Valley. Because of the extra work, Gracie always felt shattered and so it was with a sense of relief when Johnny's wound was healed and he was posted back, to heavens know where, to resume hostilities.

One evening, when Ada was nearly at the end of her tether and about to tell Daniel to pull himself together and stop thinking about himself so much, when out of the blue, Reggie Thornton appeared and suggested that they went to watch a snooker tournament at the Co-operative Hall in Bolton, the following Saturday. Being much the same age as Daniel, Reggie was too old to be conscripted and besides being an Air Raid warden, he did any odd jobs that were needed in the area. He felt a certain sympathy with Daniel, as he too had seen sights that were not for the faint hearted during the first world war, but of course he wasn't aware of the deed that had caused Daniel his on going distress.

It was as they were sitting in the Snug in one of the public houses in Bradshawgate after the tournament, that a couple of men joined them at their table. Reggie had told Daniel that he often met them there, as they too were avid fans of snooker and were often to be spotted drinking in the same bar. They were all elated, as their favourite local player had thrashed the opposition, so everyone was in high spirits.

"Shall I get you your usual, Reggie?" One of the men who's name was Tommy asked, speaking in a voice just loud enough to be heard above the revelry. It was obvious to Daniel that the man wasn't asking Reggie if he could get him a pint as they had only just started drinking.

"Aye, a couple of boxes this time. They went so quickly, I could have done with more. With Christmas coming up, everyone will want some."

"And what about you, Danny? It is Danny, isn't it? Your mate was saying you might be interested in a bit of stuff from us, seeing you've no money coming in."

"Oh... Well, I don't know about that...erm..."

"Don't take too long thinkin' about it, Danny," the other man said darkly. "We've plenty of people interested in black market stuff."

"He'll have a case, won't yer Daniel," Reggie said confidently. "If it's a matter of dosh, I'll stand it and you can pay me back later."

"Okay then. We'll have these drinks and then we'll meet you both round the back. I take it you've got the van with you, Reggie."

So Daniel began his new career as a black marketeer and his stash was hidden in his mate's lockup shed, where Reggie stored his tools and machinery and used when working as an odd job man. Daniel had one side of the lockup for his boxes of silk stockings, cans of salmon, bottles of malt whisky, cane sugar and luxury soap and Reggie had the other side and they toured around the local hostelries together, as partners in crime. Although it has to be said that Daniel avoided those places where he might have been known before in his capacity of a brewery area manager. You never knew who might be drinking there.

Both Ada and her daughters were pleased to see the change in Daniel and it was put down to the work he was doing with Reggie Thornton. Although Ada wasn't pleased when a luxury bottle of single malt appeared in her kitchen cupboard one day. She was told that it was from a grateful customer, along with a bar of Pears soap that appeared on her kitchen window sill.

She was a great defender of the rationing system. She believed that every person in the land should do their bit for the war effort, even if it meant eating powdered egg and Woolton pie, which was a thick vegetable concoction with a little cheese wrapped in a thin pastry. Though if truth was told, she ate most of her meals in the hospital canteen which wasn't much affected, as sick people had a different level of rationing. And she bought fresh food in season from the local farmers, to cook at home for Daniel and Florrie.

A whole new world had opened up for Daniel and as the months wore on, his nightmares began to disappear.

Chapter Twenty Nine

It was in the May of 1944 and Ada was surprised to see her elder daughter sitting at the kitchen table when she came home from work. She hadn't seen her since Gracie's 21st birthday in April, when the family, including Hetty next door, had celebrated with a Sunday tea. The cake, not a patch on the ones that Ada used to bake before the war, which would have been topped with pink icing, was a plain sponge made from a decent bag of flour that had suddenly made an appearance in the kitchen, courtesy of Daniel and its origin ignored by Ada for once. The sandwiches provided contained a thin layer of tinned ham, which had been saved for such an occasion when it was chanced upon by Ada in a local shop.

"You look dreadful," exclaimed Ada, when she saw that Gracie was almost yellow in the face, her hair looking lank and needing brushing and from the smell emanating from under her armpits, as she was wearing a shapeless sleeveless dress, she was in need of a good wash too.

"Have you had the flu'? Is that why we haven't seen you? Oh no, you're not suffering from the effects of working in that factory are you? I've been hearing some dreadful stories lately."

To her surprise, Gracie put her head in her hands and started crying. Big sobs caused her shoulders to shake, which startled Ada, as she hadn't seen her daughter cry like that since she was a child.

"What is it?" Ever practical Ada bent down to one of her cupboards and brought out a towel for Gracie to dry her tears with.

"I'm pregnant."

Ada couldn't believe her ears! "You're what?"

"I'm expecting a baby", came the snuffly reply, before Gracie burst into tears again.

"But you can't be. Johnny's been away since…It's not Johnny's baby is it? Oh Gracie, what have you done?"

"I had too much to drink at the work's party we had at Christmas. It was a bloke from the band who came to entertain us. I can't even remember his name. Oh, God, Mam, what am I going to do?"

"I'll have to think, Gracie." Ada's usual passiveness suddenly deserted her and as she filled the kettle, her heart began beating like a drum. It wasn't until she had poured two cups of tea out automatically, that her common sense nature began to kick in.

"Well, you'll have to go away. You'll have to go to the doctor and get him to write a note to the factory and tell them that as you're expecting a baby, it would be too dangerous to continue working there. Then you'll have to give up the house in Clay Street and advertise the furniture. You won't be able to afford the rent if you're not working. At least you're a married woman, Gracie, so there's no shame in it and they'll probably think it happened when Johnny came home."

"Which it didn't. I made all sorts of excuses when he came to ours from hospital, before going back to the Front. I couldn't stand him Mam. He wasn't anything like I remember. He was full of himself. He was coarse and vulgar and I made the excuse I was on my period so that he wouldn't touch me. He got the message when I told him I'd sleep on the sofa, so that I wouldn't disturb his bandages. What do you think Dad will say?"

"Oh, we won't be telling your father. Good grief, Gracie. You know what he's been like since he went to that bomb site in Punch Street. I couldn't bear it if your news knocks him back into how he used to behave. It's taken all this time to get him normal, thanks to Reggie Thornton giving him a job."

"You know Mam. I wasn't going to say this to you, but if we're being honest, something's been bothering me since I split up with A.J, because of Dad being his father. I've never really been happy because of it. I would have married A.J like a shot if I could. No, what it is, do you remember when I was a little girl and we went to that house in Astley Bridge? We met that woman and her daughter and you helped them settle in. It came to me only the other day, that Dad had disappeared from then on and he only came back to the cottage now and again to see us. Was that Irish girl who lived with the woman his as well?"

"Oh, Gracie, you're raking up things that don't concern you. All that is in the past and he's been a good father." Ada spoke sharply to cover her sudden fear, as she thought of the can of worms that could open.

"I knew it, I knew there was something going on! I seemed to remember now that he said that the woman was his sister, so why would he live with his sister when he had you? And when we went round to his house to sort out the furniture, he was acting all shifty. So how come we never got to see his sister or our cousin again?"

"I'm not going to even deign to give you an explanation, Gracie. It's nothing to do with you or Florrie, as to what went on in your father's past. Anyroad, you're only talking like this so's to take my mind off your predicament. We'll say nothing to your father and I'll write a letter to Moira in Gaitsgill. I take it you'll be giving the child away."

It soon became apparent that Hitler and his army were beginning to lose their momentum that year, after heavy bombing of major cities in Germany by the Allies, caused many deaths and casualties. The powers at be in England began to plan the Normandy landings, which became a turning point in the winning of the war.

Daniel at that time was in his element. Gone were his nightmares, as every day was filled with work that Reggie provided and Saturday evenings were spent touring around the hostelries, where eager customers bought their ill gotten wares. He began to take more pride in his appearance and had no time to let his mind fester. Sometimes he wondered if it all been a dream. The cash, tucked away in a safe that had suddenly come into Reggie's possession and was hidden in the lockup under an old blanket, grew larger each month, causing them to wonder whether it would be safer in the bank. Neither man were able to spend much of it, or attention would be brought upon them as they were ordinary working men. But Daniel did buy Gracie a beautiful necklace for her 21ˢᵗ and pretended it was second hand.

Luckily Daniel didn't notice that his elder daughter was a little more plump than usual. Even the wartime rations hadn't effected her buxom appearance, as she'd been having regular meals at the works canteen and had a fondness for biscuits. So when Ada announced that Gracie was going to stay in with relations in Gaitsgill, seemingly because the chemicals that she worked with were making her ill and the doctor had recommended fresh air to make her lungs better, Daniel had wished her well and sent her off with a couple of crisp pound notes in her handbag. Only Ada and Florrie were privy to the fact that Gracie was expecting and neither criticized her decision not to keep the child.

Florrie dreamt of being Mrs. Chadwick Moscrop. It seemed strange that she would be having the same surname when she married him, but it wasn't something she pondered on and always looked forward to his monthly letters, which were censored of course, but were always full of love. Chadwick, once back in his homeland, patrolled the northern part of Australia, the Dutch East Islands and over to Timor with his squadron.

It was just after the liberation of Paris, that Gracie gave birth to a baby girl whom she named Audrey after the film star, Audrey Hepburn. She'd enjoyed her time in Gaitsgill with her Nana Moscrop's family, except for the giving birth part, which she hadn't enjoyed at all. Moira had been kind and hadn't condemned her in any way. Becoming pregnant by a man who hadn't been her husband had been foolish, but it happened and the hardest part was going to be to give the child away.

It hadn't been long before the Adoption Agency, newly created by the government, as there were so many single women giving birth in wartime, knocked on Moira's door and asked to see the newly born. There had been the temptation by Moira to keep the child in the family, as another one wouldn't have made much difference, as there was a whole tribe of Moscrops in and around Gaitsgill and Dalston. But Gracie had been adamant. There was no way that she wanted to keep a child that had been conceived out of wedlock, nor farm it out to relatives. Audrey would have a better life in a loving home, where no one knew her.

Besides, she might feel that she had to explain Audrey to Johnny, if they kept her in the family and her dutiful visits up to Gaitsgill would clip her wings somewhat, if she wanted a bit of fun.

It had been agreed by Gracie and Ada, via the weekly telephone call from the red box outside the Post Office in Dalston, that on her return to Bolton, she would receive some tender loving care back at her home in Dunscar. Ada was unprepared for her daughter's attitude.

"It was awful Mam," Gracie said, after arriving with her suitcase one Friday morning and having kissed her mother on the cheek, she went to the back door and lit a cigarette. "I wouldn't have another baby for a gold clock, it was so gruesome."

"Gruesome enough to start smoking, young lady?" Ada wasn't pleased that her daughter had taken up the habit, as she had seen what smoking could do to the lungs.

"Oh, I can give it up anytime. Anyway, it was Aunt Moira's grandson, Des' that got me started. He said that smoking would keep me thin. You should have seen me, I was like a balloon."

"Well everyone puts on weight when they're expecting a baby. So the birth was that bad, was it? Good job it wasn't for me or our Florrie wouldn't be here."

"Right then." Gracie became all practical, although just for a minute her eyes shone with tears, which she dashed away with the cuff of her cardigan. "The midwife said I was to rest up for a couple of weeks. In fact, she was horrified when I said I was catching a train back to Bolton so soon. She told Aunt Moira to make me stay in bed until the end of the month, but I didn't want to hang around forever. So as soon as the baby had gone, I made my escape."

She walked back in and sat down on the sofa, then began to sip at the cup of tea that Ada had placed on the small table nearby. Ada sat beside her and put an arm around her daughter's shoulders.

"Do you want to tell me about the little baby? She would have been my first grandchild you know."

"Mam, do we have to go over it?" Gracie shook her mother's arm away crossly. "You might think me cold and uncaring, but what I did was for the best for little Audrey. How could I have brought her home with me? Johnny would have gone beserk. Dad would have probably disowned me and there was no way I could have gone to work and still been a mother to her. No, she'll be happier wherever they took her and that's the end of it."

"Okay." Ada patted her gently and ever practical, asked if she would like to lie down upstairs and did she have enough sanitary wear, as she could get some from the hospital?

"Florrie says she's looking forward to seeing you again, she's missed her sisterly chats."

If Daniel was surprised to see that his elder daughter had moved back in with them, he didn't comment. Probably putting it down to the length of time that she'd been up in Dalston so she'd lost her tenancy and he knew that Florrie wouldn't mind having her sister sharing their bedroom again. It had been agreed that Gracie could stay as long as she wanted. For the moment, Gracie needed her family for support, even if she thought she didn't need it and this way Ada could monitor her behaviour and make sure she didn't go off the rails again.

In 1945 it appeared that Hilter and his cohorts, having suffered severe defeats after their efforts of world domination had come to nothing, were brought to their knees when Hitler committed suicide.

There was universal cheering from the lands of Europe and when Victory in Europe was declared, Britain was ecstatic.

Of course there were many casualties, not just on the battle fields, but at home where cities lay stricken as a result of severe bombing, multitudes of children were made orphans and wives who had sacrificed their loved one in defense of the nation and freedom, were all alone. Someone who didn't come home was A.J McAuley, although Bunty or Nelly never tried to contact Daniel to inform him of their loss. Another was Johnny Francis, but that was from choice, not from a bullet. After his demob' and a visit to the rented house in Clay Street to find his wife had given up the tenancy, he re-enlisted and was sent to the Middle East. A letter was sent to the family home in Dunscar, stating that the allowance from her husband would cease forthwith.

Not that Gracie minded, as after a period of rest, she was training as an auxiliary nurse in Townley's Hospital and was saving her money for the next big change in her life.

It had been on April 30th 1945, when defeat was inevitable as the Allies went through Europe freeing its people from the Nazi jackboot, that Hitler decided that rather than face retribution for his evil deeds he would commit suicide. He had recently married a woman called Eva Braun and they were hiding in an underground bunker. On that day, the unfortunate dog who was ensconced with them, was given cyanide, so that the tyrant could see how long it would take to die. Thus noted, he and his wife ingested the pills and for good measure Hitler shot himself. The war in Europe was over and people all over the land, celebrated its conclusion on the 8th May.

It was time though for the ordinary people who had done their patriotic best, suffered rationing, hardship and loss of loved ones, to bring their own retribution on those who had colluded with the enemy or profited because of the war. In Europe, those women who had offered sexual favours to the Germans, usually in return for food, because of their desperation to feed their family, were publicly tarred and feathered, or stripped naked and shaved.

Investigations found that many people including farmers and small holders, had also been the main source of supplying the black market. Meat sold to butchers, who kept it for their favoured customers and had sold it on again at twice the price. It appeared that for the rich and famous there had been no deprivation, as many villains had been instrumental with supplying them regularly with luxury goods and so it led to a lot of angry muttering throughout the land.

One evening, Reggie Thornton knocked on the door of Daisy Nook and asked if Daniel would like to go for a pint? It wasn't an unusual occurrence and so Ada and her daughters settled down to listen to the wireless, which was playing a selection of Glenn Miller's music, who was a favourite band leader of that time. So it was a shock when Daniel came rushing through the door around ten minutes later, trembling all over and as white as a sheet.

"What ever's the matter, Daniel?" asked Ada, rushing over and leading him to the sofa to sit down, whilst Florrie went to put the kettle on and Gracie stood watching in concern.

"They'll be comin' to get me, Ada. It'll be my turn next. They'll lock me up and throw away the key. I'm a marked man."

"Why what have you done? And what's Reggie said to you to get you in this state? Gracie go and get a tumbler of whisky for your Dad. Ah, it's the whisky, isn't it? You and Reg' have been getting a few bottles and selling it on. Well, I don't agree with profiteering, but it at least it put a smile on your face and kept you out of mischief."

"Reggie told me that the two men who supplied us with it have been taken to the police station for questioning. It's a £500 fine and imprisonment for two years if they rat on Reggie and me."

He downed the whisky that Gracie had brought him in a couple of gulps, then stared into space as if his mind had gone somewhere else.

"They're not going to fine you £500 just for the sake of a few bottles of whisky, Dad." Florrie said, ever practical. "Ah, but it was luxury soap as well, wasn't it Dad?" Gracie said a little spitefully. "Well, whatever it was, compared to some that I've heard about, your Dad was only sticking his toe in the water. I've heard of blokes who could get you anything, if you were prepared to wait for it. Anyway, Florrie show your Dad that letter that came this morning from Chadwick. It appears that Australia has set up a Department of Immigration and are looking for applications from the people of the British Isles."

"I wish," said Daniel morosely.

Chapter Thirty

It was later when the girls had gone to bed and Ada was preparing sandwiches for Florrie's lunch, that Daniel decided to confess all, or at least as much as he could get away with. He knew that if Ada ever found out the extent of his involvement in the black market, she'd probably throw him out. It would all come out anyway if he and Reggie were carted off and they had to stand trial at the court in Bolton. There was every chance that their two suppliers could do a deal with the police.

He thought of the money that lay in the bottom of the safe in Reggie's lock up. It had only been yesterday when his friend said they must make up their minds whether to dump it in the bank or take out a lump sum and pretend that it was payment for a big job they'd done together. All those bottles of whisky, the continental cigarettes that had been smuggled over from Europe, the luxury goods that had come their way from the U.S bases. It all added up to a colossal sum, if you compared it to the measly hourly rate that they charged for their local labour.

Reggie was looking forward to buying a property, as he and his wife had rented their family home for many years. Daniel hadn't any plans at all for the moment, although he thought he might buy a car.

Ada wasn't happy. "Was it Reggie that put you up to this Daniel? It must have been, because I can't see where you would have got the money from to buy the stuff, with you not having a proper job since the bombing incident. Wait until I see him. He'll wish he hadn't been born when I've finished with him. You know how I feel about having an advantage over other people. During wartime, everyone should accept that there's a shortage of food and that there will be rationing."

"I'm sorry Ada." Daniel managed to look downcast, as he knew Ada would forgive him if he looked suitably penitent. "It was too temptin'. I didn't 'ave a proper job and was feelin' bad because I used to be a somebody. I was an Area Manager and then an Assessor for heaven's sake. Drove my own van and brought in a good wage until the bombing. All my workin' life, I've been someone who others looked up to, so I have. Then because of some little shite called Hitler, everyone had their lives turned upside down."

He walked to the back door and lit a cigarette, his hand shaking with emotion as he wondered how Ada would react to his confession.

"Let's worry about it if it happens, " she said in the usual sympathetic way she had with people in distress, whilst walking over to him and patting his shoulder. "There's no point in fretting. Worse things happen at sea, or so they say. Shall I make you a cup of tea with plenty of sugar and you can tell me all the things that you've been keeping from me?"

Florrie got off the train at Bromley Cross one Friday afternoon, clutching her handbag to her with glee as she thought of its contents. It was her papers. Her official documentation that gave her permission to live in Australia. Her journey to Manchester that morning had been full of trepidation in case her application hadn't been accepted and she would never see dear Chadwick again. Although considering the Australian Department of Immigration had been advertising far and wide in the national newspapers for people to help re-populate their nation, she didn't know why she was feeling that way.

The official that had interviewed her though, had seemed delighted with her neatly written application and had said she would be an asset. Especially after Florrie explained that she would be joining her fiance in Melbourne, who had been born in Australia and was now an airline pilot for Trans Australia Air. She had even been given an assisted passage, which meant she didn't have to spend so much of her hard earned savings to get there. A hastily converted troopship, which had been commissioned especially to take emigrants to a new life in Australia, was to leave Tilbury that November and would be sailing via Lisbon and around the Cape of Good Hope. From Cape Town the ship would sail across the Indian Ocean and dock in Freemantle, where some of the passengers would begin their new life. She felt excited, she'd be seeing places that she had never thought she would see in her life time

Florrie pulled the collar up of the thick hip length maroon winter jacket she was wearing over a plain knitted green jumper and matching tweed skirt. Her high block heel shoes made a clunking sound as she hurried along the recently laid pavement. She would have to think of what to take in the large suitcase that she'd been told she would need for her journey. Mostly summer clothes, as it wouldn't be winter over there in Melbourne on her arrival.

She couldn't wait to get home and tell her family the good news about her application. They were prepared for it. They knew she had gone to Manchester for an interview and even Gracie had said she was considering following her to Australia, if everything went well.

Daniel meantime hadn't been marched off to the police station. He had been a minor player, along with Reggie, but the powers at be were after the bigger fish who had made a fortune from the war. It was with a sigh of relief when he heard the news from his friend, that Tommy and his mate hadn't welched on them and they were free to spend their ill gotten gains.

He had wondered what to do with his life now the war was over, as he couldn't just resurrect himself like Lazarus. He had to rely on the chaos of a devastated Britain and reinvent himself elsewhere. He thought back to the conversation he had with his mate the day before. They'd been fixing a fence after a sudden winter gale had knocked it sideways.

"So what are you thinking, Danny Boy?" asked Reggie, as he knocked a nail into a wooden post. "A nice little place in the country where you and your Ada can get your feet up and retire from the hectic life we've all been living? Perhaps you could go back to Ireland or I hear the highlands of Scotland is a nice place to settle and you could buy a cottage overlooking a loch and do some fishing."

"I was actually thinking of going a bit further, Reggie, now that Florrie has applied to settle in Melbourne. I mean, I could use the money I made to set meself up over there in a little business. Import and export mebbe, I've got the experience."

"And Ada?"

"Ada can get herself a job in a local hospital there if she wants to. She doesn't have to, because we'll sell the cottage and use the money to buy a place near Florrie. Gracie could come too, now she's got her certificate. I've just got to think of a way of getting them to agree."

"Well, if that's the case, get Ada to give me first refusal on Daisy Nook. I could give her around three hundred pounds and I know if Mam is looking down from Heaven, she would be very happy to see me move back in. God Bless her."

Ada meanwhile, after celebrating her fifty third birthday earlier that year, was wondering if the years to her retirement were going to be just the same as they had always been. This second war that she had just been through had been hard won and the sights she had seen had made her weary. Perhaps she should have a little holiday, whilst she decided whether to apply for a job back at Blairs Hospital.

There was still a great deal of wrangling going on throughout Europe and she found it unsettling to hear the evil tales of men's inhumanity to his fellow man, which were slowly emerging. She hoped the Warsaw Pact, which was being considered by Churchill, Stalin and Roosevelt, would bring a certain peace to all the countries involved.

Gracie was also considering her future. She was going to miss her younger sister and wondered if she should use her recent qualification as an auxiliary nurse, as a reason to join the many jobless and dispossessed people who were going to leave the British shores.

She knew that her marriage to Johnny was over and the birth of her little baby was still on her mind. It had been heartbreaking, when part of her duties had been to help one of the nurses in the maternity ward and she'd later shed bitter tears in the sluice room.

It had been a bit of a shock, to say the least, when after dinner on the day that Florrie had got her papers and the girls were washing up, that Daniel announced that he would quite like to visit Melbourne when Florrie had settled.

"We can come over for your wedding, me darlin'. There will be a wedding, won't there? You and Chadwick haven't changed your minds."

"Why no, Dad. In fact, in his last letter he told me that his mother had already started to think about the arrangements at the church."

"I should be doing that," Ada said soulfully, looking up from where she was sewing a button on Daniel's shirt. "You're my daughter and I should be making the arrangements for your wedding. Your father should be walking you down the aisle and Gracie should be your bridesmaid."

"Well, I can't if I'm not there, Mam, but actually I've been thinking that I should apply to emigrate to Australia myself. There's nothing left for me here, especially now that Johnny's signed up for a few more years."

"Oh, Gracie, that would be wonderful." Florrie's face was a

picture of happiness, as she thought of having a relative, maybe living just up the street from her, so she wouldn't feel that she had made the move to a far off country on her own. "I can point you in the right direction to get your papers. They're crying out for young people, especially newly qualified nurses like you."

"And they'll probably need an experienced one just like yer mother, who can pass on all her knowledge learnt from down the years. What say you, Ada? Are yer up for it? Shall we emigrate to Australia with these two?"

"I think we should, Daniel Moscrop," Ada said, wondering why she hadn't thought of it herself. They could all be together in a far off land, where no one, except her brother and his family, would know them. It was a plan for the future and everyone would benefit. She laid down the shirt, then went to put an arm around Daniel's shoulder and kissed him fondly on the cheek. " A fresh new start for everyone sounds good to me."